PRAISE FOR *ARCADE*

"A keenly-observed meditation on the ins and outs of an adult video store, *Arcade* is a heartfelt love letter to a very unlikely place."
—AMY FUSSELMAN. AUTHOR OF *THE PHARMACIST'S MATE*

"*Arcade* is a novel that reads with the authenticity and honesty of a memoir. Drew Smith has written a compelling tell-all about a man coming to terms with his sexuality in an unlikely place, a peepshow arcade. I couldn't stop reading it. It's a remarkable debut novel."
— MICHAEL KIMBALL. AUTHOR OF *BIG RAY*

"Obsessive, dark, and tender, *Arcade* investigates longing and modern loneliness with care, invention, and a complete lack of fear."
— MICHELLE ORANGE.
AUTHOR OF *THIS IS RUNNING FOR YOUR LIFE*

"Intent, fearless, and funny, *Arcade* captures a prism of human sexuality, its bliss and its ugliness and its ridiculousness—all at once."
— MICHELLE WILDGEN. AUTHOR OF *BREAD AND BUTTER*

The Unnamed Press
P.O. Box 411272
Los Angeles, CA 90041

Published in North America by The Unnamed Press.

1 3 5 7 9 10 8 6 4 2

Copyright © 2016 by Drew Nellins Smith

ISBN: 978-1-939419-72-9

Library of Congress Control Number:
2016940542

This book is distributed by Publishers Group West

Cover design & typeset by Jaya Nicely

Special thanks to Steve Boren, David Duhr,
Monika Woods, and Olivia Taylor Smith.

ARCADE

A NOVEL

DREW NELLINS SMITH

The Unnamed Press
Los Angeles, CA

Sometimes I must go to certain places, if you know what I mean. I pick up the worst guys there. You wouldn't believe your eyes. Pleasure and mad arousal and terror and disgrace, all in a wild confusion...Someday I'll be beaten to death, of course. But that can also be appealing. I'm controlled by forces I can't handle.

FROM THE LIFE OF THE MARIONETTES, INGMAR BERGMAN

All sins are attempts to fill voids.

SIMONE WEIL

1

I SAW PEOPLE MENTIONING IT IN THE PERSONALS ONLINE, but I didn't know anything about it. I didn't know places like that existed. In the Missed Connections, there were ads that made clear that men were having sexual encounters of some kind there, in what I pictured as a Wild West of promiscuity. The ads said things like, "The XXX place west of town. We've played out there before. This time you came in wearing gym clothes. I had to get back to work, or things would have gone further. Tell me what you said about my shirt so I know it's you."

In a few posts, a particular highway was named. I drove out looking for it one Saturday afternoon, feeling adrenalized and nervous. I had probably passed the place a hundred time without noticing it. Aside from the red "XXX" mounted near its roof, it was an anonymous-looking building clad in corrugated metal. It could have been a hastily-erected industrial shop, or one of those oversized fireworks super centers on the side of the highway that are only open a few weeks of the year around the Fourth of July and New Year's. It looked like the worst possible place to shelter during a tornado. It would have been safer in one's car.

Pushing the door open, I felt the arcade's cool air against my face for the first time. I walked in wearing earphones, nodded at the clerk, and began looking around in a tense and jittery parody of "playing it cool." There were neatly organized racks of movies and a strange glassed-in room filled with lingerie.

I pretended to browse porn DVDs while trying to get my bearings. On either side of the main room were shadowy hallways, but from within the fluorescent brightness of the store, their darkness hid everything. The sounds of porn drifted out, sometimes momentarily blaring as though piped through a bullhorn, then receding quickly. There were things that looked like metal detectors at the entrances to the halls.

I read the signs everywhere. There were some by the front door that said not to enter if you were offended by nudity or material of a sexual nature. There were signs that prohibited food and drink, cell phones, and cameras. There were signs that said not to smoke in the building unless you were in a designated smoking area. On the things that looked like metal detectors, there were signs that said no one could enter a hallway unless they had purchased tokens at the counter. Several signs obviously made in Microsoft Word announced that if one purchased two videos, a third at the same price could be had for free. "Note:" it read, "this only applies to movies $24.95 and under."

Like a casino, there were no windows or clocks, and there were cameras everywhere. It seemed like more cameras than should have been necessary for a pornography shop, even a relatively large one.

At the front of the store, near the counter, were the magazines. Not the usual ones like *Penthouse* and *Hustler*. They carried off-brand publications I had never heard of. Then there were toys and lube and condoms and cock rings and blow-up dolls that were obviously a joke, and expensive ones that obviously were not. There were rubbery flesh-colored mounds made to resemble a woman's hips, as if her legs had been chopped off just a few inches below her pelvis, and her torso had been cut off just below her belly button. All that remained were her rubber hips and orifices. I once saw a clerk moving them around, and recognized their true heft in the way he lugged them from place to place like sandbags.

I took DVD cases off the shelves and examined their front and back covers, wondering if I was in the wrong place. I didn't know what I was looking for, what would prove this to be the locale about which I had read. I noticed the other men in the store wandering, looking at me, looking at one another. They would emerge from one of the hallways, peer around, then walk into the opposite hallway or back into the hallway from which they had just emerged. Some of the men were attractive, or anyway they had that quality I like. Most of them looked serious, as if conducting the gravest business at this porn store on the outskirts of town. I observed everything, attempting to go unnoticed in the section marked "Big Tits."

The clerk watched me. He was in his mid-thirties and wearing a fedora. He looked like a pornography director himself, with dark, lank hair that fell down either side of his face. He gestured for me to remove my earphones.

"Do you need help with something?" he said across the store.

I walked toward the counter, which was on a raised platform two or three feet above the level of the rest of the building. I gave him a confused look and said, "I don't think I do."

"Are you sure?" he said. "Maybe you should buy some tokens. For the booths."

"Booths?"

"The booths in the hallways."

"Oh. How much are tokens?"

"Four for a dollar. Three dollars minimum."

"That sounds fair," I said, "I'll take three dollars worth."

"Good man," he said.

I gave him the cash, and he slid a pre-counted stack of 12 tokens from the countertop into his cupped hand, passing them into my up-turned palm. I pocketed them without so much as glancing at them.

I went to the head of one of the hallways. There, inside a plastic wall-mounted case, twenty or so DVD covers were on display. The case was locked with the kind of tiny padlock most commonly seen securing the pages of a young girl's diary. Most genres of pornography were represented in the case, broken into three main catego-ries: straight, gay, and transsexual.

I reached into my pocket and felt the bulk of the twelve coins. I separated one from the bunch and rubbed it between my fingertips as I stared up at the DVD cases behind the acrylic panel. Finally, I lifted my hand from my pocket and I looked at the token for the first time. Brass and lightweight, about the size of a quarter. On one side, a topless woman was pictured from the waist up. "Heads

I Win" it read. On the opposite side, a naked woman's rear end. "Tails You Lose" it said.

I didn't even want to spend them. I wanted to have them as a souvenir. I wanted to frame them and hang them in my apartment. I wanted to pass them out to people I knew. If I had never seen one before, it was a safe bet none of my friends had either. Did they have these tokens in the top tier law schools where my friends learned their trades? In doctoral programs? In office buildings? Did they have them in the Montessori Schools where the teachers of my friends' children encouraged the discovery of varied interests and intelligences in settings that promoted free play and exploration? No, they didn't have them in those places. But there I was. I had them.

Standing in front of the display of video covers, looking up from the token in my hand, I noticed another sign. This one laminated and also apparently made in landscape mode in Microsoft Word, read: "This is not a Safety Zone. No standing for prolonged periods." I put the token in my pocket with the rest and entered the hallway through the things that looked like metal detectors. They didn't register my passing in any observable way.

It was a dark corridor, a hall of doorways leading into about twenty booths, each a little larger than a powder room in a suburban house. But the walls of the booths weren't made of drywall like a suburban bathroom. They were made of the same material as the cheapest furniture from Ikea or Wal-Mart: particleboard covered in plastic veneer. There were no doorknobs. The doors operated against the creaking of springs, which kept them shut. Above the doors, red circular lights were mounted. About a third of them were lit.

There was another sign in the hallway, this one announcing prohibitions against standing, loitering, and lewd behavior. It stated in capital, underlined, enlarged letters that visitors must insert a token in the coin slot upon entering a theater, thus keeping the light outside of the booth lit for as long as they stayed inside.

I pushed into an empty booth and engaged the barrel bolt lock behind me. The room was dark, navigable only by the faint light of a video screen set into the wall, just below eye level. Two black vinyl benches took up most of the floor space. They were bolted to the ground and set perfectly parallel to one another, just a foot or so apart, like pews, where two rows of people could sit looking at the screen, on which the words "Drop A Token In The Slot" blinked. There was a coin slot lit red from within, the type found in video games, that you can press to get your quarter back when something goes wrong. I reached into my pocket for one, then deposited one of my souvenir tokens into the narrow hole.

The screen screamed to life that first time, as it almost always did, with the volume as high as it could possibly go. It was doubly shocking. The noise was startling, of course, but also, like most people, I had very little experience with pornography at high volumes. I pawed at the big, dimly glowing volume buttons mounted on the wall between the token slot and the video screen, lowering the volume until it was silent. The only remaining set of buttons were the same type as the volume controls, glowing plastic circles, bright green and labeled "Vid +" and "Vid –". I tapped "Vid +", and the video on screen changed from a graphic scene of a woman having sex with a man to a graphic scene of a woman having sex with five men.

Scrolling through the options, I understood that the videos playing in my booth corresponded with the DVD cases on display behind plastic outside the hallway. They were never in precisely the same sequence as in the display case. I checked.

I sampled the videos, watching mere seconds of each before advancing to the next, when the video stopped abruptly and returned with no warning to the default screen. "Drop A Token In The Slot."

2

THINGS WERE PERMITTED THERE THAT WERE NOT permitted inside city limits. Smoking indoors, for instance. Most of the customers were men, though I saw straight couples there on rare occasions. I saw transsexuals. Always male to female—"M2F" if you're looking for one online. Once or twice, I saw single women there, but they spoiled the mood a little. I assumed the women who showed up alone were sex addicts. It goes without saying that a great majority of men are sex addicts, or would be if they could manage to get laid. Usually, the straight couples at the arcade just browsed the racks of DVDs or looked at vibrators and lubricants together. The woman would giggle, and the two of them would talk in low tones, the man's voice pitched high, as if he were interviewing a child. *You like this? You like that?* Rarely, they would venture into the video booths, which was when things could get interesting.

Single men appeared to peruse the shelves of videos, but most of them were faking. They were just waiting to see who came in the door, occasionally jingling the tokens in their pockets so guys knew they weren't really exploring Indian porn or Japanese porn or any of the other ethnicities represented on the wire metal racks around which the best view of the entrance could be had.

On either side of the main room were two dark hallways lined with viewing booths—a smoking hallway and a nonsmoking hallway. The corridors were U-shaped and ran parallel on opposite sides of the shopping space. If you entered at the front, you'd walk down the length of the corridor and exit at the back end of the store, emerging into the well-lit emporium, where you could pretend to look at DVDs for a while, or make your way to the opposite hallway to see what was happening there. Or, if you preferred, you could retrace your steps back down the same hallway through which you'd just passed to see what, if anything, had changed since you walked down it a few seconds earlier.

Things that might have changed in the interval:

1. Someone might have exited one of the viewing booths. So there might have been a new guy, a guy you hadn't run into before, walking through the dim light and the bleachy, musky air towards or away from you. If someone had exited, and you liked what you saw, you could walk towards him and look at him, or you could stay put and look at him as he approached you. And if you looked at each other in a certain way, then you might go into a booth together and put a token in the slot, and pick a movie that would play in the background for sixty seconds while the two of you shared the space in whatever way you chose.

2. A red light might have come on outside one or more of the booths. A red light lit up when the booth's occupant dropped a token in the slot, thus starting a movie and signaling to the other visitors that the booth was occupied. If you liked, you could walk up to the door and press against it. If you found it locked, you continued walking as if nothing had happened. If it was unlocked, you could enter and see what the booth held.

3. A red light that had been lit before might have been extinguished, signaling that the movie had ended, leaving the booth's occupant(s) with a few options:
    a) He/they/she (in order of likelihood) could drop another token in the slot to get the movie started again.
    b) He/they/she could exit the booth.
    c) He/they/she could stay in the booth without dropping a token into the slot, which was against the rules.

3

THE BUILDING WAS A CATALOG OF POTENTIAL PARTNERS, all moving in circles and lines and figure eights, from booth to booth, hallway to store to hallway. I was part of the catalog too. I looked at them and determined whether or not they were what I had in mind, and they looked at me and saw if I was what they had in mind, or whether I was close enough.

As a kid, everyone at my school was immensely impressed by a nearby restaurant renowned for employing an unusual gimmick for summoning wait staff. It involved utilizing a miniature flagpole with which all the tables were equipped. In order to capture the attention of your server, instead of waving your arms or crying *waiter!* across a crowded room, you sent a starched and scaled-down Mexican flag to full mast. It was my impression, even at that age, that the wait staff at the Mexican food restaurant suffered abnormal and excessive visits to their various tables, given that the control was so pleasurable and clear-cut.

Sometimes, like the waitresses called to refill half-full bowls of salsa, you ended up with people you wouldn't normally have considered, just because they had flown a flag, and you didn't have anything more pressing to do at the moment.

4

I HEARD STORIES FROM MY FATHER AND AUNT ABOUT THEIR high school days in the small Texas town where I grew up, and where they grew up before me. When they were young, all the high school students hung out at the town square, flirting and talking and showing off their cars. There were all these stories about things that happened there, pranks they played and songs they turned all the way up, who was smoking cigarettes and who was making out or leaving to go make out someplace else.

It seemed like somewhere other than the place where I was growing up, another world where there could exist this semblance of nightlife. I envied everyone who got to experience it, for having something to do in that town where I didn't have anything. Even my cousin had hung out at the town square when she was in high school, and she was only nine years older than me. Somewhere between her youth and mine, the practice fell out of fashion.

Reading about the XXX place in the Missed Connections ads had evoked visions like those I'd once had of weekend nights at the town square. I pictured men leaning against their cars, smoking, fixing their hair in rear-view mirrors, checking one another out, talking casually as if nothing might happen or everything might happen.

I imagined something secret, but also right out in the open for people who took the time to look into it or join, like Freemasonry or the Elks. When I discovered the arcade, it was sort of like that after all. I couldn't believe it.

5

SOON AFTER THAT INITIAL VISIT, I LEARNED THAT THE residents of the surrounding neighborhoods had protested the adult video store when it was first built, and apparently still bore a grudge against the place. I guessed I could understand why. They had gone to the trouble of moving outside of town thinking, naturally, that such a distance would be sufficient to insulate themselves from the city's corrupt influences, and then the corrupt influences came to them. What made it worse was that they were already very near the town dump with all its associated smells and rumbling trucks and groundwater problems and whatever other tradeoffs living close to an enormous landfill must entail.

I didn't know about the protests until I spoke to a man I'd met online. He was in his late forties and had emailed me a photograph of himself taken from inside the cab of his pickup, smiling with Oakley sunglasses pushed up on his head. He was the embodiment of my ideal. Divorced for years, he claimed that he still dated women but said the failed marriage had soured him against them. He certainly didn't date men, though he had fooled around with them off and on his whole life. What he really wanted was a buddy, a friend with whom he could hang out and go golfing and camping and fishing and to sporting events, and of course with whom he could privately have sex because, as all of them will tell you, they prefer women, but there's just something about playing with another guy. Not better, just different. *You know how women are. You know how they complicate everything.*

I'd learned over time to insist on chatting by phone before hooking up. It was prudent, I thought, to see if the guy sounded like the type who might ejaculate and then murder me in the throes of shame, or lock me in his basement for the remainder of my life, or hold me down and rape me. Or drill holes in my head and inject boiling water and hydrochloric acid into my brain, the way Jeffrey Dahmer did with his hookups to try and turn them into sex zombies.

The guy with the Oakley sunglasses was a rare find. Many of the guys I'd met online wouldn't talk on the phone. Those guys didn't want a buddy. They wanted men they'd never met before to come over and fuck or get fucked, then immediately tuck their dripping dicks inside their trousers and leave without requesting so much as a towel. Certainly without so much as the suggestion of intimacy. I once had a guy shout at me for patting his ass as I pulled up my pants to leave. It had been intended as a gesture of butch camaraderie, but he snapped that I shouldn't get any ideas. He wasn't a fag and I sure as fuck wasn't his boyfriend—in case a moments-earlier instance of sodomy had been mistaken for something more substantive.

The man with the Oakley sunglasses was the classic good ol' boy—his slow Texan drawl perfect and utterly unaffected. He wanted me to come over but worried what his neighbors would think. I'd heard that a lot and had the same fear about inviting men to my own place. Guys in our position had the idea that our neighbors—even the ones we'd never met—were tracking our every movement. The guy said he lived in a conservative neighborhood and asked what kind of car I drove. A pickup, I told him, which I knew was the right answer. He said he was going to run some errands, but that I should come by later that evening. We could turn on the football game, drink a beer or two, and see how we got along.

He told me he lived just outside of town. As he described how I would get to his neighborhood I drew the connection.

"You live close to the triple-X place."

A long pause on the line. "You don't go there, do you?" he said. The sudden tone of suspicion suggested I had lost ground with him merely by knowing of its existence.

"I went out there once. I checked it out for the first time a couple of weeks ago." It was true. I had only just discovered the place. "You've never been?"

"Hell, you couldn't pay me to step foot in a place like that. That's the kind of place you get AIDS in. I heard they got a retard there who all he does is scrub cum with a mop all day."

"Aw hell, it's not as bad as all that," I said, more careful than ever to slow and deepen my voice. Though whatever hick burg the guy with the Oakley sunglasses had come from was probably no smaller than my own hometown, the accent—natural on the tongues of everyone else in my family—had never quite stuck in my throat. But I could fake it well enough.

"I never touched anyone out there or anything," I said, knowing that opting for the double negative would have been better, but unable to bring myself to do it. "It's cleaner than you'd guess once you walk inside. But I know what you mean. It's definitely a funny kinda place. I just went on a lark. I thought it was a regular old porn shop, place to get DVDs and all. You should go see for yourself sometime. It's nothing much to be afraid of."

"Shit, I ain't afraid of it. I just know too many people 'round here to have my truck seen in the parking lot of a place like that, even if I did want to go, which I don't."

"Surely people don't pay that much attention to whose cars are in the parking lot," I said, not bothering to detail for him the building's clever arrangement, how it hid cars parked there from visibility by drivers-by.

"I guess you never heard about the protests when it first opened up. It was in the papers. Course that's been a few years back now. Maybe you missed it."

"What kind of protests? People with signs?"

"Yeah, they were out front. Women mostly, holding signs and all that. My neighbor took off work to go out there with her daughter."

"Like a little girl?"

"Yeah, a kid. Or she was then. Might be she's a teenager now."

"There were kids at the protests?"

"I guess so. At least one."

"What kind of signs did they have?"

"Just paper signs on poster board, stapled to stakes like you see on TV."

"What did they say?"

"Hell if I know. I tried to ignore all that."

"Surely you can remember one or two of them."

"Hell, I don't know. Let me think. One of them I think said something about 'Real men don't need porn.' Then another one said something about 'Shame on you, something something, devil something.' I can't remember. What are you so interested for anyway?"

"I'm not interested," I said. "Except, I guess, just because it seems funny protesting a place like that. Of all the things in the world to protest about, I mean."

"Well, maybe you'd feel different if it was in your own neighborhood."

"You do have a point there, sir," I said. "You certainly do have a point."

I wanted to ask a hundred more questions. I'd never have thought of the residents of those neighborhoods as community activists, though it did make sense that, if they were going to protest anything, it would be the possibility of gay sex in their immediate vicinity.

"Did you go to the protests too?" I said, allowing myself this one final question on the subject.

"Nah, I signed the petition like everyone else around here—the folks from the subdivisions, and those of us who still have some acreage in the area. 'Course, even though we all signed it and someone took it to a city council meeting, it didn't come to nothing. They steamrolled everything through and opened it up anyhow. Truth is, I'm surprised nobody ever chucked a grenade at the place yet."

6

LATER THAT NIGHT, THE GUY WITH THE OAKLEY SUNGLASSES gave an excuse about why he couldn't invite me over. Maybe because of my questions about the arcade, or maybe he had just jerked off and changed his mind. It didn't matter. It was better that way, in fact. Since our conversation, I had felt magnetized to the arcade. I couldn't imagine how I'd let a whole two weeks pass since my first visit.

I had thought about it over that time, of course, but it didn't really occur to me to go back. I had already achieved my aim. I'd taken those scattered Missed Connections dispatches and tracked down the source. I had been someplace none of my friends or family would ever go, smelled the smells and seen the sights.

The image of a grenade being thrown at the arcade was lodged in my mind. When the guy with the Oakley sunglasses said it, I pictured some outraged shit kicker driving by in his pickup, chucking a bomb from his window. Or his fat, country wife tossing it, hanging out the passenger side, their daughter in the backseat cheering the great pig on, a crumpled protest sign at her feet, reading "Shame on you, something something, devil something."

The idea that people like that wanted to blow it up increased the appeal of the arcade enormously. And the more I thought of it, the more I realized how little I'd seen on my one trip out, how I'd left too soon after my arrival on that first visit and with too many tokens still in my pocket. I had them in a zip lock bag hidden in my underwear drawer. After talking to the guy in the Oakley sunglasses I realized that, though I had been there, I'd barely experienced the place at all.

I took a shower and changed into a clean pair of jeans and a striped polo shirt that I didn't like particularly, but had twice been complimented on. It was the perennial scene: Junior Prepares for His Big Date, with all the usual beats, except for the slapped-on aftershave.

Entering the arcade, I nodded to the clerk. It was a different fellow than the one I'd seen on my first visit. This guy looked decidedly more normal and non-porny than the other one. He looked almost like one of my college roommates—shaggy hair, a worn and faded polo shirt, ratty jeans, his haphazard appearance a perfect opposite to the studied attempt at goth coolness I'd recognized in the other clerk.

As the rumpled clerk counted out stacks of tokens, the goth clerk, wearing his trademark fedora, emerged from a backroom door behind the counter. I overheard them as I made my way to a rack of DVDs.

"Anything else I need to know?" the rumpled clerk said.

"That's it, I think," the goth clerk said. "Oh, except there's a thing on the desk about another guy they banned yesterday. He can't come on the premises at all anymore. If you see him, call Ronnie."

The rumpled clerk picked up a piece of paper, which I could tell from the reverse side was a printed photograph surrounded by text, like a notice someone would hang on a telephone pole about his lost dog.

"I know this guy," the rumpled clerk said. "He drives a blue Honda."

"Yeah, that's what Rick said too. I've never seen him. He must only do nights."

The goth clerk shouldered a black bag and made his way out from behind the counter and through the exit door.

I stood pretending to peruse their selection of overpriced DVDs while keeping my eye on the counter and the front door. The pocketful of tokens recalled days of my youth when, left by my shopping parents to roam the mall alone, I cashed in a five- or ten-dollar bill for that clanking jackpot rush from a video game arcade's coin changing machine. Before the quarters started to dwindle, the options seemed limitless.

After several minutes passed with no one coming or going, and a few glances from the rumpled clerk, I goaded myself to the mouth of one of the hallways, where I lingered briefly before forcing myself inside. My shoulders relaxed when I found the corridor empty, save for one or two red lights illuminated above the doors. I chose an empty booth, locked the door behind myself, and popped a few tokens into the glowing slot.

As shrieking porn began to play, I used the light from my phone's screen to scan the benches for anything I wouldn't want to sit on and discovered a gift from heaven: a forgotten pack of Camels with a book of matches in its cellophane. I had been in the process of quitting for a couple of weeks by then, and had been unsuccessful, despite the fact that I had completely stopped keeping cigarettes on me. One problem was that I didn't actually want to quit at all. I loved smoking. It was the cop I was in love with who didn't like it. I was giving it up for him.

I took a cigarette from the half-empty pack and lit one. I didn't change the movie on the screen. I just sat staring up at it, filling the booth with smoke and idly rubbing my dick through my jeans.

Before I'd smoked even half the cigarette, I was startled by the sound of someone trying to enter the booth. I was perfectly silent, though of course he knew someone was inside, not simply because of the light above the door, but also due to the loud squeals of a woman in a nurse's uniform being screwed onscreen by a man in green scrubs and a surgeon's mask.

After pushing against the door several times, the person on the other side actually started knocking on it in a quiet and creepily persistent manner that filled me with panic. My eyes shot around the booth like someone in a horror movie seeking out a weapon in their limited environment. The lit cigarette was the only thing I felt I could use if it came down to defending myself. Maybe I could blind him if he somehow broke through the door.

I knew if I didn't respond, he would be forced to move on eventually, but he was still there, quietly pressing and knocking on the door when the tokens ran out and the movie ended. Suddenly the room was quiet and I heard a whispering voice that I hadn't been able to distinguish from the din moments earlier. Without rising from my bench, I leaned in the direction of the door to hear it.

"Hey," it was saying. "Hey, let me in."

"Go away," I whispered. Then I rose and quickly put three tokens in the slot. In an instant, the screen came back to life with another scene from the video, which now showed a woman having her temperature taken rectally by a physician while she performed oral sex on an orderly. I rapidly tapped the Vol+ button until the deafening moans of the medical assistant drowned out all other sounds.

Every muscle in my body was tense as I cranked myself around to see the shadows of the would-be intruder's feet beneath the door. A minute later, after they withdrew, I calmed down. But after a short time they returned. He pressed on the door, and the voice hissed something inaudible, the shadow lingering for a moment before the shoes retreated again for the last time.

I sat in the booth and smoked three more cigarettes one after another, dropping tokens in the slot each time the movie ended. Then I rose, noiselessly slid the bolt free from the lock, and peered through the open door. The hallway was empty.

I rushed towards the brightness of the store as if making my way to a protected shelter. But the eeriness of the dark hallway had carried over into the shopping space, which was still vacant and utterly silent. Now even the counter was unmanned, the clerk gone.

When I found myself alone in terrible and shameful situations, my first assumption was always that the end of the world was upon us, and I had been caught with my pants down. Had the nuclear apocalypse been announced, and here I was about to die alone, blasted apart along with one of the biggest collections of sex toys and videos in Central Texas? Had the man at my door, his voice raspy with radiation illness, been trying to warn me?

I noticed some movement at the front of the store. Just outside the exit, I could see something. It was the rumpled clerk pacing and having a cigarette in the one place where he could smoke while watching both the parking lot and the front desk.

The tokens still filled my pocket like a bag of marbles, but I was afraid to go to the other hallway and run into whoever had been at my door. I took a cigarette from the pack of Camels, and went to where the rumpled clerk was smoking.

"'Scuse me, bro," I said, a portrait of heterosexuality. "Mind if I bum a light?"

The clerk narrowed his eyes at me, but reached into his pocket and handed me his lighter. "Here you go."

I lit my smoke and gave it back to him. "Thanks. How's it going tonight? You just starting your shift?"

"That's right," he said, glancing at his watch. "Only seven hours and forty-three minutes to go."

"But who's counting, right? Anyway, I bet the time passes quick. It must be an interesting place to work."

"Can be," he said.

"You worked here long?"

By my posture, movement, and eyes, I did everything in my power, short of hocking a loogie, to indicate that these questions were merely friendly conversation and in no way a come-on. I could tell the guy was cautious and even a little annoyed, but he was too polite to tell me to fuck off.

"I've been here about six months."

"Cool. You like it?"

"It's okay."

"Seems pretty dead tonight. Does it ever get really busy around here?"

"Yeah, it gets busy," he said.

"So when does it pick up?"

"Different times. Like around nine o'clock people tend to show up. After the bars close at two. Lunch hours are busy, and I've heard that Sunday after church a lot of guys pop in."

"After church?"

"Yeah, supposedly. I've never seen that myself. I work nights."

"I heard your coworker say something about someone getting banned. I was just wondering, I mean, how…"

"Phone's ringing man," the rumpled clerk said, stubbing his cigarette out in the ashtray he'd used to prop open the door. "Gotta go."

He scooted the can out of the way, and the door slammed closed with him on the other side. I took two more drags from my cigarette, then left what remained of the pack in the ashtray and headed to my pickup with the tokens still in my pocket, more to add to my collection. Mine was the only vehicle left in the parking lot, aside from a beat up Toyota that matched the rumpled clerk perfectly.

7

ALL OF MY PROBLEMS BEGAN IN JUNIOR HIGH SCHOOL WHEN my best friend stole a porn magazine. We had a terrific indoor newsstand in our small town, owned and operated by the same family who delivered everyone's newspapers.

At the front of the shop against a blacked-out window stood the shelves of porn, a section demarcated by two magazine racks facing one another. If you were looking at the magazines nearby, you could see—and, in fact, reach—the contents of the little smut alley without actually entering it. At twelve years of age, I created a diversion, giving my friend the opportunity to lean in and snatch a magazine. I carried some smoke bombs to the clerk, then swept them off the counter so that the he had to stoop to pick them up. After I paid, my friend and I ran away, him with the magazine tucked under his shirt.

We made straight for our fort in the reedy bank of a drainage ditch near his house. It was a tremendous thrill, even if I do recall registering a little disappointment when I finally saw what he had nabbed—a small digest-style black-and-white rag printed on cheap newsprint. Sex stories filled most of its pages, and the few small photos it did contain were blurry and hard to see, printed in grainy grayscale. My friend and I took turns taking the magazine home, reading it over and over again until we had all but memorized it, in the process learning with awestruck disbelief about such things as golden showers and fisting. I was never without men's magazines after that.

A friend's older brother returned from the Navy bearing gifts. I had written to him several times, and to show his appreciation he gave me some German pornography from his travels. My favorite was a naturist magazine printed on thick card stock with full-bleed images that seemed already to be decades old. Its incomprehensible text was in German, but I could see that the magazine was arranged like a tour of a nudist colony, starting at the entrance gate. There were people hanging out at picnic tables naked and playing volleyball naked and just walking around or sitting in a circle talking, always naked. There were pictures of kids too, just standing around like everyone else. That worried me a little, although nothing about the magazine seemed particularly pornographic, even the final page, which was a photograph of a naked man lying on top of a naked woman. No genitals were visible in that picture, not so much as a breast. Hers were pressed against the man's chest. The two of them were looking into one another's eyes and smiling.

Around the same time, I paid the older brother of a classmate to take all that was left of my birthday money and purchase as many porn magazines as the cash would buy. I rode with him to the newsstand, and stayed ducked down in his car while he went inside. I was amazed at his apparent ease with the errand. He emerged with a black plastic bag and gave it to me in exchange for the twenty dollars we had agreed upon.

No one was home when he dropped me off at my house. I spilled the contents of the bag onto the floor of my room. Of the titles, I had only ever heard of *Penthouse*. The others—*Club*, *Oui*, and *Cherry*—were new to me. Years passed before I came to understand that *Oui* was the French word for "yes." I pronounced it "oh-you-eye," the same way I pronounced *US* magazine—"you-ess."

I had seen porn magazines before—the naturist magazine from Germany and Playboy-style centerfolds—but nothing that qualified as hardcore. I had also never seen an erect penis other than my own. One of my school friends had told me it was illegal to show them in print. So maybe it was the shock of seeing one for the first time that made me ejaculate, or maybe it was that I had wanted to see one for so long. The glistening example on the page I flipped to was enormous and pointed at a woman, inches from her belly. I remember shaking all over and coming in my pants, then immediately putting the magazines back in the black plastic bag.

8

THE ARCADE HAD A MUSKY, SWEATY AROMA, WITH HEAVY overtones of the scent I've seen described as "mushroomy" and "earthy," though really it's the smell of the male crotch and nothing else. It's the stink that rises from your pants as you take a leak in the middle of the summer after walking around the city all day. It's a pleasant smell, always different but the same on every man you meet.

In a forum online I saw a thread about favorite smells. There was the usual stuff about fresh cut grass, babies, and whatever, but slowly a controversial contingent arose which named the smell of their own balls as their favorite aroma. At first, it wasn't taken seriously. It seemed like the usual internet trolls saying the least constructive, most absurd thing imaginable. But as the day progressed that answer received more and more votes and notes of agreement. A conversation arose. The internet is a miracle at times like that, not just in the way it brings likeminded people together, but in the way it suggests that we are all of the same mind after all, connected by invisible trails like neural paths.

In the arcade, the smell was everywhere, mixed with a certain bleachiness. Just vaguely. Diluted. Enough to know the place was being kept up. It was a nice smell, actually, the way it hit you in the cool air the second you opened the door.

I once worked with a guy whose girlfriend's company produced scents for retail stores and restaurants. The smell of cinnamon rolls in shopping malls was the company's landmark achievement. They could duplicate the smell of anything, improve upon it chemically, and then, through patented machinery, send out their proprietary scents in invisible puffs, all but forcing people to consume impossibly high-calorie desserts as they shopped.

Smells, he told me, could make people do all sorts of things.

9

ONE OF THE GREAT MYSTERIES OF THE ARCADE WAS THAT, despite the smell of bleach, I never once saw anyone cleaning it. It was impossible to avoid imagining the chore after seeing so much genetic material splattered around, particularly after hearing the rumor from the man with the Oakley sunglasses about an intellectually disabled cumscrubber on staff. But I never saw so much as a bottle of cleaning solution or a mop propped against a wall. Maybe they tidied in the mornings, but I usually went at night, and most of the booths were still pretty clean by that time, which would seem unlikely considering what the rumpled clerk told me about there being a lunch hour crowd.

Of course, sometimes the booths were just destroyed. Though I tried to be mindful about choosing carefully, there often wasn't enough light to see what was going on inside until I started a video. Only when the screen was lit could I see the mess on the vinyl benches and on the floor. Once in a while I found myself actually slipping in cum, skidding around the tiny space praying to find traction before I landed in a puddle of some stranger's gooey discharge. Some booths had cigarette butts ground into the linoleum floor, along with wads of used tissues and paper towels from the bathroom, the smell of ass and cum as thick as if someone had been burning some vile scented candle. I hated finding myself in booths like that. After starting a movie I felt obligated to wait for the time to elapse before leaving, as if it were somehow rude to leave a light lit outside an empty booth. I practically cowered against the door counting the seconds until the minute passed. Some compartments were so horrible I wasn't able to wait it out.

I tried to pay special attention to the floors in avoidance of the shimmering puddles that made my sneakers stick to the ground for hours, that peeling-off-the-floor sound an unwelcome reminder of what I was doing with my spare time. Over the course of several visits to the arcade, I learned that there were other reasons to worry that the floors weren't sufficiently sanitized.

One session after another I went out and paid my tokens to sit alone in a booth with my door locked. After I got into the flow of the place and figured out when other men were actually there, I started overhearing every variety of interaction. I discovered that with my dick in my hand and my ear pressed against the surface of the thin laminate wall separating me from those actually involved in the sorts of activities for which the place existed, I could have something like an encounter out there—a vicarious experience completely free of any fears of infection or the face-to-face intimacy I didn't know how to process.

The sounds I heard made me feel as auditorially attuned as I'd always heard the blind were, my ears twitching at the barely detectible slip of a button through a buttonhole, every stretch of elastic, as anxious hands reached into unfamiliar underwear. No matter what I heard or for how long, I always hungered for more, staying later than I had intended in hopes of listening in on another encounter.

It wasn't easy making out the details of my neighbors' interactions. I was stuck guessing at what was happening over the racket of full-volume porn on all sides—the aural equivalent to my childhood attempts at discerning bits of pornography from scrambled channels my parents didn't pay for.

As I innocently strategized ways to overhear more of my neighbors' encounters, I realized that most of the sounds I received came not through the wall but via a small gap of about three inches at the bottom of every partition. From there, it didn't take long to realize that if I got on my hands and knees, I might be able to actually see into the neighboring compartment. I don't know why the walls didn't extend all the way to the floor. Knowing that place, it might have been to accommodate precisely that pervert's view.

The first time I worked up the nerve to try it, I heard my target making his way down the hallway, testing every door as he did. He pushed on one door and found it locked, then pushed on another and found it unlocked but empty. He pushed on another and opened the door to find someone inside with whom he didn't wish to connect. I heard a brief exchange of murmurs before he exited and moved along down the hallway, running his hand against the flat plane of doors like a kid running a stick along a picket fence. He tried my door as he passed, found it locked, of course, and then moved along to the neighboring booth, which for some reason he decided to enter and occupy for a while.

Without locking his door, the man dropped a couple of tokens in the slot. In my booth, I did the same with my volume turned all the way down and my ears pricked. Twice over the next few minutes a visitor entered my neighbor's compartment. I heard the door creak open, and could only imagine what was happening as the two of them sized each other up in the darkness before determining they were not a match. When the third man came along, there was a long pause. The two of them exchanged words in bass whispers I couldn't make out. Then the man who had just entered turned and locked the door.

Doing my best to conceal the sound of my breath, I squinted at the floor searching for anything that might give me AIDS if it got in my eye or into a tiny cut of which I was unaware. I knelt, then put my hands to the ground and lowered my face until I could make out two pairs of feet, one standing near the screen wearing a pair of black dress shoes with the dark cuffs of his slacks resting on their laces, the other wearing a pair of jeans and work boots covered in dry mud.

First they were on opposite sides of the booth. Then the guy in the dress shoes dropped a few tokens in the slot. One of them whispered something. Only the words "suck" and "you" were audible to me. I heard the clanking of belt buckles as they came undone, then the feet moved closer. There were more whispers before the man in slacks got onto his knees without, I noted, nearly so thorough a check of the floor as I had executed. The man in the work boots sighed, and I heard his belt clanking rhythmically. At last he separated from the suit long enough to pull his jeans down until they rested on top of his boots. The suit half stood to pull down his own pants, then got back into position and continued sucking. I could hear the sounds of his mouth against the other guy's dick. They both groaned quietly. I could see the silhouette of the suit's fist wrapped around his own member, his bare knees on the floor. When the movie stopped, the man in work boots reached down to search the pockets of his crumpled pants until he found a handful of tokens to cram in the slot.

I couldn't see the suit's mouth on the worker's dick, but I could see his hand working at himself, and I took out my own dick so I could time my rhythm with his. I could hear the worker getting closer and closer as the sound of the slurping grew louder and more intense. At last, the worker sighed heavily and let go, forgetting himself entirely and letting loose a series of loud exhalations as the suit kept at him until he was really and truly empty.

Then I saw them straighten up. The guy on his knees stood. "Thanks, man," one of them whispered. Then the other said, "Hey, thank *you*." They got themselves in order, pulled their pants up and tucked in their shirts. The guy with the work boots said, "Here, man, take these," and I heard the sound of him removing his remaining tokens from his pocket and spilling them into the suit's hand.

I eventually learned that by inserting my tokens at the same time as my neighbors, I could time my exit from a compartment to co-incide with theirs. It completed the scene to see the faces when I could. Often they were guys I'd already passed in my rounds. It was interesting seeing who ended up with who.

Sometimes I felt jealous watching the men make their way out of the booths, down the hallway, and out into the world. Particu-larly if I found one or both of the men attractive, or if one or both had spurned me before connecting with each other. I couldn't help wondering what it was that made me not good enough. It was a familiar feeling. I'd had it off and on my entire life.

When I was eight or nine, I watched the Olympics with my parents. The gymnasts were competing, and some of them appeared

to be almost the same age as me. I was more interested in their performances than I was in the other contests since I was in a gymnas-
tics class and was among the best in my age group. My parents, in
a presumably innocent attempt to engage me, persisted in asking
my opinions of the athletes onscreen.

Didn't she do a great job?

Did you see that flip?

What kind of score do you think he'll get?

I could feel my face reddening.

"I could do that if I wanted to," I said, the volume and pitch of
my voice rising. "If I practiced harder, I could do that too."

But I had already heard the commentators going on about how
many years the athletes had worked to perfect their skills. I had
heard about how they were selected in earliest youth and recognized to have abilities possessed by a minuscule fraction of hu-
mankind. After a few minutes more, I went to my room and bawled
thinking about all the things from which I was already excluded.

Back then, I still clung to the fantasy that I might be a prodigy.
It wasn't immediately clear what my special ability might be, but
I knew I must have one. I had the idea that everyone might be a
prodigy at something. It was just a matter of finding out what it was
you were so unexpectedly good at. I sat at a piano for the first time
believing it as likely as not that I would be able to play perfectly
without a single lesson. Same for guitar, trumpet, drums, harmon-
ica, tennis, golf, baseball, karate, and tae kwon do. It seemed to me
that the next thing I tried, whatever it was, would surely lead to the
discovery of an unaccountable superpower-like skill. I was in my
middle twenties before, defeated, I finally gave up the idea.

10

ONE DAY I DROPPED A TOKEN IN THE SLOT AND SETTLED ON
a movie and an appropriate volume, then got down to peek into
the neighboring booth. There, I discovered a dark figure on his
hands and knees peering back at me. Startled, I stood up, feeling
like a monkey who had discovered a mirror in his cage. I almost
bolted, but something stopped me, and, heart pounding, I lowered
my pants and knelt down where he could see me. He watched for a
long while before he slowly slid his fingers beneath the wall.

"Come here," he whispered through the opening. "Come here."

I felt possessed edging forward along the floor until his spidery
fingers finally grasped me. He touched me with tremendous care,
stroking me slowly and hyper-deliberately, as if measuring my
dick or performing some kind of examination of my erection. My
head swam as his hand traveled its length over and over again.

For a moment, it was as if a black cloth had been dropped over
my mind. My eyes were closed. I knew I was at the arcade, but
I didn't feel like I was inside of anything. The hand pulled and
pulled, and I rested my head against the wall separating us. Gradually, I felt everything begin to rush, all the feeling in my body
focused on that one point like the tip of a tornado.

The feeling grew and shifted, and as I drew closer to coming, the
whirlwind moved into my chest, where a panic rose. In an instant
I found myself pulled from the hold of the spider fingers. Frantic
with anxiety like a drug released into my blood, I buttoned my
pants, and pushed into the dark hallway and beyond into the main
room. I stood catching my breath and leaking into my pants at my
usual post, barely bothering to make a show of pretending to look
at DVDs. A few men exited the hallway at intervals, each of them

glancing up at me as they passed. I couldn't even guess which of them had touched me.

Later, I'd instruct myself to memorize everyone's shoes so I'd be able to know who was who at all times, but it was easy to forget to look at them, and even when I remembered to look, it was easy to forget who was wearing what.

11

CALLING THE COP WAS NEVER EXPLICITLY FORBIDDEN.
I understood that it was discouraged, yes. And I understood, obviously, that it was awkward to phone when the kid was around.
What no one seemed to appreciate was that it was at least as awkward for me as it was for the kid, and probably more so.

I knew the cop's schedule, so I knew with a reasonable degree
of certainty when he might be away from the kid. Over the years,
we'd spoken while he patrolled the town in his cruiser, so it wasn't
such a strange thing to call him, really. In fact, it wouldn't have
been strange at all in any circumstance other than our present one.

He didn't answer the first time I called, but just before I went to
voicemail I heard what I was certain was the sound of him trying to
pick up at the last moment. I didn't know what had happened, but
I was certain I recognized a crackle on the line, something going
wrong. Whatever it was, it left me with the sense that the cop had
just made it to his phone but failed to hit "talk" quickly enough,
and in some fifty-fifty lottery of digital telephonics, I had mistakenly ended up going to voicemail when he had actually intended
to take the call. I listened to his outgoing voicemail message, then
disconnected.

On my second attempt, instead of selecting his name from my
phone's directory, as I usually did, I dialed his number manually.
I'd recently found that though my phone would say I was calling
his number, when I tried him all I'd get was an abrupt end to the
ringing as if the call had connected, "Hello?" I'd say. "Hello, can
you hear me?" Then, after a short pause the line would go dead.
On one occasion, I rang seven times, and the same thing happened
each time. I never did get in touch with him that day. He later told

me that his phone hadn't shown a single missed call from me. Who knew what was going on when technology was involved? Sometimes I really did think it was conspiring against us.

I grew sweaty at the thought that this could turn into another of those episodes, and I'd be trapped calling over and over again in a loop of uncertainty. But the second time I tried him, he picked up on the third ring. When I realized I was hearing his actual, non-recorded voice my eyes welled up instantly. He hadn't forgotten me. We were still connected. That itself buoyed me, a sensation I desperately needed when we spoke, since remaining upbeat and casual for the duration of an entire conversation was all but impossible for me by that point.

"Hello?" he said. He didn't sound angry or even annoyed. He sounded, as he always did in his slow, country voice, pleasant and patient and completely balanced and calm. He was exactly the kind of police officer you would want to encounter in the real world, being in natural possession of two qualities that most police officers famously lack: reasonableness and tolerant good humor. I had come to see him as an accidental Buddhist capable of experiencing the present moment as if from a great distance of time, seeing both its depth and its absurdity. The only place where his wisdom failed him was in his insane new romantic entanglement, which was utterly beyond my comprehension.

"Hey, it's me," I said, tripping over a cheery tone I should have practiced beforehand.

"Hey," he said. "What's up?"

"Did you just miss a call from me?"

"Yeah, I was on the radio."

"Oh. I'm just trying to figure out if there's something wrong with my phone. This one's acting really weird lately."

"Huh," he said.

"Anyway. So, how's everything going? Anything new happening?"

"Not really. Just the usual stuff."

"You guys all settled in at the house now, got his stuff all moved in?"

"Yep, it's all pretty much come together now."

"That's great."

"Yeah, so far so good."

"Very cool. I mean, I still think you're completely crazy moving him in so soon, but I'm sure you know what you're doing."

"We'll see one way or the other, I guess," he said. "Listen, I can't stay on for too long tonight. I'm supposed to go talk to this guy about these scammers who keep sticking these 'we buy houses' signs everywhere."

Oh, I loved when he let slip those little details about his world. A conversation about bandit sign scammers! It was both fascinating and utterly mundane—a tiny window into his daily life. Collecting those facts, gathering them together like a great nest made of tiny shreds, I could feel that I knew him inside and out.

"But you're doing okay, sounds like," he said.

"Oh, sure, everything's fine. Everything is just normal and regular like always."

I debated bringing up the arcade. Keeping secrets seemed like a bad idea when I was doing my best to execute a complete reversal and demonstrate my ability to be a perfectly open and transparent person. I went back and forth about it. Maybe my stories from the arcade would give me the appearance of being an adventurous, independent, and unpredictable person, the kind of man he would want to live with forever and ever, enjoying an endlessly changing and unknowable future together. Or maybe it would make me seem like a typical promiscuous homo whose claims of desperate, eternal love were all talk. He might even use it as an excuse to sever ties with me, as the kid was undoubtedly pressuring him to do. Then again, maybe it would spark some jealousy in him that would grow and grow until it changed everything. I decided not to mention the arcade yet. I could always bring it up later.

"I was thinking if you're in the mood later this week, maybe you could get away and meet me for lunch. There's a place right between us. Next to that motel on the highway. That diner that supposedly has such good fried chicken?"

"I can't meet you for lunch."

"We don't have to eat if you don't want. We could just hang out. Or even just get naked and have a little fun. Not that you're not getting enough of that as it is."

Silence.

"I mean, you know, I really do miss you a lot," I said, "if that still means anything to you."

"I know you do. You've just got to calm down a little. Let the dust settle."

"I'm calm," I said. "Honestly. I'm totally calm. I don't want you thinking I'm not, because I'm doing a lot better. I mean, maybe I had too much caffeine earlier or something, but really I'm totally calm."

"Good," he said. "That's good to hear. But, listen, I've really got to go now."

"Right, no problem. I was just calling to say hi."

"Well, take care of yourself."

"You too. And we'll talk really soon. I might try you back tomorrow or the next day to see if you're around."

"Actually, don't. We're going out of town for a long weekend."

"Oh."

"But we'll talk another time soon."

"Where are you going?"

"I really have to go now. We'll talk soon."

"Okay, I wasn't trying to keep you. I was just wondering. But I understand. Okay. Have fun."

"You too. Take care, buddy."

"Okay then. Bye."

12

SOMETIMES I COULD HEAR TOKENS DROPPING INTO A container behind the screen, the sound like a quarter falling into a pile of quarters in the bottom of a plastic five-gallon bucket. Usually only one clerk worked the arcade at a time, and sometimes he'd have to go into the little hallway behind the booths to resolve a maintenance issue. Alone in a compartment, I could hear the opening of the heavy door leading into the tight passage. I could see the light come on through the coin slot, a bright white light different from the other lights in the store. Putting my eye to the slot, I could see inside. It was like looking into the workings of a pinball machine. Everything was indistinct, and it was hard to tell what was happening. I could see the figure moving around if he stood in the right place. Then, very quickly, because they couldn't leave the sales floor unattended for long, the light would go out and I would hear the sound of the heavy door closing. Then I was alone in the booth again. I spent a lot more time alone in those booths than I ever did with someone else.

13

HOME FROM THE ARCADE LATE ONE NIGHT, I DISCOVERED an email from Malcolm. I hadn't heard from him in several months. Malcolm, who didn't know my real name, my regular email address, or even my phone number, addressed me as Sam, a name I sometimes used with men. We had been in communication off and on for a couple of years, sometimes speaking for days in a row and sometimes falling out of touch for long spans of time. I considered him a kind of friend since it was undeniable he knew many things about me that no one else in my life ever would.

We'd met online during one of several periods when I felt I absolutely had to have sex with another man in order to feel like a normal human being again. I thought of it like an illness, the way vampires felt compelled to drink blood even if they didn't want to be vampires and were in fact moral beings who had been transformed quite against their will.

When we met, I hadn't had much experience, just quick and risky things, sometimes in motel rooms, but mostly in cars—hurried blowjobs in parking lots that made me come so fast out of nervousness and excitement that the experience itself was only ever a fraction as long as the drive to the agreed-upon location. For days after, I was sleepless with shame, swearing through hour after hour of insomnia that I'd never do it again.

During one of my frenzies, Malcolm responded to an ad I'd posted online. He emailed me several pictures of himself, and I replied in kind, stopping short of sending any of my face, which I always refused to do. His photos revealed an attractive, balding guy in his mid forties, hairy-chested, with about thirty pounds of extra weight and a tasteful, expensive-looking duvet cover. We traded the usual emails about what we wanted to do to one another and things we didn't want or refused to do. His was the typical "no scat or pain" requirement, whereas I detailed my prohibitions in a lengthy bullet-point index to which he replied, "Haha, nice list." I liked him. Like a zookeeper who had by chance encountered one of my species before, he seemed to intuitively know how to deal with me. Most people had no idea.

I was weirdly titillated when I learned that Malcolm lived in a neighborhood in a far-away part of the city where people with money lived. When I asked for his phone number he replied with it right away. I called, first blocking my number by dialing *67 like a prank-calling teenager, and, though I felt his gayness was audible, it wasn't too bad, and I found I truly liked him.

We talked for a long time about all sorts of things. Then, around 1:00 a.m. he invited me to his house. I still feared he might be a lunatic because who else would invite a stranger to his private residence in the middle of the night. Though I was deep into a cycle of same-sex mania, I was exhausted, so I asked if we could just jack off on the phone together.

"Sounds good, Sam," he said. "It's late and I've already got my dick out."

"So do I," I said, as if we had just discovered an unexpected commonality.

After we came, I hung up and found I didn't feel horrible the way I usually did after a sexual attack. I hadn't actually touched anyone but myself. It was nothing but fantasy. No one had officially sinned or done anything wrong. I found, too, that the pressure had been released somewhat. I didn't feel compelled to spend the next day finding someone else to have sex with. When Malcolm emailed early the next evening asking if I'd like to come over, I ignored it for several days, replying later that I had been out of town and rarely checked that particular account.

We never met in person, but talked on the phone with some frequency after that. We spoke about what was going on in our lives, and as time passed, we even talked about other men—the ones I saw very rarely, and the ones he connected with more frequently.

I felt a twinge of possessiveness at the thought of Malcolm having sex with anyone other than me, but I could never quite work up the nerve to meet him in real life. He was twenty years my senior, and he listened to all my stories and anxieties as if he knew exactly what I was going through. Every time I made what seemed to me to be a completely bizarre confession, he replied, "That's pretty normal, I think" or "That's understandable."

At some point, he began a romance with someone he'd met. At first the man only wanted to come over and give Malcolm rim jobs while jerking him off. But after several visits consisting of the same spectacular—per Malcolm—tonguing, they slowly graduated to kissing and then talking. Malcolm and I continued to chat regularly while they were dating, the two of us jerking off over the phone and eventually over online video chats in which I'd point the camera at my body and never allow him to see my face. After watching each other come in grainy, jerky video, we'd say good night, both correctly taking for granted that as soon as we'd shot our loads, the call had reached its end.

The expiration of the rim job champ's lease precipitated their impulsive cohabitation, an event that unfolded during one of our many lulls in communication. One day I received an email from Malcolm that read:

"Dear Sam, I wanted to let you know that Ron moved in with me. (Crazy, I know.) I won't be able to talk late at night anymore, and I can't have you calling whenever you feel like it. I'll miss our wee-hours chats, but we can still find time to talk if you want, and you can always reach me via email if you need me. I hope you're well. Malcolm."

I hadn't heard from him at all since then, though I can't say I missed him terribly. I had been having a parallel relationship with the cop all along, just talking and getting to know one another, until, unlike Malcolm and I, we had met at last.

Before reading Malcolm's email, just seeing his name in my in-box, I suddenly felt as if, now that the cop had abandoned the playground, some great cosmic seesaw had tilted, revealing Malcolm on the other end in his place. He wasn't the one I wished to see, but maybe he could be the key to something. It seemed impossibly strange that I hadn't consulted him sooner. I hadn't told him about my desperation and sorrow or asked his advice about what to do next. I'd always believed that people appeared in my life at precisely the right moment, and here Malcolm was again. He'd be the one to help me come up with a plan for how to prove my love and get the cop back.

Of course, the cop and the kid were on yet another in a series of long weekend getaways, which they seemed always to be taking. Before the kid, the cop never took vacation days. He had been hoarding them apparently, waiting for the right teenager to blunder into his life.

I opened the email from Malcolm.

"Dear Sam, Long time, no talk. I hope you're alive and well. I miss you! I'm alone in a hotel room in a strange city called Boston, Massachusetts. Have you heard of it? I had three or four drinks at the bar downstairs, and now I'm getting ready for bed. It's a whole hour later here. I'm in a fancy penthouse suite, which is my new home for three months or so while I whip this place into shape and help them relaunch after—I'm not allowed to tell you, don't ask, I really can't say, stop pressuring me—a (smallish) bedbug infestation and a (largish) black mold problem. Based on my first meeting with the staff today, I'm pretty sure most of them are brain damaged from the black mold exposure, but I can't fire any of them for fear they'll sue. You know, the usual! Anyway, I'm away from home for a while, and am only going back for occasional weekends, so we need to catch up. I'm going to bed now, but call whenever. I don't know anyone here, except for the brain-damaged employees. Save me, Malcolm."

I tried phoning him, even though the email was from hours earlier, but got no answer. I left a long, hyperactive message on his voicemail, trying to summarize the events of the past several weeks so speedily that I probably sounded more like a meth addict than the victim of a broken heart.

I sat down and elaborated in a pages-long email about the cop, the kid, and my heartbreak, crying as I typed and then signing off, "I'm literally crying as I type this. Sam."

14

THE FIRST TIME I ACTUALLY ENTERED A BOOTH WITH someone else, it was a couple. They gave me a look in the main room, the fluorescent tube lights glowing down on us from the high ceiling. They must have given one another a look too, to agree upon me, and then they gave me the look together. They seemed sexually serious in a way that I wasn't, as if they belonged to that class of people who devote part of each paycheck to the pursuit of sex, who devote rooms of their house to it, who join clubs and groups devoted to their favorite type of sex, who get tattoos pertaining to their sexual penchants and partialities, who have a special wardrobe that enables them to live more fully in the world of their fantasies. One of the men was wearing leather pants and a dog collar. The other looked muscular in denim and a work shirt. He had severe and asymmetric facial features. I pictured him as the oddball on some construction crew about town, while the other probably spent most of his day in a large dog kennel. Still, they were sexy in their way.

A friend once told me that when faced with a situation in which violence or sex might occur one should always try not to smile. A guy comes up to you on the street and starts asking you strange questions. You feel like he's sizing you up. Maybe he's going to mug you or hurt you or just fuck with you. It's the instinct of most people to give the guy a smile, or to let out a short laugh and say, "What is this, buddy?" My friend says that's the worst thing you can do. He says you should do just the opposite. He says to treat it like what you think it might be from the beginning. Somebody fucking with you on the street is no reason to smile.

The same rule applies to sex. My friend says you should behave the same way you would if you were being confronted by a predator. Narrow your eyes, tilt your head in an expression of humorless miscomprehension. *You talkin' to me?*

That's the look the members of the sexually serious pair gave me. This was before I'd learned the lesson of not smiling, so I replied to their look with a *Who me?* double take just shy of looking behind myself to see who else they might be checking out.

I followed the men into the dark hallway and then into a booth, all of it arranged by nothing more than a couple of exchanged glances. I felt as if I was being let in on a secret. So this was how men connected. I had no idea.

"What do you like?" the construction worker asked me, as his boyfriend dropped a couple of tokens into the slot.

"I don't know," I said. "Not much. I guess I'd like to watch you two do something."

I hadn't known that watching was what I wanted to do until I heard the words myself.

The couple accepted my request as readily as a jukebox. The man in the leather pants peeled them down until they were stretched tightly across his ankles. His boyfriend did the same with his jeans. I saw both of their dicks. They were wearing cock rings. The leather guy wore a leather one. The denim guy had a steel ring. I took myself out too. I didn't have a cock ring, but I didn't need one. The man in leather pants dropped to his knees and started sucking the man in blue jeans. I stood next to the man in jeans. With my pants down, pulling at myself, it was almost as if I was the one getting the blowjob.

I touched the man in denim. He let me reach up his shirt to feel his chest. He made to touch me too, but I brushed him away, shaking my head. The kneeling man tried next, reaching for me and pulling away from his boyfriend in a way that suggested he intended to begin doing for me what he had been doing for him. I shook my head, but he persisted in reaching for me as if I were merely being coy.

I did my best to appear somewhat relaxed as I essentially bolted from the booth in a state of what would once have been called "homosexual panic." I put myself into my pants as quickly as I could and took off, unlocking the door and leaving it bouncing against its frame.

By chance, I ran into them the very next time I went to the arcade. They gave me the look again, and I followed them into exactly the same booth as before. We started a video and wordlessly got half undressed as though it were a familiar routine. Since our first meeting, I frequently recalled the precise details of what had gone on between the two of them in front of me. I felt brazen and alert to an extreme and almost frightening degree, my eyes like vacuums, drawing it all in. This time, grasping more fully the dominate/subordinate dynamic between them, I said to the construction worker, "Can I watch you fuck him?"

He looked at his partner, then reached into his pocket and removed a condom. As he donned the rubber, the sub took off his shoes, shimmied out of his leather pants, and tossed them in a wad in the corner. He got on his hands and knees on one of the benches. The construction worker spat into his hand and rubbed it into the crack of his partner's ass. Then he slowly slid himself in. I watched their faces. It was instantly one of my favorite things, one of the favorite things I'd ever seen in person.

I stood beside the man in denim. It was the same as last time, except better. I stood watching like that for a while. The man in denim reached over and touched me, and I let him. It felt very good very quickly. I pulled away and sat down on one of the benches near his partner's head.

The man on all fours looked at me. He still looked serious. They both looked serious. It didn't seem as if they were engaged in a fun romp. I looked at both of them, and I felt serious too. I didn't know where it was going. I thought maybe we could all climax together, but only after a very long time of doing what we were doing. I wanted the experience to last. Every time the video ended, I stood to drop a fresh token or two into the slot, then sat back down.

As I took my seat for the last time, the man on all fours leaned his head directly over my groin and let loose a long dribble of saliva expertly aimed at my penis. It was a direct hit, and before I could react he began rubbing me using the spit as lubricant. I jumped into the air. This time I didn't even attempt an air of coolness. I raced from the booth, down the hallway, and out the door. I sped to my house and tore off my clothes. I got into the shower and scrubbed until the hot water ran out, swearing to God and to myself that I would never again return to the arcade.

For weeks after, I obsessed over what I had undoubtedly caught from the man in leather. I thought back on the event searching my memory for clues. In retrospect, I found it damning that his boyfriend had used a condom. I figured he only did that because his partner had something he didn't want to catch. Or maybe it was the dom guy who was infected, the one who had been touching me so much. But that didn't make as much sense. He was obviously a top, and tops were rarely the ones who got infected, I'd heard. It was usually the bottoms—or the "receptive partners" as the literature would have it. So it was the leather sub spitter who was infected. I knew it. Shit.

I Googled it for hours. I didn't think I'd catch HIV from the guy, but I thought I'd probably get whatever else he had. A friend who volunteered at an AIDS hospice said that AIDS and herpes went together. He told me that almost everyone who had AIDS had herpes too. That worried me.

Someone on the notoriously unreliable Yahoo! Answers—then Ask Yahoo!—had written a panicked plea for information after having a similar experience at a strip club just before his wedding night. A stripper had spat on his genitals at his bachelor party. I read the answers the community gave him with interest. None of them sounded authoritative. Basically, it came down to "watch and wait." I wanted to call the guy who had made the post. I Googled his user ID, but found nothing.

15

FOR AS LONG AS I'VE CONDUCTED SEXUAL RELATIONS WITH men, I've been terrified by imagined doomsday health scenarios. When I was sleeping with women I was conscious of avoiding infection in a general way, but I was never panicked about it. I never imagined their secretions as glowing toxic sludge. With men, I panicked constantly.

I was ruthless in my interrogations of potential partners. I always started by asking if they got cold sores. Never trusting their denials, I went on to explain that carriers of the herpes virus—who comprise approximately one-third of the population—might be "shedding" (a term gleaned over the course of relentless internet searches) at any time, regardless of the interval since their most recent outbreak. And, in case they didn't know or were too reckless to care, mouth sores could easily be transmitted to other parts of the anatomy.

After reading that an unpleasant tingling sensation often precedes the appearance of a sore, I imagined the prickly discomfort constantly. I also read that, following one's unwitting infection, the first sores could take months to appear, allowing one to naïvely believe he was free from danger as he unknowingly shed the virus, passing it along to partners, who passed it along to their wives or partners or fuck buddies, accidentally precipitating the breakdowns of marriages and families, and who knew what.

Fear of herpes was made worse by the fact that transmission requires so little—a kiss, a blow job, the brushing of one's member against another person's completely asymptomatic member. It wasn't as if you had to have unprotected ass-slamming anal in the back of a dark eighteen-wheeler trailer in the meat packing district or on the docks or in a bathhouse, the way AIDS had spread so quickly in the 1980s because of the insane amount of anonymous, unprotected sex being had by droves of horny and oblivious New York homosexuals enjoying what no one could have known was the twilight of hedonic bliss.

What made herpes more terrifying was its incurability. There's nothing they can do for you except give you pills that may or may not reduce the number and severity of the outbreaks you experience. They'll swab your open sores and run tests to verify what you've got. If you're lucky, it's syphilis. Get a shot of penicillin and you're fixed. And maybe it *is* syphilis. It does seem as if it's in a perpetual cycle of resurgence. But if you're unlucky, it's herpes, and you're going to have it until you die, barring the unlikely discovery of a cure.

Of course, herpes wasn't my only fear. I also dreaded and agonized over crabs, the effects of which were equally easy to produce psychosomatically. Particularly when I visited my parents or other family members overnight, I compulsively recalled my most recent sexual encounters and wondered if I had crabs that had yet to fully gestate, or were only then reaching the phase of their existence in which they begin to cause itching. For days after every weekend jaunt, I would find myself itching. I imagined calling and explaining to my parents that they should be careful handling the sheets from my room. Or apologizing that, because we all sat on the same sofa, I thought the odds were pretty good that I transmitted a genital parasite to them.

HIV seemed unlikely because I wasn't bottoming for anyone, and I always wore a condom when it came to anal sex. But the fact that it was unlikely didn't stop me from being terrified. Sometimes men would cancel whatever trysting plans we had made because of my ever-escalating hysteria, confirming and reconfirming their HIV statuses. I didn't mind when they canceled. I imagined I was weeding out guys who had something to hide, who were worried I was the type to trace it back to its source and come for revenge, like Jennifer Hills, the gang rape victim protagonist of the 1978 film, *I Spit On Your Grave*, who, after regaining her strength, terrorizes and murders her attackers, castrating one of them and leaving him to bleed out in a warm bath. Maybe they were right. I don't know what I might have done.

There were years, literal years, when I would return from a sexual encounter and check myself over and over again, convinced that every mark or blemish or spot of any kind—even if it was essentially nonexistent—was an early symptom of something horrible happening within my body.

The friend who volunteered at the AIDS hospice told me about patients with immune systems so suppressed that their genitals and anuses were completely covered in open herpes sores. He talked about their agony in trying to wipe their behinds or having their behinds wiped for them. I felt as though he was describing my future. I had seen all the medical photographs of men with genitals horribly mutilated by STIs, and the images were forever flashing through my mind, partly because I was constantly searching for them in service of my always-incorrect self-diagnoses. Eventually, they were as familiar to me as the set of 1987 Topps baseball cards I had owned and obsessed over as a nine-year-old, the ones with the faux wood grain borders.

When you're as worried about these things as I have been, you're not content merely checking yourself for signs of disease. Each time you get naked with another man, you look and look and look, scrutinizing every part of his lower half. Everything becomes a trigger for concern. You begin to grasp the maddening irregularity of human skin. It can be mottled or red-spotted. It can be irritated for no clear reason. It gets moles and tags and bumps connected to no known cause. How often I was told, "That's always been there."

"Really?" I'd say.

"Yeah," the guy always said, "for as long as I can remember. Promise."

"Really?" I'd repeat.

It's a testament to the power of something—a tremendous sex drive or an obsessive nature—that I could worry so much over STIs and still be able to say, "I did it anyway." Although it should also be said that those fears did prevent me from doing more than

I did. And the anxiety-filled weeks following my time with the leather and denim couple taught me to be more up-front from the beginning. After that, when I entered a booth with someone, I'd always whisper, "I don't do much out here" to give them a chance to leave if they were looking for something kinky or even merely penetrative. Some guys actually said, "Me neither. This place is full of freaks." They were my favorites, and I often found myself going further with them than I would with the others. If it was a ruse, it was an effective one.

Some of the guys were content to play even if it meant that not much was going to happen. The rest would leave right away. But it always felt like the right thing to do, letting people know what they could expect from me. Sometimes they didn't seem to know what I meant, but I never elaborated. Besides, I didn't know myself what it meant when I said I didn't do much out there. I knew I wasn't going to have sex. Honestly, I never intended even to let anyone touch me. But that happened with growing regularity. Then I knew for a fact that I would never let anyone go down on me. But then that happened a few times. Of course, it was a given that I would never go down on anyone else. No fucking way. Then that happened. But I always started out by saying "I don't do much out here" to manage their expectations. I never anticipated that things would escalate, but the fact that they sometimes did made it all the more exciting.

There were men who after a few minutes of casual touching and film watching would get on their knees in front of me and beg to be permitted to go further. More than once, I literally held a man back with my palm flat against his forehead.

By that time I had said the other thing I always said when I got into a booth with someone. I asked, "Are you clean?"

Most of the guys said, "Yes, are you?"

Or, "My ass? Yeah."

Or, "As far as I know, I am."

I got the feeling it wasn't a question that got asked out there a lot. The way men reacted made me think I was breaking an unspoken rule. It took a couple of seconds for them to process. When they said "Yes," I always followed up with, "Are you sure?"

I regretted resorting to the word "clean." I tried to think of another word that would be equally concise but less offensive to those unfortunate enough to be burdened with some kind of disease. I considered "neg," which most gay guys would know, but the mostly-straight guys who frequented the place probably wouldn't. And, besides, it didn't cover the variety of infections I was even more paranoid about than HIV.

The question of "cleanliness" brought to mind a scene from the Spike Lee biopic *Malcolm X*, in which Denzel Washington, as Mr. X, discovers the way he is being oppressed, not merely by the citizenry of the US or the world, but by the English language itself. He looks up the word "black" in the dictionary and sees how it's used to suggest evil and ruin, while "white" is used as a stand-in for purity and goodness.

I wanted to have a better word than clean, whose opposite is dirty, but I never found one.

16

STALKING THE COP AND THE KID HADN'T BEEN MY PLAN PER se, but obsession had always been my go-to mode, even for relatively inconsequential upsets. And given that my relationship with the cop was the exact opposite of inconsequential, I was completely swept up before I had any sense of how it might be avoided.

Before I went to work at the motel, I saw a therapist who tried teaching me to think differently, to train my brain to react in ways that would make my life better. He was forever extolling drugs that might help in our mission. He wanted to know if I'd heard of Celexa. How about Wellbutrin? Prozac? Had I heard of Zoloft? Paxil? Nardil? Had I heard of Lithium? Had I heard of Propofol? Would I consider opening myself to pharmaceuticals if it meant that I would feel happier, less worried, more in control?

I never considered it for a minute. No way was I going to be tricked by drugs into thinking everything was all right.

My shrink and I huddled over the coffee table between us, and he drew a line near the bottom of a piece of paper, making it look like a stock chart, with peaks and valleys, the line jerking upward and then downward.

"This is where you are now," he said.

Then he drew the same kind of line near the top of the page.

"This top line is where an average person is, a person experiencing typical peaks and valleys and periods of calm where everything is just flat and ordinary. And the bottom line is where you are, see? It's the same thing, except that you're starting at a lower level than most people. So your spikes into happiness are never as high as theirs. And your lows are much lower. It's a chemistry thing, you understand?"

There was something seductive about what he was saying, but I also knew that no one had tested my brain chemistry, so it was all pure conjecture.

"I'll think about it," I said.

"I hope you will," he said.

"I really just want to talk," I said.

I meant it. Even when I plopped down in the chair at the beginning of a session and announced that I had nothing to say, I talked. About people who had cut me off in traffic and conversations I had when I was fifteen years old that still embarrassed me. I talked about what I thought about the people I saw in the waiting room. I talked about my parents. I talked about money. I even talked about my sexual outings, though it was the one subject I never dwelled on. I told him my encounters with men meant nothing, that I did it out of boredom and horniness, interrupting his attempts at interrogation with lengthy, detailed stories about the violations against my personal space in line at the grocery store.

I spent our sessions covering the same ground again and again, congratulating myself on my scrupulous exactitude.

"None of your clients are as rigorous as I am," I told him.

I liked going to therapy, where my shrink eventually learned to laugh at me and call me on at least some of my bullshit. We probably would have made some progress eventually, but I had to quit seeing him when I went broke and started working at the motel. My hours conflicted with his schedule, and I didn't have the money to pay for a shrink anymore anyway. It was too bad, because after the cop ended things with me I really could have used one.

Sobbing, I told a friend it was as if part of my brain had been blocked off before the cop ended things with me. Then when he did, the dam had broken so that blood flooded the empty cavern and changed me into something other than who I had been. I would never have characterized myself as a jealous person before the cop moved the kid into his house, but afterwards it overwhelmed me until it seemed like the only thing I really knew about myself, that I loved the cop and that the kid was in my place. In a way, I had to appreciate the kid for showing me how wrongheaded I had been, but now I was ready for him to disappear again, like a cancer that revealed all my strength and courage and left me a hero and a survivor, but only if it didn't kill me first.

I hadn't understood how people were driven to do the crazy things they did before then. I thought the things people did for love in movies were over-the-top fantasies about lunatics.

Figuring out the password to the cop's email was proof that I belonged in there. I wasn't some criminal rooting around. I was a confidant with inside knowledge. I was like a dear friend plotting an intervention.

He had told me everything, so it was easy guessing which words he might choose. I was in on my third try. When his inbox appeared on my screen it seemed as if my familiarity with him had earned me the right. Though really it was just his cat's name.

Once inside, I read his email more often than I read my own, as he and the kid sent little messages to one another several times a day. I scoured the internet to see if there was some way I might intercept their text messages too, but no. It was for the best. The emails kept me busy enough. I watched videos of them having sex that they'd taken on their phones and emailed back and forth. I looked at photos of them in bed and sitting around the cop's house. I thought about them all the time, imagining their lives together in vivid detail, picturing every stage of their respective days, what they were doing, when and where.

17

MALCOLM AND I TRADED EMAILS FOR A COUPLE OF DAYS but were unable to coordinate our schedules until one Saturday night when he was in his penthouse in Boston at the same time I was at home.

"I can't believe the emails you've been sending me," he said. "I never would have thought you'd get this hung up on a guy."

"It surprised me too," I said.

"Have you told anyone else?"

"A few friends."

"What have you been telling them?"

"The whole thing. That I've been having a secret relationship with a cop in a small town and that I'm in love with him and that I'm going to do whatever I can to get him back."

"So you're basically just coming out to everyone all of a sudden?"

"I mean, I guess. Honestly, the gay part seems like the least interesting element. And the truth is I'm telling people that I'm not really gay or whatever, but that I've fallen in love with a guy."

"I don't get the distinction."

"Well, like maybe I'm just gay for him, not gay in general."

"But that can't be what you really believe."

"I don't know. It's more complicated than that. I definitely know I like screwing women sometimes."

"Right, but I mean…"

"I just don't want to think about all this other stuff at the moment. The cop thing is enough."

"How have your friends reacted?"

"They've been supportive, I guess. Mostly, everyone just seems surprised. I've been crying a lot, which I didn't used to do. It seems to disarm people."

"So everyone basically understands that you're gay?"

"Like I said, I'm just telling them about the cop. Listen, I don't even care about this part of it. I don't even care if I'm gay or whatever. What I'm interested in is getting him back. I really need your help. I know you'll be able to help me if you'd just try. He's moved this kid into his house, and now I think maybe I've fucked up everything and I don't even have a chance."

I started crying.

"I'm sorry, Sam. I wish I were in town. I'd come over and take you out for a drink or something."

"Thanks. I really just need your help. Do you think you could help me?"

"How?"

"Help me strategize or brainstorm or whatever. You know how gay stuff works."

"I'm happy to try, and flattered to be your gay expert, but if you want to know the truth I don't have the greatest track record myself. When did he move the kid in?"

"Five weeks ago on Wednesday."

"Have they known one another long?"

"Six months or so I think. They were just fooling around off and on, and I guess things got more serious."

"Is the kid in trouble?"

"What do you mean?"

"Is he being turned out by his family or something?"

"No, I don't think it's anything like that. I think he goes to the college nearby, and they've been fucking for a while. And the kid needed a place to move or something, and he moved into the cop's house, and they're pretending to everyone that he's the son of one of the cop's college friends."

"Really?"

"Yeah."

"Because the cop is closeted too?"

"Yeah. He lives in a small town. You know how it is. He used to be married, but now he's divorced. No one knows about him there. And, by the way, I didn't want to put this in an email, but I'm seriously thinking of killing myself if I can't get him back."

"Oh please, Sam."

"I'm serious. Do you think you can help me? Do you think there's any chance for me?"

"I don't know what you've done so far. Have you done anything crazy?"

"I don't think so, I haven't even seen him since he moved the kid in. We've only talked on the phone. I just can't believe it would be the same with him as it was between us."

"The kid is how old?"

"Nineteen."

"And the cop?"

"Forty-two."

"Yeah, some guys get really into that stuff, you know. You're what, twenty-six?"

"Twenty-eight."

"So it's no contest age-wise."

"What does that mean?"

"If he's into really young guys, and you're almost ten years older than the kid, there's not much you can do. Is the kid like a skinny twink or something?"

"Not at all. He's like a dumpy kid from Odessa."

"Oh! Well that could be good for you."

"That's what I keep thinking. And I'm quitting smoking and I got some running shoes. And I've told the cop all that so he knows that I'm really improving and all."

"Listen, telling him too much of that kind of stuff is going to make you seem like a needy weirdo. I had a boyfriend once who did this kind of thing after I split up with him."

"Did it work?"

"It actually sort of did, but only after he chilled out and left me alone for a while."

"Did he remind you of the good times you had together?"

"Maybe. I don't really remember. Is the cop kind of dumb?"

"Not at all. He's a smart guy. Why would you ask that?"

"I mean, small town Texas cop. I wouldn't say most of them are geniuses."

"I don't think he's like a big reader or anything, but he's a bright guy for sure."

"Then he probably sees through whatever shit you're doing to manipulate him."

"But don't you think it's a good sign that he's still talking to me on the phone?"

"Yeah, I'd say that's a good sign. But you should stop calling him for a while."

"But then we won't ever talk."

"You've got to give the guy some room to breathe. Moving a new boyfriend into your house is kind of a big deal. Especially a teenager. God, his life is probably crazy enough without you stressing him out more."

"What if I've done that already?"

"I think the answer either way is to leave him alone for a while and work on yourself."

"But how do I get him to call me?"

"I've never even met this guy, Sam."

"God, I don't want to not call. How long do you think that would take for him to call me?"

"I have no idea, Sam."

"Well, estimate, Malcolm." I was crying into the phone.

"Between one and two weeks."

"Are you kidding? Why not say 'between this year and next year?'"

"I'm basing this on absolutely nothing, Sam."

"Okay, so answer this: do you think there's any way they'll last? Do you think the relationship can work?"

"I mean, just based on what you've told me, I would say no. I don't think things like this typically last."

"What's the average duration? I mean, it's already been weeks, and I don't think they're getting tired of one another at all yet."

"They're not going to get tired of one another in a few weeks."

"So how long do you think they'll last?"

There was a long pause on the line during which I was perfectly silent. I pictured Malcolm's eyes trained at the ceiling as he tabulated factors in his head.

"Six months, max. It'll be a miracle if they make it longer than that."

I took in what he was saying. Six months sounded right. It was the maximum duration of a fling, a period you could look back on years later and laugh saying, "You think *you* had a midlife crisis? Maybe you've forgotten that I moved a teenager into my house."

I kept a wall calendar hidden under a pile of papers on my desk on which I was marking the date and time of every conversation I had with the cop. I also noted every other relevant development I could track via his email—their trips, spats, dinners at restaurants.

"Six months from when they moved in together?"

"If I had to guess, I'd say that's about the limit of it."

Looking at the calendar, I told myself I could bear anything for six months. I flipped through and marked the date six months from the day they moved in together.

"You're going to have to find a way to calm down and just let this go for a while."

"I'm going to quit smoking and take up running."

"You said that. Listen, Sam, it's getting late, and I have to be up early. We can talk again tomorrow if you want."

"You need to go?"

"Yeah, I should."

"Don't you want to jerk off first?"

"I'm not too much in the mood actually. This has been kind of heavy."

"Oh, come on. It'll help me sleep."

"We can if you want to, I guess."

"Yeah, if you're cool with it."

"Sure. Okay, Sam. Let me get my dick out."

18

ONCE I WAS REASONABLY CONFIDENT THAT THE LEATHER and denim couple hadn't infected me with any diseases, I started wishing to see them again. That was the way it was out there. You'd run into someone two or three times, and it would seem inevitable they'd always be around. Then you'd go out one night at the time when you always ran into them, and they wouldn't be there, and then you'd never see them again.

It was that way with the Marine. I met him out there on five or six occasions. He wasn't at all my type. My age, fit, with just a patch or two of hair around his nipples and at the center of his chest. A couple of times it was shaved, but usually it wasn't. He was a handsome guy, and he had a mysterious aura of sensitivity, which I found strange for a Marine.

I met him on a Thanksgiving night. Everyone I knew had left town to be with their families, but I didn't get holidays off at the motel. I was avoiding my family anyway. My sister had told my parents about me and the cop after I made the mistake of confiding, and they had left two angry-sounding messages on my voicemail, which I ignored and deleted.

A couple of friends expressed pity that I was alone on Thanksgiving, but I didn't mind. The cop was home alone too. He had to work and had encouraged the kid to go visit his family in Odessa. The kid had left on Tuesday, and the two of them had been emailing several times a day since. The kid was having his share of family problems too, it turned out, and the cop was emailing him things like, "I know it's hard, but you have to do your best to strengthen familial bonds." And "You only have one mother." And "Try to see things from the perspective of your father." I thought I detected a kind of preachy, parental tone in his emails to the kid, but it was hard to know if he was trying to sound wise or just rational. I fantasized that maybe he'd phone me out of loneliness or boredom, but he didn't, so I went to the arcade after work.

I liked going to the arcade on holidays, seeing how things were different. You could treat the arcade in a collect-them-all kind of way. You could see who was there during the Super Bowl. During a citywide motorcycle rally. During lunch hour. After church. While an enormous convention of Realtors was in town. On Christmas Day. It was always different.

The Marine was into chests, and when we met he insisted I take my shirt off, which I had never done out there. He wanted us to press our chests together, which we did. The letters "USMC" were tattooed on both his arms. He was the first person I ever kissed at the arcade, and it happened on the first night I met him. I never would have thought I would kiss out there, but he asked if I wanted to, and I found that I did. It was the kind of kissing that was so engrossing I couldn't think about anything else, and even the self-critic in my head was silenced. I felt lucky that we established those things in our first meeting, the kissing and the pressing our bare chests together because then we got do them every time we saw each other. We never wasted time not doing those things.

We always came when we were together, which was another thing I had never done at the arcade before meeting the Marine. Usually, I'd just watch and play and then go home and jerk off remembering it all. But with him I always let it go further. I could feel him getting close, and I'd let myself get close, and he'd let go, and we would lean forward with our pants around our ankles so we could hit the floor or the little garbage can, splattering anything other than our trousers and underwear. In the dark, you could hear the sound of your wad hitting the trashcan liner or see the glittering light reflected off the tiny fresh puddles on the floor. Coming with someone at the theater was a compliment. It meant you weren't going to go on cruising around for someone else to play with.

Once, I told him I thought we should get together someplace else, and he gave me an email address and said to write him. I could tell it wasn't his real email address. It was the address he used for fooling around with guys. Everyone had one of those. At least one. His was somethingsomethingMarine@hotmail.com.

The subject line of the email I sent read, "Dispatches from the Booths." I kept it short and light, but the Marine didn't reply.

After that, I didn't see him at the arcade for a while, though I always looked for him. Then one day weeks later he was leaving just as I was arriving. He saw me, but he didn't put his car back into park and go inside with me. He reversed out of the spot and drove away. Right after him, banging through the door, came a short, dark haired guy who could have been my stand-in on a movie set.

I did see him in the booths one last time after that. I told him I had tried to email him and he confirmed that I had his correct email address. "Maybe it went to your spam folder," I said. We had a nice time together, and I sent another email afterwards. He didn't reply, and I never saw him out there again. I liked to imagine that he had post-traumatic stress disorder or that he was recovering from a love affair with a fellow Marine who died in combat. I liked to imagine he had managed to live for thirty years without ever learning how to check his spam filter. I liked to imagine that I'd bump into him again at some point, but I never did.

19

HERE WAS SOMETHING THAT COULD HAPPEN: YOU HOOKED up with someone and had an unexpectedly incredible experience, the kind during which you both ran out of tokens and started feeding dollar bills into the machine just to be together a little longer, the kind that could only be credited to pheromones or some unknowable chemical magic. When it was over you exchanged names—real or fake, didn't matter—and you even touched one another on the stomach or over the bulge in their underwear as you both got dressed again. You fantasized about it later and imagined running into him, how both of you would smile and shake your heads like, "Here comes trouble!"

And then you did see him again finally, and he smiled and nodded, and walked past you or into a booth with someone else. It was worse when there was no one around and you could see he was just waiting for someone, anyone else, to show up. And there you had shown up, and he kept waiting, watching to see who was coming in each time the door opened. You walked by him again to try and jog his memory, but he just gave a short, dismissive nod, a combination of recognition and rejection.

20

IT WAS THE COP'S FAULT THAT I DISCOVERED THE ARCADE at all. I never would have heard of the place if I hadn't been reading the Missed Connections section of Craigslist, which I checked compulsively in hopes that he would post something there for me. The ads called to mind a movie I'd seen on television dozens of times in my youth, the 1985 film *Desperately Seeking Susan*, in which Madonna, a fashion-forward rock hussy / petty criminal, communicates with her one true love via coded personal ads in a tabloid newspaper. It was easy to see how Rosanna Arquette became fixated on their ads, following their story, and eventually becoming entangled in it herself.

I loved reading the ads. The people posting in Missed Connections were my people, their ads filled with stories like my own, sometimes with so much at stake and sometimes as trivial as could be imagined. They were always trying to reconnect with the people with whom they'd had these passing encounters or arrangements that had failed for any number of reasons. They'd go home and fantasize about them. They'd have sex with their wives or girlfriends or boyfriends, and their erections would be a tribute to those strangers who in fleeting episodes in odd locales stirred something in them. Occasionally, you'd see pleas to reunite with former long-term lovers. I scanned the ads so often that I came to recognize repeated postings from the same desperate people, who, one assumed, would never find satisfaction there.

Most Missed Connections ads had titles like "Laundromat Parking Lot, May 18th" or "Silver Daddy at the XXX theater" or "Bathhouse Jock with Steelers Tattoo."

After rehashing their encounters in gooey prose, their authors would say things like, "Tell me what I was wearing so I know it's you." Or "Where did you pinch me before we parted ways?"

Most Missed Connections ended with one of a few heartbreaking codas in acknowledgment of the astronomically bad odds of reconnecting:

"I know this is a long shot."

"You'll probably never see this."

"If you happen somehow to read this, please get in touch."

Such is a seldom-considered risk of casual encounters. You can end up having the best sex of your life with someone you'll never see again. You think you couldn't have feelings about someone you blew at a rest stop, who jerked you off and kissed you in an airport bathroom, or who hugged you from behind and reached into your pants in a dark booth at the arcade. But then you do, and those experiences rise to the surface again and again, as fantasies and memories and standards that your loved ones will never meet.

I picture a lie detector with its spindly metal arms marking straight lines on an endless scroll, registering encounters with gentlemen and sleazebags, guys in sports coats or swimsuits or windbreakers. I picture the metal arms shuddering here and there with the passing men, then bursting to life, drawing lines so abrupt and jagged they cannot be reconciled with what came before. That's what it was like with the cop.

I met him on a website for connecting straight men and women looking for casual sex. I had initiated a membership there because I was looking for male/female couples that might agree to sleep with me. Threeways seemed like a reasonable middle ground in which I could demonstrate my heterosexuality while being in very close proximity to other naked, engorged men.

I had a surprising run of good luck meeting people on the site. In one episode I met a couple in a motel room. After I spent a while sliding in and out of the guy's wife while she blew him, he pulled away from her and went behind me where I couldn't see him. I thought he had gone to the restroom, but then I felt his grip around my balls and his other hand pushing my ass, as if he were driving me into his wife, as if I were a male sex doll he was piloting. Later, he put his fingers inside of her while I was fucking her, curling his fingers against my dick.

The husbands sometimes had things in mind that they didn't want their wives to know about until the critical moment. One man messaged me without his wife's knowledge prior to our meeting. He wanted me to get his wife on all fours on the bed. He wanted me to stand next to the bed and fuck her from behind while he slid under her and went down on her. Then he wanted me to come in his mouth when I was ready. I met with the couple. Neither of us mentioned to the wife what had been agreed upon earlier, though the husband and I shared several looks of complicity. The wife was clueless, but totally agreeable to whatever we asked of her. They had gone out for drinks before meeting me, and she alternated between ravenous passion and spaced-out bleariness throughout the encounter. What I remember most of her in retrospect was the taste of wine coolers on her breath, a flavor I hadn't encountered since junior high school. The husband and I were as wide-eyed as if we were on speed, maneuvering his moaning wife like a slightly overweight doll. I spent the evening completely focused on what I was supposed to do. When I finally got her into position, her husband moved beneath her. Barely even acknowledging her vagina, he surprised me by sucking and licking my balls until I got so close I pulled out and whipped off the rubber just in time to glaze his beard. He went to the bathroom afterwards and while he was out of the room his wife thanked me over and over again. "Thank you so, so much," she said. "You don't know how long we've had this dream."

In two other episodes, I met with couples without touching or being touched by the men at all. Once, the husband, who had a ponytail, sat on the end of the bed jerking off and calling his wife a whore. I didn't come that night.

The other time, the husband got naked with me, but was only interested in watching me have his wife anally. She seemed to want the same thing. I met them at their house in the suburbs, and they showed me with pride a large collection of dildos. I did fuck the wife in the ass, but felt bossed around and micromanaged by both of them. They seemed to have such a specific thing in mind, I got the idea that the encounter was being filmed. I spent much of the experience scanning their room for innocuous-looking items that might conceal a spy camera, ultimately fixating on a shelf of teddy bears whose dead eyes could easily have been recording everything.

I treated the website as a part-time job, as any single man had to do in order to have sex with the couples there. In joining the site, I joined hordes of local males locked in competition for the same few willing vaginas. Inwardly, I reassured myself of my commitment to high standards of attractiveness and class, but I often caught myself in deluded cycles of rationalization, forgiving poor grammar and spelling as coincident with the kind of reckless abandon to be expected of the types open to atypical sexual practices. When necessary, I told myself that their photos weren't truly representative, the subjects were likely attractive but unphotogenic. Other times, I had to work myself into extended sessions of fake self-reproach, railing against my own shallowness in order to persuade myself to message people on the site that my desperate horniness would permit me to fuck but who I would never want anyone to know I'd gone to bed with.

One got the impression that the couples' inboxes were packed to capacity with thousands of eager entreaties. In order to receive even the most perfunctory of introductory replies to a message, you had to be smart and charming and have pictures of your dick that made it look absolutely enormous. You had to become great at reading people based on their profiles and send them emails feigning casual detachment while pretending to be precisely what they desired and nothing at all like your true self. I relied upon the few marketing tricks I knew, along with recommendations I'd read about excelling in job interviews—namely, mirroring in your portrayal of yourself your target's language about what they desired. I can hardly endure thinking back on the countless occasions I labeled myself "laid back," a description given in such bad faith that it would be laughable to anyone who ever encountered or even observed me under normal circumstances.

During a long dry spell, it occurred to me that I should investigate how other single men went about charming the couples I was failing to attract. That's when I had what I thought was a brilliant idea. I sent the same message to about a dozen other men looking for MMF (or MFM) threesomes, my hand shaky and nervous as I copied, pasted, and hit send over and over again. I reassured myself that no matter how they replied I had obligated myself to nothing. In a way, it was like a performance art project.

"I know this is a long shot, but have you ever considered fooling around with another guy one-on-one? Nothing hardcore, just fooling around. Jerking off, looking at porn or whatever. Regular masculine str8 guy here, but it's hard meeting women on this site. Seems like they're deluged. I know how to keep a secret if you do. Might be fun."

I received only one reply, from a small town police officer who lived not terribly far away. Burly with the classic cop moustache, the utility belt and holster draped over his closet door, the commendations for community service and bravery adorning his entry in Wal-Mart picture frames. He was perfect. One day in bed I told him if I could have ordered someone from a catalog it would have been him, and he said he felt the same way about me.

We spent hours and hours on the phone, far more time than we ever spent together in person. Face-to-face meetings only happened on rare occasions when I felt I could escape without being questioned by anyone about my whereabouts. I considered it a successful outing when I didn't have to lie to anyone, when no one noticed or questioned my absence. That was maybe half the time. The other times, I lied. I was always collecting lies when they occurred to me, so I could use them when I needed them.

In all those hours of talking, many of them as he circled his town in his police cruiser, I heard a world I never would have known. I heard his CB crackle and I wondered how he managed to make out what the people on the other end were saying. I learned about the side jobs he had in his off hours, doing security at events and picking up cash drops for busy restaurants around town late at night.

He told me about everyone with whom he had ever been to bed, including his ex-wife. He had even slept with a handful of guys from his small town and on the little trips he took by himself to Reno and Acapulco. He had played with other cops, men who went home to their wives afterwards, the way I went back to my empty apartment an hour's drive away.

21

MALCOLM WORKED DURING THE DAY, AND I DIDN'T GET OFF until late at night, so coordinating phone calls was difficult. Occasionally he would make an effort to stay up late to talk to me. For his trouble, I told long stories in which I recalled every single detail about my times with the cop, hoping he would verify that the connection I perceived was far stronger than whatever he might be experiencing with the kid, whose cluelessness and lack of sophistication might be charming for a short time, but not much longer, surely.

"The last time I called him was Friday," I told Malcolm.

"I know," he said.

"Do you still think your idea is the right one? Maybe I could email and just check in. Just something casual."

"I don't think you could do that without sounding very, very desperate."

"Maybe you could write it for me and I could just edit it."

"We're not there yet, Sam," he said.

I hadn't told him about the arcade yet. Not because I was hiding it, but because our time was limited, and I only wanted to talk about one thing.

22

WALKING TO MY CAR AFTER MY SHIFT ONE NIGHT, I REALIZED
that the motel was laid out almost exactly like an over-scaled version of the arcade. The parking lot was where the brightly lit store
would be, and the motel rooms were the booths. At night, you
could see which rooms were occupied by the light leaking out between the faux-wood blinds. They were frequently lit only by the
TVs inside, just like the booths with their blue glow. You wouldn't
even have to press against the door to see who was open to having
visitors and who wasn't. You'd just look for Do Not Disturb signs
hanging from the doorknobs.

Naturally, I had occasion to mess around with a couple of guests
in my time at the motel. Even the girls from housekeeping got
lucky once in a while.

Once, it happened that when I was fooling around with a guest
just after my shift I got a call from the security guard. He had noticed that, though I had clocked out twenty minutes earlier, my car
was still on the lot. He was worried that something had happened
to me, that I had been kidnapped or assaulted. I told him I was still
around the property, and that I was okay.

"Oh," he said. "In that case, I'm sorry to disturb you."

The next night, when he came on duty, he entered the lobby as
usual to say hello before beginning his rounds.

"I figured out whose room you were in last night," he said. "It
really surprised me. After you left, he came out to smoke a cigarette wearing a silk, paisley robe. A big guy like that wearing a silk,
paisley robe. It was really funny. Whatever you did, it seemed like
he must've had the time of his life. He was out there smoking and
looking up at the moon like he'd just about fallen in love."

"I doubt that," I said.

"No, really. It's funny," he said. "Of all the guys in the place."

I had seen the robe myself when I was in the room. It was almost a kimono, but short, above his knees. It looked like something from the 1970s. He had called down to ask for a few extra hangers at around eight o'clock, not long after he checked in. I told him I'd bring them up to his room, and he had said, "There's no rush. You can bring them when you get off your shift."

"That's not until eleven o'clock," I told him. "Surely you'll want them before then."

"No, eleven is fine. You can just drop them off then. Thanks."

I spent the rest of my shift wondering what would happen when I got to his room. When he checked in he told me he was a construction bidder who had come to town to bid on big concrete jobs, to see if he could win them for his crew. If he was successful, he said, he'd be around a lot more.

When I dropped by his room with the hangers on the way to my car, I knocked on the door and he called out, "Come in!" exactly as I had suspected he might.

I opened the door as he was exiting the bathroom, pretending to be caught off guard, cinching shut the robe too late for me to miss that he wasn't wearing anything beneath it. I quickly entered the room and shut the door behind me as if guarding his privacy.

"I'll just put these hangers here on the dresser," I said. "Sorry to have bothered you."

"No, no, just let me find my wallet," he said. "I at least want to tip you."

"You don't have to do that," I said. Then, nodding toward his midsection, I said, "Nice robe."

He laughed and said, "You like it? My wife got it for me as a joke, but then I started wearing it for real. Now she hates it. It's nice though. It feels nice against your skin. You know?"

"I've never worn robes," I told him.

"Oh, you should try it," he said. "It's real different. Not being dressed, not being undressed. It's like this in-between feeling. You know that feeling? In between two things?"

"Sure," I said.

"You could try it on if you want."

"The robe?"

"Why not? You're off work, right? It's just us guys."

It was a game some men liked. This was what guys had done in locker rooms since the dawn of time. When it ended you didn't know what had just happened.

"Right," I said. "I'm off work."

"So, why not then?"

"What the hell? I'll try it on."

I unbuttoned my shirt and put it on the bed. I took off my undershirt and put it on top of my other shirt. Then I hesitated to see if he might think that removing that much would suffice, but he didn't give any sign that he thought I was done, so I sat on the foot of one of the two queen-size beds and untied my shoes. I took them off. Then I undid my pants and slid them to the floor.

I stood there in a pair of white boxer shorts and socks and looked at him.

"All of it, or you won't get the full effect," he said.

I made an expression of reluctance, and he said, "You don't have to be embarrassed around me, buddy. I was in the army for almost twenty years."

I hooked my thumbs into the waistband and slid them down over my thighs, kicking them off onto the puddle of fabric made by my pants.

Then I was in front of him naked except for my socks. He looked me up and down.

"Boy," he said, "you take care of yourself, huh? Work out and all?"

"Not really," I said. "Just a lucky metabolism, I guess."

He spread the robe and showed me his gut and everything else. He patted his stomach, and said, "I thought I'd never have one of these, but you get older and it's not as easy."

"Well, at least you wear it well," I said.

"Feel it," he said. "It's pretty solid, actually. Not all flabby like some guys."

I reached across and touched his stomach with my palm.

"Don't worry," he said. "I'm clean. Fresh out of the shower."

Then he slipped off the robe and held it so I could put my arms through the armholes. I put it on.

"It's too big for you," he said. "It doesn't land where it's supposed to, up here." He touched my thighs to show where the robe should have stopped. Then he rubbed my arms through the robe. "See how good it feels? That silk?"

I said that it did feel good. And when I made to cinch the robe closed he spread it with his big hands and said, "Leave it open. It looks better on you that way."

He was just my type, but I was embarrassed that the guard saw him. He brought it up a few more times, always saying how surprised he was to see the man, and how he just couldn't picture the two of us together.

23

OF COURSE I RELATED TO CLERKS AT THE ARCADE, WHOSE jobs weren't unlike my own. Except theirs wasn't like the usual service industry gig where one could make small talk with the customers. The clientele didn't wish to be distracted from their pursuits, and the clerks didn't want to give the appearance of hitting on them anyway.

A moviegoer's relationship with the clerks at the arcade was a strained one. I felt I could see myself through their eyes each time I bought tokens. It was easy to understand why they might have thought of me as a disgusting, skulking, filthy, infected piece of human garbage. It was easy to see why they might hate me and want to make my life difficult. There were a few times they actually gave off that impression, but not very often, actually. Usually the clerks were relaxed and even fairly polite.

They were just ordinary guys, of the relatively unambitious variety one might expect. Sometimes friends of theirs would bring them dinner or come to visit. The visiting friends always seemed like unsavory characters, creating the impression that the clerks at the arcade were the most stable and reliable among their peer groups. One of the clerks was an obese white guy who I only ever saw out there very late at night. Then there was the rumpled clerk who looked like my college roommate. And the guy with the fedora who looked like a pornography director. Another was a tall, Hispanic man who wore attractive, tailored clothes. The least pleasant of them sported a badly dyed pink reverse mohawk and belched loudly and repeatedly while on duty.

When not doling out tokens, a clerk could pass his shift in any variety of ways. He might spend some time stocking the condom and lube case, or heating his supper in the microwave, paging through a magazine, or watching TV. Often, the clerks just sat listening to the radio, glassy-eyed and blank as deactivated robots. It was interesting what different people listened to. One guy only listened to heavy metal, another only played Tejano music. Sometimes they kept it reasonably quiet, but sometimes the music would be so loud you could hear it in the booth just as clearly as you could hear the porn.

One night, I entered to find the rumpled clerk watching a football game.

"Hi, I just need four bucks in tokens please."

"Coming up."

I peeked over the counter to see his TV set. "What's the score?"

He glanced at the screen. "Twenty-seven to seventeen."

"How much time left in the quarter?"

Another glance. "Looks like about four minutes."

"I watched the first quarter at my place," I lied. "Didn't think it'd shape up to be such a good game."

"Yeah," he said. He dropped sixteen tokens into my palm. "Here you go."

"I almost bet on the game. Now I wish I had."

The rumpled clerk looked down at me with total apathy, wanting nothing more than to return to his zoned out state.

I don't know why I cared what any of them thought of me, but I did.

Stepping up to buy my tokens, I could see their omniscient view of the place. Big TVs were built into the structure of the counter, each one divided into four smaller screens showing black and white video feeds taken from all the cameras in the place. Waiting for my tokens, I could see the men walking around the hallways, snakily moving from one booth to another, pressing against the doors with their lights lit. You could see all the parts of the store. Visible were the bald spots of everyone browsing or pretending to browse the magazines and movies. Visible was the parking lot from three different angles.

A large plastic jar sat on the counter. Once a display for condoms, they'd converted it into a tip jar. I always tipped the clerks, even if it meant I didn't have enough tokens to stay long. The mandatory minimum was three dollars in tokens. If I had five dollars, I'd get four dollars in tokens and tip one dollar. If I had four dollars, I'd get three dollars in tokens and tip one dollar. If I had only three dollars, I didn't go. Tipping was like paying the mafia. You knew it didn't protect you from everything, but you hoped it protected you a little.

What you didn't want was to become the target of one of the clerks. You didn't want to be banned. You didn't want to be humiliated. You didn't want to get berated over the public announcement system, the microphone for which looked like something from a 1970s principal's office or NASA's first moon landing. It was at the end of a flexible metal arm, cranked up to one's mouth the moment before making an announcement.

I heard all sorts of announcements, but most of them amounted to "stop breaking the rules" and "start spending money," both of which seemed to me completely reasonable requests, though compliance wasn't always as straightforward as one would imagine.

You were in a booth, or you were strolling around in the hallways, or you were pretending to examine the tiny photos on the back of some DVD you would never consider purchasing for $4.95, let alone $24.95. You were somewhere playing around or looking for someone to play around with, or courting in some bizarre way another guy with whom you knew you would soon be fooling around. You heard the sound of something being turned on, something electronic popping to life. And this voice came over the speakers, which were planted all over the place, alongside the video cameras. When I was first going out there, it always made me jump.

"Start dropping tokens," the voice said. "If you're in a booth you must drop a token. Light up those lights, or get out. The rest of you, find a booth and drop a token."

The issue arose constantly. Men, diverted by passion and lust, grew inattentive in booths and forgot to drop tokens. Or else they deliberately tested the limits of what they could get away with without spending any money. If I failed to drop a token while in a booth, it was an honest accident. I got the impression that everyone else hated them, but I kind of liked when those announcements came on because suddenly I'd start hearing coins dropping into slots all over the place. Red lights popped to life in corners I'd written off. There were people in all the places where, moments ago, there seemed to have been none. It was like having night vision for sixty seconds, enabling me to see all that had been hidden before. Then, just one minute later, the lights started to go off again. Some people would leave their booths to roam around, and others would re-up with more tokens, but a lot of them would just go dark again until the next announcement.

Sometimes the clerk said, "I've got too many cars out here to have only two booths lit up. Don't make me come out there." That one worked well to shake out the sleazebags who didn't want to pay. I don't know why I was so disgusted with the ones who refused to buy more tokens. I understood that they might have been broke, but they should have found another way to get laid. When I was broke, I didn't go to the arcade.

When the clerks became particularly peeved, they exercised their pre-nuclear option by switching on the lights in all the booths. One moment, you'd be ensconced in a comforting blue glow in the warm darkness, and the next, as if the victim of a flash grenade, you'd find yourself blasted by harsh white light. It never lasted long—usually just a second or two, but it was weird when it happened. If I was alone, I got this rare, fully-lit glimpse of the interior of the booth. I could see the floor and the walls, and the little hooks where you were supposed to hang your clothes. I could see the black vinyl benches. I could see cigarette butts on the floor. I could see dropped tokens. I could see the little black trash can, and, if there was something in the trash, I could see what was inside. But I couldn't look at anything closely or for long because before I could even focus the lights were off again.

If you happened not to be alone when the lights came on, you were confronted with that person at extremely close range. He was very, very—sometimes tragically—visible. You saw him, and you saw him see you. Whenever that happened to me, we both put

24

FOR EACH TIME I GOT WHAT I WANTED, I WAS REJECTED innumerable times. It's always a numbers game, as any barroom seducer will attest. Of course, I rejected my share too. That's how I started to see that it wasn't personal. It really wasn't. Though when I was the one on the receiving end of the shaking head or averted eye, it could certainly feel personal. That sharp edge had to be ground down in me.

When I first started going to the arcade, rejections made me sick. My face got hot. I had to find a clean booth, start a movie, and sit down for a minute. There was a whole class of men I thought I should be able to land with no trouble, and when I couldn't, I didn't understand why. Not because I thought of myself as particularly good looking. I didn't, and I don't. But I had this sense of my place on a scale of attractiveness, and I imagined that everyone I placed below myself on that scale should be within my grasp. There were older guys and very fat guys, people who looked truly abnormal, who took one look at me and were absolutely not interested.

It took many visits for me to learn that when someone at the arcade rejected you, it was simply because you were not his thing. And there was no way you could ever be the thing for which he was looking, because you were another thing entirely. It had nothing to do with some imagined attractiveness quotient.

Sometimes there would be a man at the arcade so classically, George Clooney-good-looking that it was almost unbelievable. Everyone wanted him. They'd all be pseudo-casually walking up and down the hallways, ducking into booths to see if he'd follow. They'd brush against him as if by accident, and then stare him in the eye. Sometimes you couldn't believe which one he chose. It could be shocking. Some pear-shaped, duck-footed guy in a salmon-colored polo, pleated shorts, and a pair of flip-flops. You'd see them connect, and the guy he had chosen would be just as shocked as anyone. And the handsome one would be shy and surprised when the duck-footed guy wanted him too. Sometimes it really was like watching a love connection. A while later, you'd see the pudgy guy emerging from their booth, tucking his shirt into splattered shorts, clearing his throat and making his way to the exit. You hoped he got the guy's phone number at least.

25

BEFORE DISCOVERING THE ARCADE, I'D ALWAYS HEARD THAT homosexual communication was all in the eyes. It turned out to be so true and obvious, I still can't fathom how I was missing it all that time. They looked you in the eye when they wanted you and to determine if you wanted them. And if you held that simple eye contact for just a few seconds, they knew, and you knew. But if they wanted you and they looked into your eyes, you could simply not return their look, and they almost always understood. Or they should have anyway. The persistent ones were the worst.

26

I'LL SAY THIS ABOUT THE COP: ANYONE ELSE WOULD HAVE seen it coming. When I returned from a short vacation, he told me he had fallen in love and moved a nineteen-year-old college student into his house. It wasn't the first time I had heard of the kid. I had known of his existence as an occasional sex partner, but I hadn't known to think of him as an actual threat.

I was standing outside my apartment building when I called him. The way he was talking, I could tell the nineteen-year-old was with him. The streetlight beneath which I was standing suddenly went dark, in an instance of what is known as "the Street Light Interference Phenomenon" by the sort of crackpots who think feelings can interfere with the world around them.

"But I'm in love with you," I said to the cop.

"Well, that's certainly the first I've heard of that," he said.

It was true that whenever he asked me out to dinner or to a movie I told him he should find a gay guy to do that kind of stuff with. Still, we had laid together in the incredible darkness of his bedroom—working nights meant he had sprung for high-quality blackout shades—and talked about how we would still be seeing one another when I got married to a woman someday. Now he was breaking our deal.

He had to get off the phone after that. I went to my apartment and spent the next several hours throwing up.

27

I PASSED MOST OF MY TIME AT THE ARCADE IN THE STORE, the neutral zone between the hallways. I stayed beneath the fluorescent lights, where I felt safest, pretending to look at the boxes of dirty movies while almost everyone else stayed in the corridors, only emerging to cross to the hall on the opposite side. That's when I'd see them and they'd see me.

Sometimes I'd follow a man into the hallway, hoping he'd go into a booth, drop a token and leave the door open for me. That usually worked. But sometimes I misread signals. I'd follow a guy into the hallway, and he'd peer at me through the shrinking crack of the closing booth door with what I perceived as a beckoning gaze. I'd walk to the door, ready to join him, and then hear the lock being engaged on the other side. Or I'd push the door open and he'd give me a look that made clear I had mistaken the meaning of his glance. When that happened, I had to stroll on and into a booth of my own to watch a little of a movie by myself, because once you entered the hallway you were supposed to go into a booth and drop a token. No loitering. Those were the rules.

A lot of men preferred staying in a booth to roaming the hallways. They'd stake their territory, then keep the lights outside lit by dropping tokens into the slot whenever the movie stopped. Unless they already had company, you could count on their doors being unlocked.

Some were "straight" guys who didn't actually seem to want anyone to come inside, though neither did they lock their doors. They behaved as if they didn't understand what was happening when someone entered to join them. They stared ahead at the screen, barely acknowledging me, rubbing themselves a little over their pants. It was confusing when they kept feeding tokens into the slot, which, under normal circumstances was a sign that your booth-mate wanted to keep things going. When those guys did it, I didn't know what it meant. Sometimes they would turn around and frown and raise their hand and say "No, thanks" after we'd stood together in silence for five minutes or more. Sometimes we would watch the movie for a while and they would finally whisper, "Lock the door." If you hadn't locked the door quickly enough, another guy might already have come in, and all three of you would be there watching the movie, about which none of you really cared, all waiting for something to happen.

It was a letdown when they dismissed me with a "no thanks," because the longer I was in a booth with some repressed, self-hating man in Wrangler jeans with the gold band on his left hand, the more I wanted him. Standing in silence together, I could envision Sunday dinners with his parents, from whom he'd never lived more than ten miles except when he went away to an agricultural college.

It was a great feeling when a guy like that said, "Lock the door." Those guys, the silent movie watchers, they just melted when you touched them. I'd undo their belts for them if they'd let me, and then their pants, and then reach into their white undies, and they'd just quiver. They really did. Waves radiated out of them.

Other men stayed in their booths with the red lights burning, glancing up when anyone came in and rejecting all who entered. A guy like that would usually just shake his head when he saw that you had dared to enter his space. The worst part was that, though they were rarely men I wanted to fool around with, they always gained the upper hand by rejecting me first. No matter how accustomed to rejection one grew, there was still something depressing about seeing a hideous troll of a man turn around in the booth and, lit blue by some perverse pornography, register a look of unqualified disappointment upon seeing you.

Some men implemented velvet rope tactics, keeping their red lights lit and then standing in the doorway, beckoning chosen guys in the form of hissed whispers, or rejecting undesirables in the same way as they headed down that part of the corridor. Those gatekeepers always struck me as the most jaded and depressing of the arcade dwellers. I never connected with any of them, even when I was invited. It just seemed discourteous not to let people come in and be rejected or embraced in whatever meager privacy could be mustered.

The old pros were my least favorite of the arcade's characters. There were always one or two of them around. I was in the minor leagues compared to the real regulars. One middle-aged man who drove a sporty silver Mercedes was guaranteed to be there during daylight hours. He dressed like a regular professional—always in slacks and a button-down shirt with stays in the collars and slick leather shoes—but I can't imagine how he could've held down a job with his rigorous dick sucking schedule.

I'd hear him in the booths sucking guys off, at which he must have been incredibly skilled, because their reactions were frequently atypically vocal. You'd think he'd be in heaven, but he seemed so bored with it all. He'd come out of the booth and go back to scouting the hallway for fresh guys as soon as he was finished. He'd buy a soda from the machine and drink it while he walked around, washing the last guy out of his mouth with a Big Red.

My whole life I aspired to be a "regular" someplace. The limitations of the town where I was raised had, years earlier, introduced me to the sense that the world was nothing but an oversized play whose actors were all known to me. It was more than a mere TV fantasy having a waitress who knew your order the moment you sat down, or having a gas station attendant who put your brand of cigarettes on the countertop when he saw your car pull into the lot. I didn't know until I left how I'd miss being a member of that play's cast, and how often I'd try to duplicate the feeling at some neighborhood restaurant or bar in whatever city I had adopted.

For a time, I enjoyed the thought of becoming a regular at the arcade. Then I saw what the real regulars were like, how they were hunters with darting eyes, alert to every move. I saw how practiced they were, and how pleasureless their interactions.

28

MOST TIMES WHEN I WENT OUT THERE NOTHING HAPPENED.
I spent three dollars on tokens, one dollar tipping the clerk, then
roamed around looking for a good time that never materialized,
and eventually left. But the possibility was there. It was a better bet
than a lotto ticket. Even if I only watched the rituals and saw the
ongoing narrative of the place unfolding, that itself was a happening. I never felt ripped off.

You discovered something about yourself out there. A new
branch of your personality emerged, the way it does when you
take a new job or meet your boyfriend's parents or go to French
class. You're a different person when you hang out with your red-
neck cousins who you only see once a year at Thanksgiving. When
I went to the arcade this untapped part of myself—a little knot of
roots—came to life, and a personality grew around it that never
would have existed if I hadn't gone there.

You didn't have to go to prison or volunteer in Mogadishu. You
didn't have to join the Navy to have a different part of yourself
come to life. You could do something small on the outskirts of
town that no one knew about but you.

29

I FELL INTO A BRIEF PHASE OF AGGRESSIVELY POSITIVE thinking after watching a badly produced pseudo-documentary about *the law of attraction*. Regardless of the idea's inherent implausibility, I found myself desperately invested in the new age fantasy that I could reach the life I most desired through a more affirmative version of the anxious forecasting that already occupied most of my time. Unable to control the cop through any other means, I undertook the acquisition of my ideal life with him by projecting it into the future as if its eventuality were a guarantee.

When asked by the few friends whose calls I still sporadically answered, I told them that the cop and I would get back together soon and that everything was going perfectly between us.

"Oh!" came the surprised replies. "So he ended things with the kid?"

"Well, they still live together," I said. "But it's winding down."

"Wow, that's great. You must be so relieved. So, this is really happening. You two are really going to give it a shot?"

"It's sure looking that way," I said through a tense smile. "I can't really get into the details at the moment though." As if it were a contract, the particulars of which hadn't quite been hammered out yet.

The system was designed to punish negative thinking of any kind. "Energy flows where attention goes," the motto went. So whenever I caught myself returning to dark thoughts, I instantly became despondent and upset, reprimanding myself for destroying my future with the cop before schizophrenically snapping back to a collection of cheery visions for as long as I could. Then reality began seeping in again and the process repeated.

I managed to keep it up for a week or so, during which time their emails revealed no sign of a weakened relationship between the cop and the kid, no matter how hard I searched.

When I finally abandoned positive thinking I had to explain to anyone I'd spoken to that, in fact, nothing had changed and I hadn't spoken to the cop in weeks. None of them had bought it anyway, least of all Malcolm, who had been the unfortunate witness to most of my phony levity and optimism and the subsequent crashes.

"Maybe you could just try focusing on learning the lessons of this experience so this sort of thing doesn't keep happening to you."

"Like what lessons, for instance?"

"You know, all the obvious stuff. Like being more open and honest about who you are. Being the kind of person that someone else would want as a partner. Not hurting yourself by looking at things that make you feel bad, like his email."

"Maybe you're right," I said, quickly cataloging a few lessons I might learn and how the acquisition of such lessons might lead to a happier future with the cop. Maybe people who believed the universe to be random and unjust simply failed to grasp its basis in lesson-learning reciprocity.

"So you think if I learn all the right lessons, the cop might come back to me?"

"No, that's not what I was saying at all."

"But it definitely could happen," I said.

"I don't think there's a magical component to this at all," Malcolm said. "I don't think the universe cares or is tracking you karmically or anything like that. I just think trying to grow and learn these lessons would be better for you in the long run. That's all I'm saying."

"But what good is that?" I cried. "I have to live today, not in some distant time. What good is learning lessons that may or may not help in some uncertain future?"

There was a silence on the line, and Malcolm, who had told me at the start of our conversation that he had had a long day at work, sighed into the receiver.

"Tell me this," I said. "Do you even believe that things would work out between me and the cop if I got a second chance?"

"How could I possibly know that, Sam?"

"Well, what do you think just based on your gut?"

"If you want to know the truth, I honestly doubt that it could ever work out between the two of you."

Before I realized what I had done, I hung up the phone.

All night, I lay in bed thinking about what he had said and trying not to. Wondering if Malcolm was furious or just tired of me. Wondering the same thing about the cop.

The following evening I rang Malcolm up, and almost wept when he answered as usual. He didn't even bring up what had happened the night before. He showed mercy. Who else could I count on for it? Not my family. Not God, who, no matter what I had been told my whole life, *did* in fact give people more than they could handle. There was no mercy awaiting me at work. And none, of course, at the arcade.

30

IF YOU WENT OFTEN ENOUGH YOU WERE BOUND TO OBSERVE an exhibition of genuine hostility by one of the clerks, usually over the loudspeakers. You couldn't imagine the horror on the faces of their targets until you saw it yourself. Once, I witnessed a man walking down the smoking hallway idly reading text messages on his phone. The Voice, angrier than I'd ever heard it, came over the loudspeaker, "Hey, you in the blue shirt! No phone! Put it away or get out!"

The guy with the phone convulsed, looking skyward, then fumbled with his phone and dropped it on the floor. It shattered, shooting bits in every direction. He picked up what he could, and didn't spend even a second inspecting it. The moment he laid hands on it, he was in a booth. An instant later the red light outside was aglow. We were all relieved it wasn't us. Of course, we had all done exactly the same thing any number of times. The guy with the broken phone left immediately after his sixty seconds of pornography elapsed, and I never saw him again.

I was once yelled at over the loudspeaker in the parking lot, where I mistakenly imagined myself untouchable. The lot, shielded from the street by the building itself, was a world of its own which could be read like tea leaves. There were the cars I recognized, of course, like the silver Mercedes of the ever-present Big Red-drinking letch. Then there were cars with vanity plates. Government cars. Utility vans belonging to the city. Plumbing trucks. A/C repair vehicles. Economy cars with rosaries dangling from their rearview mirrors. Mid-range cars with bumper stickers boasting some kid's academic or athletic acumen. Pickups were promising. Luxury cars weren't necessarily.

I once saw in the parking lot a pickup piled with boxes, a faux-leather sofa dangling over the tailgate. As if the truck's owner had been in the middle of moving when overcome by the irresistible urge to suck a dick.

Sometimes I arrived and found that I was the only one there. Or there were just two cars in the entire lot. The question of "enough" arose. I sat in the parking lot and asked myself: *What makes it worth it?* Because there were certainly times when it wasn't worth it, when the arcade felt like an empty chat room, and I wondered what I was doing there, what I had ever been doing there with three dollars in tokens.

I was in my pickup pretending to speak on the phone. The act was for the benefit of the clerk. If he were paying attention to the video monitors, he'd see I was occupied and not merely lurking. The parking lot had just three or four cars in it, but I figured I'd go in if any promising prospects arrived. All my friends were out of town for the weekend, and I had the whole day to myself with nothing to do.

The P.A. system crackled to life the way it did on *M*A*S*H*. I hadn't even known before that moment that there were speakers outside.

"Hey, you in the truck, no loitering. Come in, or take off."

I debated it for a moment, and then made a show of disconnecting from my imaginary call for the cameras. I went in. Naturally, it was the disgusting belching clerk with the pink reverse mohawk.

"Sorry about that," I said. "I was just wrapping up a conversation."

"Yeah, right," he said.

That was the only time I heard that particular announcement out there. I wondered who else had gotten it and if they really were on the phone at the time. I didn't know how anyone could be expected to explain such a thing to the person on the other end of the call. I tried imagining a plausible lie to use in precisely that instance, but came up with nothing.

31

SOME NIGHTS I WENT TO THE ARCADE AND, LIKE SOME
hideous troll, repelled everyone in the place. I'd request the key to
the restroom from the clerk so I could check my face in the mirror
and sniff my armpits. No matter how good I got at rejection, those
nights were tough.

Other nights everything seemed to work in my favor. I'd arrive at
the same time as some trucker or cable installer or pig farmer. As I
made my way to the entrance, our eyes would meet, and he'd enter
just on my heels. The clerk would be one of the nice ones who let everyone do as they wished without hectoring them over the speakers.
Attractive men would shuffle about, smiling when they saw I was
buying tokens.

I'd pretend to peruse the movie selection, and the most alluring
man would come by and feign interest in a DVD on the rack I was
browsing, brushing against me as he reached for an installment in
the *Barely Legal* franchise and making a *hmmm* sound, as if considering the tiny photos on its cover. I always knew it was an act because
with his other hand he'd be subtly jingling the tokens in his pocket,
like all the guys did when they were trying to figure out who was
who and whether they had a shot. If I felt like it, I'd jingle my tokens
back at him or brush against him a little. Or if I was feeling bold, I
might have said in a low voice. "I've seen that one. It's pretty good."

And he would say, "Yeah? If you like this one, they've got some
pretty good movies playing here in the booths."

"Is that right?"

"That's what I've heard, anyway," he'd say.

"I don't know," I'd reply. "I just got here. I haven't even gotten
the lay of the land yet."

"It's dead, man, believe me. I was getting ready to leave when I saw you come in."

I could see that his idea of "dead" was different than mine, but it didn't matter. He'd lead the way, and we'd find a booth together.

He'd receive my warning—that I didn't do much out there—in stride. He'd confirm and reconfirm his disease-free status. Maybe I'd help him get off, or watch him get himself off. And then he'd go and I'd stay. Maybe he'd give me his extra tokens, and I'd use them to find someone else to hang out with.

On the best nights, men kept showing up until the place was absolutely filled. I liked it best when there were more guys around. The building swelled with optimism and the feeling that satisfaction was underway or not far off. The clerks were relaxed, and they didn't seem to care what anyone was doing because plenty of tokens were being dropped in the slots. Those were great times.

32

AN INCREDIBLE PERCENTAGE OF ARCADE GOERS WERE married or lived with women. Others lied, claiming to date women, although many hadn't slept with one in years, if ever. It was something anyone who could pass for straight did on occasion. There was a particular prestige about appearing to be straight.

Some of the men there genuinely were straight—not perfect "zeros" on the Kinsey Scale, of course—but were unable to have their appetites met by their wives and girlfriends, or didn't have the time and energy (and often money) required for pursuing even non-prostitute partners of the opposite sex. Or they simply weren't traditionally attractive or sufficiently socially skilled to acquire female companionship. But they had learned at some point that playing around with guys could be fun too and that willing male partners were infinitely easier to find.

Whatever their actual orientations, unlike in the gay community at large, most of the men at the arcade were trying their best to appear unmistakably straight.

If you thought about it too much, you had to think about the lives of the men you were with, the lives they were living and lives they weren't living. You had to think about who they weren't being and at what expense to themselves and the people around them. Then you had to think about who they were pretending to be, the people to whom they were lying. You thought about the wife, the girlfriend, the parents who may have wondered, or maybe never wondered, not even for a second.

33

NOTHING MADE SENSE AFTER THE COP ENDED THINGS
with me. My friends were calling and I wasn't answering the
phone. I was lying on the floor crying or reading crazy stories online about how women claimed to have gotten their boyfriends
back through a wide range of manipulations including witchcraft.
Even though I lived alone and had for years, I was still clearing
my browser history every time I looked up anything even vaguely
homosexual in nature.

I called the cop over and over again feeling certain that we hadn't
yet reached an irreversible stage. I pictured him walking into his
house after a conversation with me and confronting the kid, who I
always imagined sitting on the couch playing video games.

"It's over between us," he'd say.

"What do you mean?" the kid would say.

"Just what I said. I'm in love with someone else."

The kid, dropping his gamepad, would stare up at the cop bewildered. "You don't love me?" he'd sob.

"I love someone else. You know who."

"I begged you not to talk to him anymore."

"Yeah. Well, look on the bright side," the cop would say, "at least
we haven't unpacked all your boxes yet. We'd better hurry. The bus
to Odessa leaves in two hours, and I'm meeting him for supper."

I was more than a decade younger than the cop, and I couldn't
even imagine spending the night with a nineteen-year-old. Young
people were so dumb and inexperienced. I didn't even want to be
nineteen when I was nineteen. As a kid I'd wanted to dye my hair
gray when the kids in my class were dying theirs green and plum
and fire engine red.

When he did feel like taking my calls, the cop expressed a seemingly bottomless astonishment at the sudden intensity of my feelings. He had always thought he was the one with the stronger attachment. So had I. Sometimes I wondered if he only took my calls to hear me in this weakened state, to hear anyone so heartbroken over him.

"If things ended with the kid, would you still give me a chance?" I asked him more than once. "I mean, I haven't blown it completely, have I?"

"You haven't done anything unforgivable," he said, really seeming to think about his answer as he always did. "You haven't done anything at all, really. It's just that I started to believe you when you told me who you are, and I kind of got off at the next exit."

"See? That's where you went wrong," I said. "You never should have believed me."

"Well, that's just too complicated for me. I want to be with someone who says what he means. I want to be able to tell someone that I love him and for him to say 'I love you too.'"

"Oh, I didn't mean it in a complicated way. I love you. See? I can say it."

"Sounds pretty complicated from here."

I knew what he meant. From their emails, I could see all the things about the kid that he loved, all the unreserved passion and excitement, the way the kid could let himself be taken care of without seeming needy. It wasn't something I knew how to compete with.

"Okay," the cop said, "I need to hang up now. I'm almost to the house. We're going out to dinner."

"He's waiting for you?"

"He's there at the house, yeah."

"You don't tell him when we talk, do you?"

"Of course."

"Don't do that!" I said.

"We're a couple. You have to get that through your head. I tell him everything."

"How could it be that you were just you alone a few months ago, and now you have to tell someone else every little thing you do?"

"I don't *have* to do anything. Look, I don't expect you to under-stand. It's just the way it is now."

"Okay," I said. "That's okay. Have a really great night, okay? I'm not trying to stress you out. I just want you to be happy."

"Sounds good," he said. "Goodbye."

"Wait!" I said.

"What is it?"

"Nothing. Forget it. Goodnight. Talk to you soon. Tomorrow, maybe? Okay?"

34

ONE OF THE CLERKS AT THE ARCADE STARTED FLIRTING with me, and though he was not at all my type, I got a kick out of him liking me. It seemed like a compliment since he had so many men to choose from. He was an attractive Hispanic guy, short like me. I always felt glad when I showed up and he was there. He was friendly, and we'd chat for a few minutes before I took my tokens to the hallways. The flirtation began when he would give me my tokens and drag his hand against mine as he withdrew. That always made me roll my eyes. Eventually, though, I'd curl my fingers to meet his.

Once or twice I went into a booth and got hard watching the kinds of movies I watched out there. Something, for instance, in which construction workers were instructed to strip and masturbate by the disembodied voice of the cameraman. I'd get myself all wound up and excited. Then I'd arrange my erection so that it stuck up above the waistband of my pants, beneath my t-shirt. I'd walk into the main store, and, when no one was looking except Bruno, I'd lift my shirt to show him my dick sticking out of my pants. He'd look and widen his eyes. He'd smile and laugh and shake his head.

Then Bruno showed me his dick, which would get hard after I showed him mine. It was always fast, just a glimpse. It was a brand new way of using the arcade. I liked that he was stuck behind the desk. It felt as if all that sexual energy and momentum could encircle us both and then be expressed in other parts of our lives, like a Newton's Cradle.

After seeing my dick one day, he said, "Pretty big. Not as big as my boyfriend, but nobody is."

He knew my taste in men. I'd walk in the door, and he'd say, "Man, you might as well turn around and go home. You should have called first. There's nothing out here for you. Just a bunch of pretty boys."

Or he'd say, "Oh, shit. Look who just showed up. You're gonna be in hog heaven with this bunch of bruisers."

Sometimes I would stand by the counter and chat with him.

He'd say, "Why don't you go fuck that one right there? The guy in the running shorts."

And I'd say, "I'd never do it with that guy."

Then we'd watch on the TV screen behind the counter as someone pulled up in a plumbing truck wearing jeans and boots, his gut pressed against his work shirt. "Here's my guy," I'd say. He'd come in and buy his tokens from Bruno while I pretended to browse DVDs. A few minutes later, I'd find the plumber, and we'd go into a booth together.

Bruno never believed me when I told him I didn't really do anything in the booths. I'd tell him I was there to watch, that I didn't let the guys go down on me, and that I didn't go down on them. "Hands only," I'd say. "If that."

"Yeah, right," he'd say. Or, "Please."

I felt safer knowing he was watching me on the cameras to see where I was going and with whom. There were times I let things go further than just watching or just touching. Bruno acted like he knew, but I'd lie and say nothing happened.

Late one night I found him working the counter, blasting Tejano music on the store's sound system. I bought some tokens, tipped him his buck, and spoke with him for a minute or two before someone else came in and I moved along.

Later, as I pretended to browse DVDs, he signaled for me to come talk to him. When I got to the counter, he whispered that I should meet him by the soda machine next to Big Tits in two minutes. That worried me a little. It meant he was coming out from behind the counter. I'd never seen him come all the way out before. He'd opened the swinging half-door a little so I could get a look at his lower half, but he'd never actually emerged.

By then, it had happened many times that I had flirted with someone, male or female, and had my bluff called. I would have laid it on thick by then. I'd have put everything I had into it. I'd have hinted and cajoled and been witty and clever and shown off in every way I knew. At last, he or she would give in, perhaps even thinking "Let's just do this already." Usually it was only then that I realized I had never really wanted that person to begin with. Suddenly, I was put in the position of spurning the advances of someone who thought they were granting my wish. It didn't make sense to anyone, least of all me.

The pattern was familiar at the arcade long before Bruno told me he was coming out from behind the counter. I'd see some guy in the store pretending, like me, to flip through the DVDs, and we'd be looking at one another. He'd smile a little or nod toward one of the hallways. Or he'd grab his crotch as if adjusting himself.

I'd feel myself becoming attracted to him almost against my will, just because the sexual tension was so gripping. But when the acceptable time limit for pre-booth courtship had elapsed, he'd stop pretending to look at DVDs and start signaling towards the dark hallways. The longer I stalled, the weirder I appeared. I'd come off as a tease or someone who didn't know what he wanted.

I couldn't just go into a booth with him. I had to build up to it. It wasn't enough to be attracted or interested. I had to feel overwhelmed and controlled by irresistible lusts in order to finally give in.

The false alarms surprised even me. I'd follow the guy into a hallway. I'd be walking behind him. I'd watch him go into a booth. It was understood that I was right on his heels, that his door would creak open in two seconds, and we would be alone together. Sometimes something in me would let me go. I'd follow him and we would be in the dark booth together. But other times, at the final moment I'd veer off in another direction. When later I saw him outside in the store, I greeted his bewilderment with cheery blankness, as if encountering him for the first time in my life.

I waited in Big Tits until Bruno came out from behind the counter. He made like he was going to get a soda, then ducked into the area next to Cum Shots—a category which long confounded me, because I've always understood pornography to be an industry growing ever more granular, appealing to smaller and smaller segments of idiosyncratic perversion, and here, one of the biggest sections in the store was basically devoted to sex itself, or sex endings.

"Come here," he whispered.

I went over to him. He reached down and undid my belt and opened my pants. "Someone's going to see us," I said.

"Who cares?"

"Let's at least go behind this shelf."

"Stay where you are," he said. "This is the only place in the store where the cameras can't see us."

"Oh!" I said, excited by this bit of insider knowledge. "Is it being recorded or something?"

"Yeah, and the owner can see all the cameras live from his house."

He took my dick out of my pants. "Does he do that? Watch from home?"

"Sometimes," he said.

I undid Bruno's belt and his pants. It was the first time I'd ever touched him, apart from the curled fingers. It was exciting the way it was happening with no warning.

All the arcade's customers were in the booths or in the hallways. I kept thinking someone would walk by. I didn't know where things were going. I thought we'd have to stop soon, but Bruno didn't seem to be slowing down. He got on his knees in front of me.

"We can't do this," I said.

"Just let me taste it."

I let him, then I stopped him again.

"Someone's going to see us," I said. "We have to stop."

"I don't care if they see," he said. "They can watch if they want to."

The idea sent a rabble of shocks up from my hands and feet, flooding into my chest and stomach. I was surprised he didn't care. I was surprised about the whole thing, but I was surprised about that especially. I would have expected him to view it as a potential threat to his authority to be seen blowing a customer on the floor of the store. At the same time, it was kind of amazing to think of being seen with him that way. The idea made me harder.

At that moment, someone did exit the hallway nearest us, and I let go of Bruno's head and let him draw me into his mouth just in time for the guy to glance over. When he saw us, I could feel myself surge towards the edge. I had been nowhere close, and then I was right there. I stopped Bruno again with my palm pressed against his forehead.

I looked down at him.

"Come on," he said. "Don't stop."

I let him go again. His hands were gripping my ass, as he pulled my entire dick into his mouth and throat. Several feet away, the man watched us, stopped in exactly the spot where he had been when he first saw us, like someone trying not to disturb a woodland scene he'd happened upon.

I could feel myself getting close again, rocking my hips towards his mouth. I wanted to come in his mouth, but I was afraid to for some reason.

"We have to stop," I said. "I don't do this stuff out here."

Bruno pulled back, and my dick rested against his chin as he looked up at me.

"You really don't want to finish?"

"I can't, man. Someone's watching."

Bruno didn't even look around to see. He didn't care. He just smiled and shook his head and rose from the floor. "Your loss."

I put myself away, and he reached and touched me through my jeans. Then he started to put himself away and let me touch him too.

The guy who had come out of the hallway was still watching the two of us. He went to a nearby shelf and pretended to look at DVDs. Someone came in the front door, and Bruno went and bought a Coke from the machine and returned to the counter as if he had only popped away for a moment. The guy bought some tokens and went into a hallway. The man who had seen me with Bruno followed the other man.

It seemed wrong to hit the hallways after that, so I went to the counter.

Bruno smiled and said, "I knew you were full of shit."

"You think I do that with everyone?"

"I don't know. Probably."

"Oh, right. What about you?" I said. "How often have you done that?"

"That was a first, man."

I didn't press it. I didn't want to think of him sucking off a bunch of other guys just like me. I didn't want to feel jealous, and I was afraid I might have, as irrational as it would have been, given that I had no interest in having any kind of romantic association with Bruno beyond our recent encounter, or maybe another similar one.

We joked about when we might have a chance to finish what we'd started. I went home after that, twelve tokens in my pocket. I fantasized about it for a few weeks, and I didn't run into Bruno in that time. I thought I'd see him again and we'd go back to the place between Big Tits and Cum Shots and give the guys a show if they wanted it.

When I did finally see him, it was on a busy night. We were barely able to speak at all, and there was no opportunity for him to leave his post.

After that, I never saw Bruno again. It was too bad. I liked him. Now someone else was learning to run the arcade. The new guy was a bouncer type in his forties with a big beard, long hair, tattoos across his knuckles. The heavyset clerk who usually worked overnight was training him.

I had earphones in my ears, as I often did. And, as always when in public, I wasn't listening to anything at all. I heard them discussing the procedures of the place, how everything worked. I wondered where they had advertised the job. Craigslist, I assumed. I wished I had known about the opening. Maybe I would have applied. Although I already had a hard enough time explaining my job at the motel to friends and family without extended disclaimers and excuses and feelings of inferiority and shame.

Swept up in a daydream about a peepshow career, I missed when the clerks' conversation transitioned from arcade protocols.

As I stood pantomiming looking at DVDs, I gradually realized they were talking about me.

"I don't know much about any of them, frankly," the heavyset clerk was saying. "That guy usually tips at least, which a lot of guys don't do."

"Huh," the bouncer said.

"Everybody's different. Some of the clerks are friendlier than others. I mean, none of us are gay, so there's that difference from the start. I think that's intentional on the part of J.R. Not that he's like discriminating against them or whatever. I mean, I don't know if a lot of gay guys have applied for jobs here, but I don't think he'd be interested in staffing the place with a bunch of homos if he could avoid it. J.R.'s pretty smart about getting the most out of people, which can be a good thing and a bad thing, if you know what I mean. Anyway, supposedly there was some trouble with the last gay clerk a while back, so he pretty much stopped hiring them."

"Sounds about right," the bouncer said.

The heavyset clerk went on. "But in general, speaking only for myself, I'd say you don't have to work here long before you notice that there are a few different types of customers, and it's pretty rare that someone just goes and breaks the mold."

"Like what kind of types?" the bouncer asked. "Like aggressive guys?"

"No, not aggressive. Like a few of them are really flamey and over the top. And some of them are real reserved and conservative. Not what you'd usually think of. Some of the guys are here all the time, like they're real junkies for it. I mean, some of them you just see over and over again, every day. Some of them want to talk to you and kind of try to be your friend or whatever."

"Well, that shit ain't gonna work with me. I'm not looking for friends out here."

"People get the idea pretty quick if you're not a chatty type. Most of them are actually alright. A lot of them just like being here. For some of these guys it's funny, it's like their favorite place to be."

"Sounds pretty fucking desperate."

"Yeah. Like I said, everyone's different, and for sure Casey's style is going to be different than Ray's style, is going to be different than Jason's style. And they're all different from my style, which is still different than what J.R. would say about how we should be running the place. But if you ask me, it's a good idea to try to avoid getting too judgmental about people. My ex-wife was a stripper, so I know how that stuff goes."

"Oh yeah?"

"I'm sure I've had my moments or whatever, but I try to be respectful and cool with everybody. I mean, people know I'll drop the hammer if I have to, but I try to avoid it."

The bouncer seemed to be thinking. "I guess if there was a place like this with women roaming around looking to get fucked, I might check it out," he said. He laughed at the idea.

"Of course, man. That's the thing. The thing is, these guys that come out here are getting laid like three or four hundred times more than most straight guys. And they're sure not all lookers. I mean, that guy over there with the headphones. I've definitely seen him go into booths with people, just like anyone else. And, you know, like I said, no judgment. I mean, he's not a freak or anything, but he doesn't exactly look like the type to get a lot of action, you see what I mean? So I guess there are a lot of those types out here too. Sort of average guys, I guess you'd say."

"I guess you see all kinds of shit out here."

35

MAYBE THE CLERKS THEMSELVES FELT JUDGED ABOUT THEIR unconventional service industry jobs, as I often did at the motel. A lot of the guys who went to arcade had respected positions in the fields of their choosing. When guys like that were at the arcade, it was understood that they were slumming. They'd show up wearing suits and shirts pressed by wives or dry cleaners. Guys like that thought they were doing the clerk a favor if they acted like his pal for five seconds or asked about the book he was reading.

I grew up in small-town upper middle class society, thinking the same way, projecting myself into a future where I too would learn the names of my servers in restaurants so I could use them excessively in a show, not of genuine respect, but of some studied and disingenuous facsimile of regard for one's "peers." That's why I always made up names to give the guests when they asked for mine. The joke was on them when they kept thanking Mitch or Jeffrey for helping them with their stopped sink or for explaining how to get an outside line on the telephone in their room. Or when they complained that Ivan wasn't very helpful when they had a problem connecting to the Wi-Fi.

Once, my manager came to the lobby before leaving for the night and said, "Have you been telling people your name is Champ?"

"No," I said, "but I told someone my name is Chip."

"That solves that mystery. A woman in 254 complained that there weren't enough pillows in her room, and that Champ acted put out by her request for one or two extras."

"She asked for seven extras," I said. "In addition to the eight that were already on the two queen beds in the room."

"What the fuck?"

"Exactly. I had to make two trips. And she was the only person in there."

But she remembered my name, or tried anyway.

I could never have predicted those kinds of conversations when I was younger. For all my progressive leanings, well into young adulthood I still believed that the most intelligent people were the ones who had money. If you were smart, I figured, you'd find a way to get your hands on it or else you'd just end up with it. I probably got that wrong impression from repeated viewings of *The Big Chill*, in which Tom Berenger's character says to his old college friend played by Kevin Klein, "Who would have thought we'd both make so much bread?"

Of course, I learned it doesn't flutter down quite the way I thought it would.

I read that empathy is the highest form of emotional intelligence, and that most people won't ever experience it. It's not simply that most people won't have a clue what it's like to see the world through someone else's eyes. Most would never even be inclined to try.

I became preoccupied by the subject of empathy soon after starting work at the motel, where I interacted with people all day but felt invisible, not to mention broke and hypersensitive and too aware of the difficulty of bridging the class divide over the course of some fleeting encounter with a vacationing guest.

My friends from college were all financially secure by then. To them, my situation was a novelty. Over dinner Jarrod said of me to his wife, Lara, "He's the poorest of our friends now, isn't he? It used to be Wayne, but then he got that great job in New York."

Later that evening we were talking about the punk bands from our youth that were reuniting and touring. Jarrod said, "What do they have to lose? They're probably just working at Home Depot or something now."

I said, "There's nothing wrong with working at Home Depot. I think I read they have really good benefits for their employees, actually."

They didn't say anything, but I felt something pass between them over the table, an unexpressed eye roll, a bookmark in the conversation they might talk about later as they got ready for bed. Or laugh about. "There's nothing wrong with working at Home Depot," Jarrod might mimic later that night, as he flossed and Lara brushed her teeth. Then they'd laugh. I wondered if they thought I was a class warrior.

A few months earlier Jarrod had been laid off from his job. When Lara called to tell me that he'd found another, I said, "That's great. Did he have to take a pay cut?"

"Actually this job pays about $15,000 more than the last one," she said. "Of course, at our level, that won't make any difference to us."

I vacationed with wealthy relatives who grew angry after hearing me say on more than one occasion that I couldn't afford something.

"Stop saying that!" my aunt finally snapped.

"What should I say when I can't afford something?" I said.

"Say, 'I prefer not to spend my money that way.'" She was literally holding a silver spoon in her hand as she spoke, poised over a bowl of lobster bisque.

They were footing the bill for the trip, and were generous and lovely people, so I left it at that, but I spent months thinking about her suggestion whenever my dire financial situation arose in my mind.

A vacation home? I prefer not to spend my money that way.

A new laptop? I prefer not to spend my money that way.

A pair of running shoes? I prefer not to spend my money that way.

Dinner at Whataburger? I prefer not to spend my money that way.

A Bartleby for the age of consumption.

I never judged the clerks at the arcade, even if they did judge me. I understood implicitly that they were not just guys working at a sex arcade. They were men with jobs who wished to be doing something else with their lives, or who were actively doing things with their lives that the job at the arcade made possible, even if their ambitions were as simple as feeding themselves and enjoying, as much as they could, their brief existences on the planet.

36

IN MY OWN CAREER AS A CLERK, I FLATTERED MYSELF THAT I had a particular skill for reading people. Like the Fifty States puzzle I had as a kid, it was as simple as slipping them into the right slots, the appropriate cliché categories and tidy archetypes. I'd read that there were only seven basic plots that all works of fiction could be divided into. It seemed like bullshit, but the longer I worked at the motel the more it seemed true of people themselves. Maybe there weren't even seven different types.

On my worst days, it was as if I had a compulsion to develop opinions about people and then to subtly let on what they were. When I liked someone, I was straightforward, complimentary, and open. When I didn't like them, I joked dryly. I'd describe someplace I felt they should visit while they were in town, then hint at how much I detested the place and its denizens. Or if they were arriving to join a big group, all of the members of which seemed to me to be essentially the same, I would say, before they could tell me, "I bet you're with the people in rooms 140 and 141." Though I was always right, I could see their frustration at being perceived in a way that was counter to the way they thought of themselves, as members of a group rather than as individuals. But given the way I went about it, it would have seemed silly for them to defend themselves openly. They would have looked sensitive and paranoid.

I'd like to think it wasn't ever anything devastating or even memorable. Just a bit of discomfort quickly forgotten, a minute of bad customer service. But even after I stopped, I still searched for a way to place myself on the same level as everyone else from behind the front desk. I was always surprised at the nakedness of people's feelings towards perceived underlings, and I was equally surprised by how much it got to me. At least five percent of the customers appeared not to think of me as an actual human being. Five percent doesn't sound like much—I guess I should have been grateful for the ninety-five percent—but it could feel like a lot, particularly since I worked at a budget motel at which many of our customers weren't much better off than I was. I could only imagine how much worse it would have been at one of the nearby boutique hotels or the great towers of wealth where Malcolm was trying to whip into shape a workforce made up of people wearing actual suits and ties.

One of the great gifts of the arcade was the way it put us all on the same level. Of course I could tell which men were rich or poor or middle class, but it didn't matter out there. After the three-dollar threshold, we were all the same. I went to the arcade when I was flush with cash, and at other times when I was so hard up for money I debated whether or not I could really drop a fiver on the venture. It didn't change anything. It didn't change my luck. It was the first and only level playing field I'd ever been on. I liked the idea that most of us never would have met or interacted if it hadn't been for that place, divided as we were by our jobs and incomes.

37

I DROVE TO THE COP'S HOUSE ALMOST AN HOUR AWAY. I didn't know what would happen once I got there. I wanted to look at it, to see the exact brick house inside of which he lived, even though it was identical to any number of brick houses, not just in his neighborhood or mine, but in the United States and the world. I didn't know why I was going there, and I tried not to think about it.

As I drove, I played the same two maudlin albums of bad radio music I listened to ceaselessly during that period, albums which had come out that very year and which seemed to capture my feelings so precisely that I had the standard, ludicrous notion that if only the cop could hear the songs on those records he might reach a state of empathy and comprehension of my position so complete that he would return my love.

I could imagine a fantasy in which I took a portable stereo to his house. I could imagine his impatience as I insisted that he would understand everything perfectly if he would just listen. I could imagine loading the tracks and watching his arms slowly uncross as the songs played. I could imagine invisible lightning bolts of mutual understanding traveling between us. Sometimes I thought the scene played better in a car, but then I'd have to pull over in order for us to embrace.

The first time I drove to meet him I told myself that at any moment I could exit the highway and turn my pickup around, to return to my apartment and my normal life where I would be a straight person who didn't fool around with men ever, under any circumstances, no matter what. When I arrived, he answered the door, and I remembered learning about the receptors in our brains designed especially for molecules that fit perfectly into them, no matter how complex and odd their shapes.

After that first visit, I played particular albums on the way to meet him with the intent of using classical conditioning to mark the experience by the sound. Then I could have the same feeling by playing the songs later, the way people who have traumatic experiences at great heights can become phobic about skyscrapers. Driving out there, I felt good and excited and eager. I also felt a little preemptively sad, because I could already see that it would soon be over. Whenever I saw a pickup like mine going in the opposite direction I imagined I was seeing a future version of myself heading home an hour or so hence. The landmarks along the way were like friends cheering me on, telling me I was that much closer to the house of the cop, where I never once thought about killing myself. I kept looking at my phone, always afraid it would ring and somehow interrupt me and ruin everything.

When the cop saw me getting out of bed over and over again to check my phone, he started frisking me when I came inside and making me leave it in my pickup, parked at the curb in front of his house. He got out a legal pad and we sat down at his kitchen table together to make a list of excuses I could use if I returned to the cab of my truck and found that I had missed calls.

First, we made a list of the people most likely to call and ask, "Where were you?" or "Why didn't you pick up?" Then we mapped out a list of people those people didn't know, but who I also knew. That was excuse number one. "I was on the phone with X. S/he's having a rough time because of some personal stuff." Since they didn't know one another but did know *of* one another, they'd never have an opportunity to test the alibi.

Then we had to come up with an excuse explaining where I was in case someone needed me urgently. I'd have to explain that I was an hour away. We agreed that no matter how pressing the issue, I would wait until I was within half an hour of my home to call.

"In fact, don't even check your messages until you're within a half hour of your house," he said.

We came up with a list of locations around town that could reasonably be half an hour from my house. There were lots of places from which I might have had a hankering for ice cream or a particularly good cheeseburger. Then, if I had to call, I could say, "I'll be there in thirty minutes," which would raise far fewer suspicions than an hour.

I could also say I was out for a drive. I really did go for drives to unwind in those days. Gasoline was so cheap then that going for a relaxing drive seemed like a free activity.

At the bottom of the page, the cop wrote, "I'm out for a drive."

"Don't you get tired of this stuff?" he said, when we were finished. "I do."

"I mean, of course I do. On one hand. But on the other hand, it's nice that you're my secret. It's nice having a secret."

"You'll see," he said. "It gets old eventually."

He'd said it before, that he was sick of all the secrecy. That he didn't like lying to people. That he was basically an honest guy with ideals and all that. I knew he'd never come out to anyone though. His stepfather? With that backyard shed for woodworking, and those horrible racist jokes? No way.

But then he did, for the kid. Or at least he had come out to some people. He told me about it on the phone, how he told his sister. How he told a guy he knew at the restaurant where he had sometimes worked security during big events. He told me his mother said she was glad he had a new roommate, and that he should try to be happy however he could because life was short, but that his grandmother, who would only be with them for a short time longer, didn't need to know every detail, and that sometimes ignorance was bliss. He took the kid to family dinners calling him his roommate. And the kid had friends over to the house. They played video games and drank margaritas from the margarita machine the cop had bought, and they all laughed so hard someone had to run to the bathroom to pee, like girls at a sleepover.

The day we wrote the list, the cop stopped me before I could walk out the door.

"Don't forget your excuses," he said.

He went to the table and tore the top leaf off the pad and brought it to me.

"I can't take this with me," I said. "What if someone finds it?"

"Right," he said.

He opened the drawer in his kitchen where he kept all his manuals and warranties. He put the paper under the stack there and said, "This will always be here when we need it."

Then he kissed me and sent me home.

I liked to imagine what would happen if I got into an accident on the way home from his house or on the way to it. I hoped it would be a gruesome scene and that I would die tragically. No one would know what I had been doing there an hour from my place in the middle of nowhere. It wouldn't make sense, and no one would know how to figure it out. No one knew the truth about where I was going except for me and the cop. Maybe he would show up at the funeral and everyone would wonder what it meant, what any of my life had meant. Or maybe he wouldn't know, would never hear, and would think I had simply disappeared. He would be heartbroken and remember me forever as a mysterious and wonderful thing in his life.

I didn't know why I suddenly felt I had to drive out to his house. It was important to prove to myself that I could get there without directions. That it was ingrained in my mind. I really did know. I could locate it with no problem in that sea of houses that all looked basically the same. This exit off the highway, take a right over the freeway, the road dead ends next to Noah's Ark Self-Storage and a barbecue joint called Adam's Rib, a right, the second right, wind around through the neighborhood, but stay on that street, and at the very last right before the road ended, there he was.

Anything could happen once I got there. Maybe I'd know just what to do at the critical moment. Maybe I'd abandon my still-running truck at the curb, with the driver's door open as I marched to the door and pounded with my fist. What then? I didn't know. But those were the kinds of bold moves I had read about and seen in movies that won people back, that made people think twice about all the passion they were abandoning if they were really saying no to this person.

I thought maybe I would see them, the cop and the kid, like in a film. I'd be parked on the corner or directly across the street, but they wouldn't notice me. Through the windshield, I'd glimpse their perfect life as they loaded the car for a picnic. Or maybe one of them would be leaving for work and the other would rush out with the forgotten lunch pail and a front yard kiss.

I could crack the house open like a dollhouse and see inside all the rooms, thanks to my familiarity with the place and all the photos they were emailing to one another or linking to in private galleries to which I held the passwords.

When I arrived at his house, I didn't think. I got out of my truck and strode to the door. I knocked and waited, feeling as though someone else was steering me, feeling that I had some right to be there. It was my list of excuses somewhere in that kitchen drawer. The kid had no right to them.

I knocked one more time. No answer. I got back into my truck and drove away, replaying the event in my mind, amazed that I'd summoned the courage to do it. I had no idea what would happen next or what else I was capable of.

38

JACK AND JOAN INSISTED ON TAKING ME TO LUNCH. I DIDN'T want to go. I felt obligated because everyone was worried about me, and I was starting to fear that my friends would stage some sort of intervention or appear at my doorstep unannounced. Or, worse, show up at the motel. I hadn't seen Jack and Joan since a month earlier, when over the course of a frantic tour of my friends' homes I had enacted the same breakdown in living rooms all over the city, bursting into tears then blurting out everything about the cop and the kid and my own uncertainty about everything, including whether or not I should go on living.

I told them I had lost my mind and that my only remaining connections to the cop were our sporadic, unsatisfying phone calls. I even confessed reading his email "once or twice." I told them that I was doing everything I could to get him back, but that I hadn't made any progress at all. In my mania, through tears, I even tried soliciting their advice, but they were all too shocked by the sudden revelation of my homosexuality and a secret romance to help me strategize. And besides they'd never met the guy and had no idea what might work.

It seemed to me in those moments that even if they had met him, my friends would never really understand. They were all so *normal* in the end. I couldn't expect them to grasp passionate secrets kept for years and the kind of love that wasn't cause for celebration but made one's own father say things like, "I always knew there was something wrong with you, I just hoped it wasn't this."

My coming out happened in such a rush of confusion that my friends were left bewildered and panicked on my behalf. It didn't help that after each explosion, I was quick to beat it out of their homes, only rarely answering phone calls thereafter.

I didn't feel like talking to anyone other than the cop and Malcolm, who was still working at the hotel in Boston and still taking my calls whenever he had time. I couldn't imagine why. I was beginning to wonder if there might even be something suspicious in his tolerance for my hysteria and the insane repetition of my queries. *Would the cop ever call? Would he love me again? What did the kid have that I didn't have?* Malcolm's patience certainly wasn't normal, and he never gave any reason for it. In a movie, it would have been revealed that, years earlier, he had lost a love in a similar fashion and now was committed to getting it right vicariously through me. But no such explanation emerged.

Jack and Joan wanted to pick me up at my place. I said I'd rather meet them. They tried pressing the issue, but I was firm. They gave me the name and address of a place I'd never heard of and said I should meet them at eleven-thirty. The tone of the conversation was hyper-cheery, with Jack cautiously avoiding any questions about my private life apart from a, "Hey, how are you?" when I first answered.

I arrived at the address twenty minutes late, and found that Joan had picked the brightest venue possible, a new restaurant named Glass for its primary construction material. It was essentially a greenhouse with some tables. Clear on all sides, even the ceiling was made of windows. Plants everywhere. I spied Jack and Joan, sunlit at a table beneath a drooping fern hung from the ceiling.

I felt like Nosferatu invited out for brunch. My whole life took place in darkness then. The late hours at work. My shadowy apartment with the blinds closed. The arcade.

I walked to their table, regretting that I hadn't worn sunglasses. Jack and Joan looked like alien creatures to me, so clean and happy, like the type of merry vacationing guests that sometimes stayed at the motel.

"Hey!" Joan said. "We were getting worried."

"Sorry I'm late."

"No big deal," Jack said, shaking my hand. Had he hugged me before finding out the truth about me? I couldn't remember.

Joan stood and wrapped her arms around me. "Isn't this place adorable? We've heard such great things about it. And they have deviled eggs, which I know you love."

I looked down at the monogrammed handkerchief apparently meant to serve as a napkin, and the amber-colored prescription bottles from the 1920s that contained, I presumed, salt and pepper, despite their labels reading "Cocaine" and "Morphine."

"Cute," I said. "Very, very, very, very cute."

"Well, it's no Taco Bell," Jack said.

It was a joke among friends that I had lowbrow tastes. It was true that I was a devoted diner at Taco Bell. I always had been, all through college and the subsequent years, when my friends were experimenting with farm-sourced meats and wild-caught salmon and, at last, veganism, which they had all abandoned by the age of 26.

A tattooed waitress came and I ordered a thirteen-dollar pimento cheese sandwich and their only option for a soft drink, an all-natural, caffeine-free lemon soda.

"So, we have news," Joan said.

"Oh?"

"You tell him, Jack."

Jack smiled at Joan, and Joan smiled back. They both smiled at me. They seemed more like aliens than ever. All this smiling. Maybe I was the alien. The alien vampire pervert homo.

"Well," he said, "we're pregnant."

"Oh my God," I said. "Are you keeping it?"

A short silence passed.

"People don't announce it when they're not keeping the baby."

Had the timing been different, I might have mentioned that, very drunk about six years prior, Joan *had* announced a soon-to-be-terminated pregnancy with an ironically festive air. Less than a week after the procedure we had gone out for an occasion she dubbed the Roe v. Wade Happy Hour.

"Can you believe we're having a baby?" Jack said again.

"I hate it when men say 'We're pregnant' or 'We're having a baby.' It's not like you're doing any of the work, Jack. When you tell people, maybe try 'We're expecting' or just 'Joan's pregnant.' I hope I'm the first person you're trying this out on."

"You're not. We told our families first. And about a dozen other people."

"Then my intervention is in vain."

"You have to admit, it's pretty cool," Joan said, her voice at a chirpy lilt. "The first baby of two of your dearest friends."

"I can't even imagine it," I said. "But congratulations, I guess."

"Thanks a lot," Jack said. "Guess who we're not asking to be the godfather."

"Don't be mean, Jack," she said.

"What does everyone else do?" I said. "Do they like squeal and spring out of their chairs and hug you both and say stuff like, 'Oh my god, you're going to be a mommy and daddy?'"

"Not exactly, but, yeah, something along those lines," Joan said.

Jack was getting mad. I'd known him long enough to recognize the sneery little smile he got when he was thinking something mean and debating whether or not to say it. I imagined him thinking, *This is why the cop doesn't want to be with you, you fucking faggot asshole.*

"We were hoping our news might cheer you up a little," Joan said.

"Really? You did?" I couldn't imagine a world in which someone else's breeding would mend my completely destroyed heart.

"I guess we were wrong."

"Sorry," I said. "But good for you guys for cloning yourselves or whatever."

"Wow, thanks," Jack said. "Really touching."

"Okay, enough of that. Do you want to talk about how things are going with you?" Joan said. "Have things changed at all with the policeman?"

"Maybe they've changed. I guess they've changed for the worse."

"I'm really sorry to hear that. I was hoping that the reason you weren't calling was that you were making some progress and had been going out to see him or something."

"No, nothing like that."

"Do you want to talk about it?"

"I don't think I can," I said. I didn't want to weep in a corny, fashionable restaurant.

Then Joan reached out and put her hand over mine on the tablecloth and I began to cry.

Even before bringing us our meals on deliberately mismatched, non-dishwasher-safe antique dinnerware, the waitress had to give me two more monogrammed handkerchief napkins. I kept thinking that one of them would have the cop's initials, and it would be a message of encouragement from God or the universe, but it wasn't to be.

Jack took pity on me and hugged me at the end of the meal saying, "I hope things get easier for you, man."

"Thanks. And good luck with the pregnancy stuff," I said. "You forgot to ask, but yes, you can name the kid after me."

In the parking lot, I looked at my phone. One missed call. From the cop. My heart seized. My hands were shaking as I stared at the screen. The call had come forty minutes earlier. My fucking phone hadn't even rung. It had been nine days since we had last spoken.

I called him back, forgetting everything I had rehearsed with Malcolm in preparation for that moment. He didn't answer, so I hung up and called him again. No answer. I called again, then again. I left one message on the fifth attempt and another on the seventh. I couldn't understand why I was being punished. I wanted to smash my face with my fists, to snuff out my own life by wrapping my seatbelt around my throat, to die and evaporate. I wanted never to have existed. I rested my head against the steering wheel, trying to keep my focus on deep breaths like I'd read to do online. It really was true that I wasn't fit company for anyone but the rejects out at the arcade.

39

BEING BANNED WAS MY GREATEST FEAR. THERE WERE SIGNS that threatened it. One said "We reserve the right to refuse service to anyone for any reason." Another, posted in both hallways said, "Customers who fail to follow the rules will be banned from the premises." Among the listed prohibitions were lewd behavior and loitering, which was essentially a list of the only two things I did there. I couldn't guess how I would end up getting banned—I was always on my best behavior—but I had a feeling it would happen eventually.

For most my life, I've had a similar horror that I might somehow end up in prison by a freak accident or misunderstanding. I'm not certain about the fear's precise origin, but I have a feeling it might have been coincident with the original airing of the prison-centered HBO series, Oz. I was 18 the year it premiered. Though I was finally able to buy cigarettes legally and to vote, I was preoccupied by the realization that, whatever might happen, there was no longer any possibility that I would be tried as a minor or find myself in juvie. Whatever I might do, however dumb with inexperience I was, the justice system saw me as fully formed.

A girl with whom I worked briefly in my early twenties once broke down and confided that if she was behaving strangely it was because her brother had recently been released from prison and had moved into her tiny apartment, bringing with him an incredible variety of problems. He'd been raped in the penitentiary and was HIV positive now, she said. She also explained that she did his laundry, and that he routinely experienced heavy anal bleeding. She wore rubber gloves to handle his clothes. I was so chilled I could barely remain composed, let alone comfort her. After that day, the subject of her brother was never raised again, though I thought and wondered about it all the time.

The character in *Oz* with whom I identified was a buttoned-up attorney imprisoned for driving drunk and killing a young girl on a bicycle. He was—as I would be—a poor candidate for prison life. In the first season, he's raped and made the property of his cellmate, the head of the Aryan Nation in the prison, who tattoos a swastika on the attorney's ass. As the series progresses the attorney undergoes a transformation. In a final-straw moment, he bites the tip off of a would-be rapist's penis, a sequence that I found especially powerful and shocking, given that penises were the primary reason I was watching *Oz* at all. It was arguably the premier place to view naked men for a few years in the late 1990s.

I'm sure if anyone ever bothered to do a survey of the gay population, it would be confirmed that a large percentage of *Oz*'s viewership was tuning in thanks to a different type of penal fascination. Never was there an episode without a shower scene, and there was always plenty of gay sex, both consensual and nonconsensual. During its original run, when I was still deeply in the closet, even to myself, I wondered if the title was a reference to the famous collective homosexual fixation on Judy Garland and *The Wizard Oz*, from which the euphemism "friend of Dorothy" originated.

I am sometimes in awe of all that I have been exposed to culturally that I never would have discovered if not for the pursuit of sex or sexual gratification. I think of all the movies I watched when I was young simply because I thought I might glimpse a nude body. I was like one of those men in the 1960s and 1970s watching Swedish films for the breasts and bush, who meanwhile were inadvertently absorbing Ingmar Bergman's entire filmography and being confronted with his ideas about God's silence in a random universe. Or watching the *I Am Curious* films and experiencing the disintegration of traditional editing and story structure just to see some sex and nudity. No doubt, countless intellectuals were born in those theater seats nursing hard-ons and accidentally becoming smarter.

Maybe Edgar Wallace was wrong when he described an intellectual as "someone who has found something more interesting than sex." Maybe an intellectual is someone who, while in pursuit of sex, happens upon something to fill the time he couldn't manage to fill with sex.

I must have been exposed to at least *some* great art in the search for sexual gratification *Porky's? Emmanuelle? Caligula? Cruising?* I don't know what might qualify. I remember having a whispered conversation with a guy at the arcade after a particularly intimate and fun encounter. He said I should read Stephen Pinker's *The Better Angels of Our Nature,* and I did, wishing very much to believe, as Pinker postulates, that mankind is improving.

40

THERE WAS A HARLEY-DAVIDSON MOTORCYCLE PARKED BY the door when I pulled into the lot, and I got the idea that I had to connect with its owner. He was easy enough to spot once I was inside. It's never a mystery with those guys. They're all such brand junkies. Everything Harley-Davidson. The whole basis of the culture is supposed to be this anti-corporate rebellion and free-spirited journeying out into the world of adventure and unpredictability, but these guys are absolute slaves to the brand name. All of their clothes say Harley-Davidson on them some-where. Their credit cards, wallets, baby clothes, teddy bears, cof-fee mugs, shot glasses, Christmas ornaments, their pocketknives, pencils and pens. It's not sufficient that everyone in the family is labeled, they must be tagged from head to toe in apparel sanc-tioned and produced by Harley-Davidson, Inc. No other adult fashion phenomenon rivals it.

The part that gets to me most is that the whole thing suggests a tremendous amount of disposable income, which flies in the face of the working man image of motorcycle culture I had growing up, in particular as portrayed in the 1985 based-on-a-true-story film *Mask*, starring Eric Stoltz as Rocky Dennis, a teenager afflicted with Craniodiaphyseal Dysplasia, a disorder that made his skull grow in unusual ways, so that his head was enormous and oddly shaped. In the film, Cher plays his mother, a biker chick surround-ed by her biker friends. Outsiders themselves, Cher's gang of biker friends serves as an unconventional family for Rocky, accepting him without reservation despite his radical deformity. The same movie could never be made today. The guys with Harleys would be weekend warrior types in the highest tax brackets. They might attend a benefit for Rocky, but would never become a surrogate family to him or even otherwise acknowledge his existence.

The Harley guy at the arcade was mid-forties, relatively fit, short hair. He looked like the kind of guy who might hold season tickets to his college football team, who drives an expensive pick-up that he washes obsessively when he isn't on his bike. He was wearing a Harley t-shirt, naturally. When I found him among the racks of movies in the store and asked the time, he checked his Harley-Davidson wristwatch. He was actually a little too classically good-looking to be my type, but he was close enough. We went to the hallway and found a booth. He touched me a bit and I touched him. It was always an uncertain moment. No one knows where things are going at first. I could tell he wasn't getting what he wanted.

"To be honest," he said, "I just came out here to get a blow job. Would you mind?"

He was so attractive and unusually well-mannered, I considered it for a moment.

"Actually, I don't do that out here," I told him finally, getting myself back into my pants. "You won't have a hard time though. You look great."

I meant what I said, that it wouldn't be difficult finding someone willing to go down on him even if it meant no reciprocation. There are innumerable men who are happy to fellate other men regardless of whether they will receive services in return. In online ads every day, scores of men make the same offer. "You come over, watch some porn. Straight or gay, I've got 'em both. Pull down your pants and let me give you the best blowjob of your life. No recip required."

These insatiable cocksuckers have transcendent experiences giving head. They're happiest when they're at it. It's amazing. You can't believe it when you connect with one of them. It's simultaneously incredibly fun and mildly terrifying, particularly when you imagine all the legs they've sat between on the floor, just there to perform a service. *Don't mind me.* There are thousands of videos online of truckers and roofers and deliverymen plopping themselves down on the sofas of these types of men. Their pants are down, their shirts are on. Squeals are audible from an off-camera TV, the sounds of a female porn performer. Sometimes the guy will have a remote control in his hand, fast-forwarding to the good parts. Or a cigarette or a beer. They exert the full force of their will in striking the image of straightness, which they pull off surprisingly well considering that their genitals are in the mouths of other men.

Later that same week, I had an encounter with a second biker at the arcade. He was equally easy to spot, though he was far from the weekend warrior type. This one looked like he might actually have been a friend to old Rocky Dennis and Cher back in the *Mask* days. I could see a crowd gathering in one of the booths. I tried it and found the door unlocked. Four guys, all with their pants undone and cocks in hand. On the floor knelt the biker, a thin middle-aged man with a ponytail and a long, gray beard. He wore no shirt and a sleeveless denim vest with a big patch sewn onto the back, reading "Lone Wolf – No Club."

He was at the center of an incredible scene. The lone wolf brought men to climax one after another. No recip required. Men entered and left the booth. It smelled strongly. Our pheromones filled the air. I stood in the corner and watched. It was disgusting and vile and fascinating. The biker seemed to be in the throes of something. A born again Christian might have taken it as proof that possession was a reality. We all kept feeding tokens into the slot. I didn't know where any of it was going. It went on and on.

I stayed and watched until no one was left in the place that hadn't been in that booth. It had been a long time and a lot of men. I kept expecting myself to leave in the next minute, and the next, and the next. But I stayed. Before that, I hadn't known something like what I'd witnessed could spontaneously occur.

In the end, I was alone with the lone wolf. I couldn't get a handle on him. He seemed almost like a machine to me, but I knew he was a real person with a framed photo of his mother in an apartment or trailer home somewhere. He hadn't said anything the entire time, and he didn't say anything now. He stood up as I was putting my dick in my pants, his knees hurt from being on the floor for so long.

He was a mess. With his pants still around his ankles, he sat on one of the benches and took a red handkerchief from his back pocket. He tried to clean himself up.

"Thanks for letting me watch," I said.

"No problem," he said, his voice gravelly and parched.

41

I TRIED TO REMEMBER EVERYTHING ABOUT THE COP.

The time we sat naked on his back porch. I sat on his lap, and we looked out onto a field that hadn't been developed into anything yet but would eventually become rows of tract homes. The only time I was ever naked with another man outdoors. Then I lit up a cigarette and he winced and pushed me away.

"That stinks," he said. "Go sit over there."

I remembered that once when there was something wrong with his hot tub, he had spread newspaper over his dining room table and sat a bunch of greasy parts and a little motor on it.

"You really know how to fix stuff like this?" I'd said.

"It's not hard. You just have to be patient and think about what you're doing."

I had been at the cop's house on his sister's birthday one year. He had baked her a cake before I arrived. He left it on the counter to cool during our visit, and was icing it as I was leaving. He wore a gray bathrobe. One of those big plastic cake covers sat on the countertop. He put some frosting on a spoon for me to taste. The cake was a hideous pink color, and the icing had the flavor of melted rubber and sugary strawberry.

"I like it," I told him. "You're a good cook."

"Thanks. I changed the recipe up a little."

A *Reader's Digest* sat nearby, open-faced against the countertop marking the recipe he had adapted.

I remembered precisely where we had stood in his kitchen. I could have found the exact spoon from which I had taken that single, revolting taste, if I could have somehow gotten back into that house of his to dig though the utensil drawer just for a minute.

We were talking on the phone again, but only because he occasionally answered when I called. Malcolm warned that I was blowing it, but it felt so good to hear the cop's voice, I couldn't stop myself.

He didn't seem fascinated by the depth of my emotion anymore. And I was trying harder to imitate a calm and reasonable person when we spoke, because he was obviously fed up with my blubbering and arguments against the absurd age divide in his relationship.

I knew his feelings for me must still be in there somewhere, retrievable by the right combination of words or gestures, the way I imagined that if a maniac had a gun to my head, there must be some move I could make, some phrase I could use that would change the situation entirely. The hard part was figuring out what that thing was before having one's head blown off.

One evening, after trying and failing to disconnect from a phone call with me for several minutes, the cop said, "You ever think maybe you made our thing out to be a bigger deal than it was?"

I was shocked he would suggest such a thing. "I don't know how you could say that when we saw each other so many times and told each other so much."

"Bud, I think we're probably still in the single digits when it comes to face-to-face visits."

"You think we hung out fewer than ten times? Seriously?"

I began listing the different occasions we had been together. Maybe it really hadn't been more than ten.

"But we talked on the phone all the time," I said.

"I know we did," he said. "I used to always like it too."

"You mean before you moved the kid in?"

"I asked you not to call him 'the kid.' You know his name."

"I didn't mean to say that. I'm sorry."

"It's okay," he said. "Anyway, I got to go. I'm almost home.

"Sorry again," I said.

In every phone call, I had to apologize. First for everything, then for something specific.

42

IT WAS JUST AFTER I ARRIVED. THE FIRST BOOTH I ENTERED.
The light was on, the door unlocked. I pushed in and saw a movie
playing with the sound turned off. On the bench, a colossal fat man
on all fours, his rear end pointed at me.

I didn't leave. I stood and took it in, all the folds of fat around
his body. He must have showered just before he went to the arcade. The compartment smelled like Ivory soap and Right Guard
deodorant. The scene was like some outrageous art installation.

The man stayed perfectly immobile as I surveyed every inch
of his body that was visible from my position. His little scrotum
dangling between his legs, his enormous thighs. When the movie
stopped, I put in another few tokens so I could look a little longer.
Next to his foot was a condom in its wrapper and a small bottle of
lube. I was glad to see the condom, at least.

His breathing quickened while I was watching. He must have
been growing impatient. Just as I was about to leave, he moved.
Slowly ducking down, he pushed his ass higher in the air then
reached back and, without looking to see who had entered, spread
his cheeks.

43

ESPECIALLY AFTER THE BOUNCER TOOK THE AFTER-HOURS
shifts, some nights at the arcade took on a peculiar and ominous
dimension. It felt as if anything could happen, as if there were no
grownups paying attention.

On the rare occasions of my childhood when my folks returned
drunk from some party, I became overwhelmed by anxiety. It
wasn't simply that I felt vulnerable. I felt as if all the evil forces in
the world that had been waiting for an opportunity to smash their
way into my life had been granted complete access. I felt a twinge
of the same some dark nights at the arcade. You knew you could
get away with more if you had the balls to try. You could sneak out
your bedroom window if you wanted, and no one was going to
catch you, but no one was going to save you either.

Nights like that, the guy up front was just there to sell tokens, not
monitoring anything besides the register. Men were hanging out in
the hallways smoking cigarettes, leaning against the pressed wood
walls with one foot flat against the vertical surface like James Dean.
The hall transformed into a promenade, where you found yourself
walking back and forth before groups of loiterers who were openly
sizing you up, or trying to draw you into something, or pointedly
ignoring you. I always behaved the same way, wandering slowly,
acting a bit like I'd just lost something or had forgotten something
I was trying to remember, or as if I was on the hunt for the perfect
booth, and was operating purely on feel, a dowser missing his di-
vining rods. I felt foolish and self-conscious when groups of guys
were clumped together talking in little cliques. They'd be quiet for
a second as you made your way past but then inevitably they'd
whisper something right after, and even if it wasn't about you it

seemed like it was. Nights like that, the place felt haunted. *The Amityville Peep Show.*

After watching scary movies with the friends of my childhood, we could create nights in which the air itself felt barbed with fear and excitement, a buzz in our little chests as we talked about our scariest nightmares and the times we thought we saw a ghost or heard one just outside our windows, saying Bloody Mary into a dark mirror. Telling the story of how someone broke into my aunt's house while she was in the shower and stole her jewelry, leaving behind a trail of muddy, bare footprints. We talked about Ouija boards, and the girl at school who did tarot card readings in the lunchroom and had Sharpied a pentagram onto her three-ring binder.

When I was a kid, I was obsessed with the mysteries of the world. I checked out every book in my small town library on the subjects of Bigfoot and the Loch Ness Monster. I read about UFOs and the Bermuda Triangle and Stonehenge. I thought about telekinesis and astral projection and psychic powers and what it meant when something popped into my mind for no reason. I could never understand why everyone else wasn't as fascinated. When I learned about germs, I remembered the way we had to watch eclipses through a special apparatus we made from a paper towel roll. I became fixated on the idea that we were surrounded by things no one knew about because they hadn't yet thought of the right way to see them.

Close Encounters of the Third Kind played on TV when I was a kid. In the film, the government knows of the existence of extraterrestrials and is in the early stages of establishing contact with them. Despite denials from the authorities, the connection is already clear to many citizens who have experienced firsthand UFO sightings and, in some cases, abductions.

I watched the film over and over again and memorized the three types of encounters.

Close Encounter of the First Kind: Sighting of a UFO
Close Encounter of the Second Kind: Physical Evidence
Close Encounter of the Third Kind: Contact

After a close encounter of the first kind, Indiana lineman Roy Neary, played by Richard Dreyfuss, becomes inexplicably obsessed by a figure that intrudes on all his thoughts. In the movie's most iconic sequence, he molds a mound of mashed potatoes into that inscrutable shape, as yet unaware that he is replicating the Devils Tower National Monument in Wyoming. Staring at the form, not knowing what to make of it, he says to his frightened family, half out of frustration and half as a revelation, "This means something. This is important." The scene led me to experience a swell of emotion I couldn't begin to describe or understand.

I rented *Close Encounters* in adulthood and found that it held up. I still liked it for more than nostalgia's sake, and when Richard Dreyfuss said, "This means something," I got choked up, even though over the years I've heard so many negative things about Dreyfuss, who developed a reputation as a difficult and unpleasant person later in his career. My opinion of him softened briefly when I read that he had spoken publicly about being diagnosed with bipolar disorder. But I've noticed that people who are horrible because of their mental disorders are still horrible people, and I don't know quite how to think about that.

Watching *Close Encounters*, I could imagine just how it felt looking at that mass and not knowing what to make of it. I knew how exhilarating and terrifying it could be to have things happen to your mind over which you had no control. Things you wanted and didn't want at the same time.

44

AS A BOY, ALL MY FANTASIES CENTERED ON THE WISH THAT someone would molest me. I grew up in an era of panic about the fates of latchkey kids, and adults were always talking about the different kinds of touching, and how some of them were bad. I knew it was wrong to feel titillated by those discussions, but the idea of some older man sneaking into my room and touching me seemed so exciting and great. I'd lie in bed thinking about it until I shook all over.

When I wasn't praying to have a big penis, as I did every night, I prayed to be molested. It was a great blow to my ego that no grownup ever tried forcing me to perform oral sex on him. Wasn't I as good as all the other kids who were supposedly being raped pretty much around the clock? Even then, I had a sense of the limited time at my disposal. I knew I could only attract child molesters for a scant few years. I wondered if there was a signal I was supposed to learn to let people know I was a good candidate. I wanted them to know that I would never tell, that it would be our secret. They wouldn't even have to threaten my family or me, unless they wanted to, in which case it would be fine.

Of course, I didn't understand what molestation would entail. I only knew that, even not knowing what it was, it sounded like exactly what I wanted. I thought the word "fondle" was the sexiest word in the world. I didn't even care who it was. I just wanted some creepy old pervert to spread his trench coat in front of me, or to pose as a trusted member of the community and to lure me into an innocent-looking relationship. Then, on some overnight camping trip, he could teach me how to fuck.

Particularly influential on my earliest sexual fantasies was the "very special" two-part episode of *Diff'rent Strokes* in which Arnold and his best friend, Dudley, are seduced by the owner of a nearby bicycle shop, a lovely-seeming man who happens also to be a pedophile. In the show, the kindly cycling enthusiast seduces the boys with ice cream, and then wine. He shows them naked photographs of himself. In the end, of course, his plot is discovered before anyone can get really and truly molested, but it did give me an idea of what kinds of things I could anticipate if I could attract the right man.

The 1989 airing of the TV miniseries *I Know My First Name is Steven* gave me my first misgivings about my dreams of molestation. The story, based on the real-life kidnapping of seven-year-old Steven Stayner, made me call into question all my fantasies. Stayner had been held for more than seven years before escaping his captor with another boy named Timmy White. The name of his abductor, Kenneth Parnell, has stayed on my mind all these years.

Walking home from school just a few months after seeing *I Know My First Name is Steven,* a stranger actually did pull his car to the curb and offer me a ride. I shouted, "No!" and ran home, hysterical and constantly checking over my shoulder. The driver hadn't given chase. After that, at night, I sometimes masturbated to the fantasies of what might have become of me had I said yes and had gotten in his car and been carried away. By then, I was already resigned to the notion that a kind, older friend posing as a regular straight guy would never molest me.

Those types, men posing as regular straight guys, would be infinitely easier to find as I got older.

45

WHEN I TOLD MALCOLM ABOUT MY BOYHOOD DREAMS OF being molested, he said, "I think that's normal," as he did about almost everything.

We were catching up after more than a week without speaking. He'd decided to take a break from his struggles at the hotel in Boston to go home and spend a few days with his partner, Ron. They'd been missing each other, he told me. Neither of us mentioned the possibility of meeting in person while Malcolm was in town, and it was a given that he wouldn't be available to speak again until he was back in Boston.

All that week, I felt slightly on edge. Every time I went to the store or to get gas, I was hyperconscious that we might run into one another. Not that he would've recognized me. He still hadn't seen my face or even learned my real name. I didn't know the proper way to react. I figured I'd just pretend not to know him.

I had a fantasy about flying to Boston and staying in his empty room to restore the balance. He had described his penthouse suite little-by-little over our talks, and I had a vision of a sprawling, past-its-prime retreat with a giant oak desk, a king-size bed, a big flat-screen TV in the master bedroom and an old tube TV in the living room, a stocked minibar, and a cart from room service shoved in a corner. In the living room, a dated sofa, the floral print of which I'd seen over a video chat when the two of us jerked off together. A balcony looking out onto some historic harbor.

Malcolm said it had been a glamorous place once, and named some stars who had stayed in his room: Candice Bergen, Judd Hirsch, Lonnie Anderson, Dixie Carter. Fred Savage had stayed there with his parents. They were all people who had been on TV decades earlier. The company he worked for bought it cheap and were relying on Malcolm to bring it back to its "quote unquote former splendor." He'd done the same thing in other cities all over: San Diego, St. Louis, Philadelphia.

I had to admit I admired him. I'd always appreciated him for his help, and I even liked the guy, but hearing about his job I realized that I respected him too.

"Do your coworkers know about you?" I asked him.

"Know what about me?"

"That you like guys?"

"Yes, they know, obviously."

"Why 'obviously?'"

"Because I'm obviously gay."

"You think people know just when they meet you?"

"I'd say unless they're pretty clueless they figure it out relatively quickly."

"On the phone you don't sound too… too swishy or whatever. Are you more like that in real life?"

"Like am I a big queen?"

"I guess. You know. Do you do the floppy wrist thing? Or like big gay gestures or something?"

"No, I don't think I do that."

"But people still know you're gay."

"Right."

"Do you wear bracelets? It seems like a lot of really gay guys have a thing for bracelets and rings."

"I don't, no. Ronald does, actually. But I don't know if that's really a gay thing."

"Oh, it definitely is." The one gay person I had known growing up was a piano player in my hometown. He had given me lessons, and when his thin, gold bracelets would occasionally get stuck in the keys he'd let out a short little yip, scandalized every time it happened. "The bracelet thing is definitely gay."

"You're the expert, Sam."

"Don't get annoyed. I'm just asking questions."

"I'm not annoyed. But I do have to hang up soon. Hurry up and fill me in on the news about the cop and the kid before I fall asleep. What did I miss?"

"Not much. They've been going back and forth about this permission slip the kid's folks supposedly have to sign for the kid to go on that cruise, since he's under twenty-one."

"I'm sure his parents were really into that."

"They didn't even ask them."

"They forged it?"

"Yeah. It didn't even have to be notarized or anything, apparently. So they just signed it with his parents' names."

"Makes sense."

"You don't think it's weird? Morally? That he's a cop forging documents for his underage lover?"

"God, Sam. I've probably done worse things in the last month than that. He's getting him onto a cruise, not enlisting him in the army. Anyway, the kid's nineteen years old. He's not a child."

"I guess so, but it's still illegal. I feel like maybe the cop is brainwashed or something. Don't you think he probably had to take some kind of oath swearing to uphold the law?"

"'An oath to uphold the law?' I swear, I've never known anyone whose standards were so high and so low at the same time."

And I still hadn't even told him about the arcade.

46

THE GUYS WHO APPEARED TO HAVE A GENUINE INTEREST in the videos and products at the arcade confounded everyone. You couldn't be sure who was actually looking to fool around. It was even more disconcerting when a straight couple came in to check out dildos and cheap negligées, as if taking a shot at spicing up their sex life or beginning in earnest their earliest dalliances into swinging. The wives looked at us baffled, and the husbands narrowed their eyes as they pieced together what we were doing out there. Whatever sick shit they were involved in, at least they were straight and probably fucking in beds like normal people instead of in shabby, cramped coin-op booths on the outskirts of town.

If there was a crowd that seemed especially judgmental though, it was the groups of girls who came in giggling and goofy, there to buy supplies for some bachelorette party. They filled their arms with balloons made to look like dicks, the cake pan in the shape of an enormous cock, and the pin-the-penis game marketed alternately under the names "Pin the Macho On the Man" and "Pin the Junk On the Hunk." The girls always gave looks of outright disgust to all they saw at the arcade, as if there might be any threat of us coming on to them. I did my best to mirror their horrified expressions, imitating them to themselves. But that was strictly for my own entertainment. I don't think they understood anything.

It was incredible how quickly we put on masks for the shoppers, donning phony versions of ourselves the same way my friends and I had at junior high dances when we'd catch sight of a chaperone we knew—a teacher we liked or one of our friends' parents. Our collective abandon was shattered the second they looked at us. Whatever we might have been from the inside, from the outside, we understood, we were nothing more than a bunch of dumb kids jumping around.

It bothered me that we behaved differently when other people were at the arcade. It bothered me that we had to be different at different times. I wished we could always be ourselves—or at least that version of ourselves—if only out there. After all, they were the intruders, not us.

At least outsiders brought with them the advantage that the clerks never used the PA system when they were around. They never got on the loudspeakers to tell people to find a booth or to drop tokens or get out. They never targeted guys for having their cell phones out. You were protected as long as there were straight shoppers about, like a kid who can rebel against his stepfather as long as his mother is nearby.

The few men who actually came in looking to buy DVDs carried with them the erotic possibility that they would somehow become curious right there in the store. Perhaps one of them would become reminded of some terrific sexual encounter he'd had with another male in his youth. Or maybe he'd just say, "Hell, let's see what all the fuss is about."

Meeting the cop on that straight website was proof that things like that happened. He was the straightest-looking person in the world. He didn't even have that appearance of over-the-top masculinity that can betray some men as gay. He just looked like a normal guy. And even though his profile said he was straight and seeking women, I had been in bed with him, had once even fallen asleep with him, the two of us rousing an hour later and me hurriedly dressing and racing out the door without even kissing him goodbye.

One evening, I watched a cowboy in long, lean Wrangler blue jeans. No one knew whether he was the kind of guy to buy tokens or if he was a regular porn consumer. Even the clerk couldn't tell. He wasn't making any announcements over the loudspeakers. I stayed in the cowboy's general vicinity, and when he looked up, I'd look up too and give him a friendly smile.

After a while he made his way over to where I was stationed in Double Penetration.

"'Scuse me," he whispered. "Sorry to bother you, but do you happen to know how this whole thing works?"

"Oh, sure. It's real simple. You just go buy some tokens and then you can go in the hallways and use them to watch videos in a booth."

"I see. Is that what you're doing?"

"Yes, sir," I said. "I'm just hanging out here for a minute. Taking a break. I'm just about to go back in there actually."

"Is that right? Well, I think I'll go get myself some tokens too," he said.

"Good idea. Maybe I'll see you in there."

I let him have a few minutes with his tokens, roaming the halls. I figured the crowd that night made me look good by comparison. Then I went and found him. He entered a booth, and I went in right after him.

"Have you really never been here?" I whispered.

"What?" he whispered.

I reached past him and put a token in the slot. I turned down the sound on the video. Our faces were lit. I put my lips close to his ear. "Is this really your first time?"

After that, I saw him out there twice more. Once, he asked me to follow him back to his house. His wife was gone for a week caring for her ailing mother.

47

TALKING TO MALCOLM MADE ME REALIZE THAT I HAD
settled for too long in my dead-end job. Hearing about his real,
grown-up career, I saw how little I had to offer the cop. I couldn't
go into that relationship as his equal any more than the kid could.

But it wasn't just that. I could no longer bear the hundreds of
insane things that happened each day at work, the slights against
my humanity and the way the job made me resent such a wide
swath of the populace. People appeared to have no clue how truly horrible they were. A guest who sneezed on my hand without
apologizing. A woman holding a speakerphone conversation over
the entire course of her check-in. A man who drunkenly vomited in
his bed and then called down to tell me to come change the sheets
right away, who then vomited on the other bed while I did. That
particular guest left a review online claiming that I was rude and
acted put out when he found that the sheets in his room were dirty.
It came to me as a grand revelation that a new career might change
everything, might be the first domino in a string of successes that
ultimately returned me to the cop's arms.

Almost as soon as I resolved to begin searching for another career, it appeared that I might have one, thanks to one of the regulars at the motel. He came to town every few weeks in a suit and
tie, and each time I saw him, it was the same routine. He checked
in around 8 o'clock in the evening, then went out for supper. After
eating, he came to the lobby to talk to me before going to bed. He
wasn't flirting or anything. He was a regular, straight guy, tall and
white with short gray hair and a perfectly regionless accent.

He had a boring business he liked talking about. He sold gratings for outdoor spaces. Gratings and benches for commercial

applications. It wasn't stuff anyone would have at their house. The things he sold belonged in parks or on the campuses of huge corporations. It was a normal, dull job, but it was his own enterprise, and he got to do whatever he wanted. Despite his independence, he always seemed anxious and worried when he talked about his work.

One night after supper he entered the lobby while I was checking someone in. He took a seat and waited for me to finish up. He looked glum and distressed.

"What's wrong?" I said when the other guest left.

"Oh, just work stuff. I'm pretty sure the rep I hired here in town is about to quit, and I'm going to be stuck finding her replacement. She just started six months ago. I haven't even finished training her really."

"Yeah, I remember when you mentioned hiring her."

"She's pregnant now. I was afraid this was going to happen. You're not supposed to discriminate, but Jesus. I swear, you're asking for it if you hire a woman under forty-five."

"Oh," I said. "Sorry to hear it."

"Of course she won't just quit now. It's never that easy. She says she thinks she'll probably just take a month or so off after she has the baby. But, she says there's a chance she won't want to come back at all."

"So maybe she won't quit."

"She's definitely going to quit. Believe me. I've seen this before. She's just stringing me along in case she hates motherhood or has a miscarriage or something."

"What can you do?"

"Nothing. I just have to wait. And she's going to get progressively worse at the job in the meantime. I'm going to have to be in town a lot more for a while."

"You should just give me the job," I said. "Then you wouldn't have to think about it anymore."

"Haha. Right."

"You never know. Maybe I could do it."

"Hell, it might come to that."

"It doesn't sound that hard. I'm actually a really fast learner."

"Food for thought," he said.

Then someone came in the lobby, and he waved goodnight and went to bed.

I didn't think anything would come of it, but when he checked in a few weeks later, he started telling me about the job and all that it would entail. He showed me the website for his company, which looked professional and polished and almost comically uninteresting.

"You'd have to wear nicer clothes," he said, "if something like this ever worked out."

"Oh, I know," I said. Even given the casual nature of the motel, I was surprised that management never complained about my chosen uniform: dark jeans and a white undershirt.

"Not to get your hopes up," he said. "Who knows what'll happen."

The next time he had a reservation, I wore a short-sleeved shirt instead of the t-shirt he usually saw me in. I didn't want to overdo it. I mentioned some of my experiences in real estate in a way that seemed relevant to the conversation, casually dismissing my failures as the result of the faltering economy. I tried not to appear pushy. I could see he was thinking about it.

When I mentioned the job to Malcolm he said, "It sounds really boring."

"I know. But maybe I'd be good at it."

"Maybe."

"You don't think so?"

"You don't strike me as the sales type, to be honest."

"Maybe I could learn. Maybe it's like acting, and I could just sort of act like a salesman."

"What exactly are you looking for in a job? Like, what's your best case scenario for a new career?"

"I haven't really thought that far. The best-case scenario is just that I look back on this entire era of my life and laugh and say, 'What a weird time that was. I can't believe I did that.'"

"I'd say that's a safe bet no matter what you do next."

48

I DIDN'T RAISE THE SUBJECT OF THE ARCADE WITH ANYONE in my life. There was no way to explain it. I could imagine what people would think if I tried. I hated the idea of being judged for anything that happened there, or anywhere else. When I was younger, I'd told a friend I wanted him to speak at my funeral using the eulogy Kevin Kline delivers at the beginning of *The Big Chill*.

I'd watched the movie a thousand times as a kid and always liked his simple tribute for his departed friend: "There was always something about Alex that was too good for this world."

It worried me knowing that if everyone knew the truth about my life, they'd never believe there was something about me that was too good for this world.

The fear of running into someone I knew at the arcade never left me. Every time a man directed his eyes at me for longer than a moment, I thumbed through a mental rolodex trying to match the face to a memory, straining to recognize him and to determine whether he appeared to be recognizing me. When it finally happened that I saw an acquaintance there, it turned out to be an ostensibly straight married friend of a friend, a guy I didn't see often but who I knew socially.

I had exited the nonsmoking hallway and was standing near the Teens section when I looked over and recognized him standing not far from Orgies. It was obvious from the way he was bolting through the store that he had already spotted me and was trying to avoid being seen himself. I watched him rush towards the exit. Then, just before making it out the door, he turned to look at me. I tried to return my gaze to the shelf of DVDs quickly enough to allow him at least the fantasy that perhaps he hadn't been observed making his escape.

I was nervous about seeing him again socially, but when I did go out to a rare dinner and found that he and his wife were among the guests, the subject didn't arise. He did, however, direct a few funny looks at me that I didn't know how to interpret.

Encounters like that brought to mind the game of Global Thermonuclear War depicted in the 1983 film *WarGames*, in which a young Matthew Broderick teams with Ally Sheedy to teach a military supercomputer the concept of mutually assured destruction. No one wanted to be caught at the arcade, so being caught by someone you knew was (one hoped) an act that cancelled itself out. Or, as the computer in the film discovers in its attempts to find the best way to annihilate its enemies while securing the fates of the American people, "The only winning move is not to play."

Even greater than my terror of being recognized was my fear of getting into a car accident in the parking lot. I always drove slowly and checked my blind spots over and over again. I tried imagining what I would do if I smashed into some guy's pickup or if he dented my bumper. Would we take our cars somewhere else and re-stage the accident there so as to avoid explanations to our partners and wives and insurance agents? Would we just say, "Forget it, man," and leave without trading information, with the plan of pretending that we had been victims of parking lot hit-and-runs?

"I was in Home Depot for five minutes, and when I came out, it looked like this," I imagined telling a skeptical insurance adjuster.

It also occurred to me that I might go outside one night and find my car's battery dead. I could picture myself trying to stop every guy who had just ejaculated and wanted nothing more than to get away from that place, every guy I had just ignored or spurned or refused to make eye contact with, or who had asked me to go down on him and to whom I had said, "I don't do that out here."

"Could you please give me a jump start?" I'd say.

"I don't do that out here," he'd reply.

49

I NEVER HAD A BRUSH WITH THE POLICE AT THE ARCADE, but I couldn't help wondering about it. I'd watched enough *COPS* to have a passing familiarity with police methodologies for dealing with people involved in victimless sexual crimes. I'd seen the attractive female officers dressed as hookers and the way they manipulated men into saying exactly what they needed in order to get the arrest. They had to get them to explicitly draw a link between a specific amount of money and a sex act.

There was once a controversial episode of *COPS* in which a police officer dressed up as a clown and drove a minivan with magnetic signs attached to the sides advertising himself as Coco the Clown. He picked up hookers while wearing full makeup, a purple wig and an insane Dr. Seuss hat. He appeared to deliberately prolong the experience for the hidden cameras in the van, offering balloons and throwing confetti at the young, desperate, and obviously drug-addled sex workers he picked up. In the course of one particularly revolting arrest, he sprayed crazy string at a sex worker in the moments before her arrest. I read that the episode was a subject of dismay among clowns, who felt the contemptuous depiction of Coco reinforced negative clown stereotypes. Later, the police department admitted that the producers at the network had proposed the idea and they had merely gone along with it.

One can't help but grow cynical imagining the brainstorming sessions in police stations all over the country, as officers devise new and interesting ways to lure criminals into committing minor offenses so that they can be arrested. Like all those episodes in which the cops planted expensive, unchained bicycles in low-income neighborhoods and then sprang from the backs of vans to arrest the kids who inevitably came along to steal them.

In the episodes with phony hookers, the police ended up with so many would-be johns, they sometimes had to establish minia-ture processing centers in parking lots, where they fingerprinted the men at folding tables as they sat in aluminum chairs. Some of them cried and pled their innocence, but others just looked incon-venienced.

I never knew what kind of crimes I might be committing at the arcade. Public lewdness? Public nudity? Would I have been hand-cuffed if the police burst into one of the booths and discovered me masturbating with a stranger? I wondered if I would have gotten a ticket, or ended up before a judge in a room full of people. I could imagine being seated in a courtroom with the other guys who were at the arcade at the same time I was. Maybe we would have flirted and traded phone numbers. More likely, it would have been like those moments when the clerk flashed the lights in the booth. We'd have all looked at one another shocked that *this* was what we had to work with out there.

I worried I might end up listed as a sex offender, that my neigh-bors would protest my existence in their otherwise-perfect neigh-borhood. I worried that my house would appear on one of those interactive maps that parents check when they're concerned about their kids getting raped by sex maniacs residing in the vicinity. I worried I'd have to confess to the cop before we moved in together. I could imagine the effigy burning in my front yard and everyone gathering around taking photos of it with their phones.

I imagined the booths were relatively safe in terms of legal risk. The places where one really had to be careful, I think, were the ones set up like regular movie theaters, auditoriums where everyone was sitting with everyone else in rows while trying to fool around with themselves and each other. I never went to one of those the-aters, but it was a place like that where Paul Reubens, a.k.a. Pee-wee Herman, got caught.

I loved Pee-wee Herman when I was a kid. A lot of people my age did. He was a tremendous influence on me growing up, his creativity and *joie de vivre*. I was twelve or thirteen when he was arrested for indecent exposure at an adult movie theater in Sarasota, Florida, less than an hour away from the Tampa-based Coco the Clown stings. Soon thereafter, I ordered a t-shirt from a tiny ad in the back of *Rolling Stone*. The shirt read "Free Pee-wee" on the front. On the back it said, "We're all pullin' for you, man!" Though I never wore it in public, I treasured that shirt for years.

It was awful when he got busted. At thirteen, I was already convinced that masturbating was the worst thing I could possibly do. Hearing that a childhood hero had been convicted as a criminal for jerking off, seeing the way his mug shot appeared all over television and even in the newspaper my parents read, was strange and upsetting. I felt personally implicated when, over breakfast, my father shook the newspaper in my direction and said, "Look what your hero did."

The mug shot didn't look like him. It looked like someone who was the exact opposite of Pee-wee Herman. He looked like someone from another time, some roadie from the 1970s, some drummer, some weirdo who would get caught jerking off in a movie theater. It was such a dramatic public shaming. Overnight, he was out of work, and everything associated with him was a joke and a collector's item. I could empathize. I could imagine myself being outed in the same way at school or in church. I thought about it when I jerked off. Or, actually, the second after I ejaculated.

In the booths, my rule was that I always let the other guy take his out first. I got that from drug movies in which the dealer always makes the new guy snort a little of whatever they're selling to prove that he is who he says he is and not some cop, which he always turns out to be anyway. I figured if I was looking at another guy's dick, then odds were good he wasn't going to bust me.

I wished I could have asked the cop's advice. He would have known whether I could have been arrested and on what charges. Maybe he would have said that I was too good for that sordid, degenerate place. No, not degenerate. Not sordid. Scummy, he'd say. Or sketchy.

50

MR. GRATE AND BENCH CALLED TO MAKE HIS BOOKINGS
for the next three months, making several reservations at once
as he had the whole time I worked at the motel. He was already
booked for a reservation the following week, when he could have
secured the other nights in person, but he always said he liked to
be at his desk with his calendar spread out in front of him. I noted
all the dates and made his reservations as cheerfully and efficiently
as possible, and when he offered to read off his credit card number,
I told him not to worry about it.

"I know where to find you," I said.

"That's right," he said.

"How's it going with your pregnant employee, by the way?"

"That's what I'm going to come and find out," he said. "The
numbers out there don't look great, but I've seen worse. Partly it's
just the time of year."

"I hear you," I said, but I had no idea what he meant.

Though only minutes earlier, a woman in her sixties had repeatedly and unapologetically passed gas in the lobby while
waiting on her cab, I demonstrated laudable restraint by not
grasping the phone with both hands and screaming into the receiver's many tiny holes, "Help! Help! Get me out of here! Hire
me, I'm begging you!"

I almost couldn't imagine having a different job and no longer
being a clerk, with its lowly title, bad hours, and meager pay. I
couldn't quite conceive what I might do with vacation pay and
national holidays off work. It seemed obvious the cop would find
me more appealing if I had a normal schedule and a more middle
class presence in the world.

I wondered if I'd become just another business-casual salesman type, like Mr. Grate and Bench. It seemed risky somehow. Maybe I'd like it too much. Maybe I'd want for nothing and turn out to be the best grate-and-bench salesman in the world.

If I am that, what then won't I be? That's what I wondered.

But of course I'd have to take the job with its normal hours and normal clothes and its total lack of any edge. At dinner parties, people would ask what I did, and instead of choking out that I was a desk clerk, I'd say that I handle outside sales for a major distributor of quality site materials.

Mr. Grate and Bench said his employee's pregnancy was just a couple of months along.

"But you know how it goes," he said. "They all think they'll probably want to keep working, but they never do. I've been through this with my wife before. Both of them."

This he confided in a way that made me certain he still thought I was a straight guy and could be spoken to without resorting to diplomatic, PC bullshit.

"I'd say there's a seventy percent chance she'll hang it up. So much for my new area rep."

The second he said it, I could picture my business card. Area Rep. I wondered if I'd go back to apologizing for it the way I used to when I was in real estate. "I mean, come on," I'd tell myself, "Everyone has to make a living."

51

EVEN WITHOUT KNOWING ABOUT MY EXPERIENCES AT THE arcade, most of my friends believed I had a sleazy sex life. I'd made an unwise confession years before that wound up being widely circulated among our group. Long before I came out to anyone, including myself, I was engaging in occasional threeways with a married buddy from work and whatever willing women we could find. We were both on record as being "completely straight," but things occasionally went slightly further when we managed to meet a game female.

We had some success together, and met a few regular women when the ads I posted yielded fruit. When we couldn't find someone who would lay us for free, we sometimes met with a hooker who used the name Champain. The misspelling was hers. A deliberate play on words, perhaps, but I doubt it. S&M was never on the table.

Champain was in her early 20s like me. She always said she liked playing around with the two of us. More than once she said that the things she liked best were "Fast cars, chicken fried steak, and getting fucked by two men at the same time." The way she said it, repeating it word for word on multiple occasions made me believe it really was some kind of motto for her. While I'm certain she was a complex person with as rich an emotional life as mine or anyone else's, she was decidedly unintelligent, even by our severely reduced standards.

We met her at her apartment once. She said she never had guys over, but we'd seen one another a few times by then, and she trusted us. Her place bore evidence of a potentially unhealthy obsession with the Looney Tunes character Tweety Bird. He was the primary decorative motif. Everywhere, paraphernalia in his honor. Stuffed dolls and books. Framed pictures on the wall. She had a kid who was with a babysitter. It was the first we'd heard about him. At one point, she suddenly stood and shut the door to his room. The place was tidy and organized. I thought it would be different. She was a ditzy girl who actually seemed to enjoy having sex with men for money. I realize this is the sort of rationalization used all the time in the exploitation of women, but it really did appear to be true.

While my buddy fucked her that night, I stuck my fingers inside of her and felt his dick sliding along my hand. When Champain couldn't see, he reached back and gave my dick a quick squeeze that I recalled frequently for the next several years.

That night, when we left her place, she was in a state of mild crisis. My friend had lost his condom inside of her. Though he didn't seem concerned, Champain was in an absolute panic. She couldn't find it. Female anatomy being the mystery it is, I couldn't begin to imagine where it might have gone or where to recommend she might search for it. Walking to my pickup, my friend pointed out her car to me, recognizable by its dangling Tweety Bird air freshener. I've long held that a great deal can be determined about one's level of taste based on what, if anything, is hanging from his or her rear view mirror. The less the better. Ideally, there is nothing.

A week or so after the lost condom incident, my friend came to my apartment.

"Don't freak out, but I have something to show you."

He undid his pants.

I started getting excited. I didn't know what was going to happen.

He was in his underwear, and he pulled them down to reveal his dick.

"Come closer," he said.

I did. He pushed his pubic hair aside and showed me a small, open sore on the skin just above the base of his penis. He had already been to his doctor, who, without running any tests, gave him a shot of penicillin and said it was either syphilis or herpes. If it was syphilis, the shot would clear it up. If it was herpes, it would go away on its own after a while.

For some reason I was the one who had to call Champain, who sobbed and screamed into the phone that she knew for a fact that she was "one hundred and fifty percent clean." She repeated the phrase over and over again.

A week later she called to tell me that she had been tested and everything was fine. My friend's sore cleared up, and he never found out what caused it.

I told a friend about one of the episodes with Champain. In a toe-dipping half-confession, I downplayed it dramatically, making it sound like a one time, isolated event. My friend reacted with interest and made a variety of inquiries for further details, so I answered his questions, careful to make the whole thing sound not as though the pursuit of these kinds of experiences was a part-time job, which was essentially what it had become, but like something that happened by a bizarre happenstance, organically and completely unorchestrated. *You'll never believe this funny thing that happened to me.*

Though my confessor was a friend I loved and trusted, he could not be relied upon to keep a secret of that type. A week later, I was dining with Dan and Beth, a couple my confidant and I had in common as friends. I thought they were behaving strangely, but it wasn't confirmed until Dan said, suddenly, "Look, we're not supposed to mention it, but Mike told us about what you did, and we're both having a really hard time acting normally around you. So maybe we should just cut the evening short while we process this."

Of course I knew, but I said, "What do you mean? What did Mike tell you?"

"You know what he's talking about," Beth said. "With the hookers and your pal from work. We think it's completely disgusting, don't we, Dan?"

"Yeah, we do."

"That was supposed to be between Mike and me," I said.

"Well, I think he felt like he needed to talk to someone about it," Beth said. "And I don't blame him."

"It's not that big of a deal," I said. "I mean, we're talking about some threesomes. I didn't invent some new perversion or something."

"With a hooker and a married man?" Beth said. "Are you kidding?"

"I had no idea you'd be so judgmental about something like this."

"Hey, don't call Beth judgmental just because some people take marriage more seriously than others," Dan said.

"You don't even know the guy, let alone his wife. They're practically separated. What do you care?"

"It's just a shitty way to behave," Dan said.

"Exactly," Beth said. "It's fucking uncivilized."

"We're not saying we don't want to be your friend. We're just disappointed." Dan said. "I think we need some space from you right now."

And with that I was out the door.

Furious, I called the friend who had betrayed my confidence. I shouted into the phone, threatening to bust his lip, as if I were Norman Mailer.

I didn't see Dan and Beth for a few months, during which time the rift had to be explained to our other friends, so of course everyone ended up hearing various bastardized versions of the story about Champain and my friend from work.

52

IT'S HARD NOT TO OBSESS OVER THE STUPIDITY OF YOUNGER days. I wish it were different and that I could view my former self nostalgically, as an innocent upstart trying to make his way. Instead, my reminiscences play back like scenes from a horror movie.

Surely he won't go into the basement alone. Not after finding the body in the kitchen. But of course, he—my former self—always does the wrong thing, no matter how oblivious seeming, how laughable.

The scariest part is looking back at the painful lesson learned by my sixteen-year-old self, knowing that he'll make essentially the same mistake again at twenty-two, then again in a slightly more imaginative, but equally stupid way, at twenty-nine. It can arrive at such a point that one begins to question the tastes of his friends and loved ones.

The only thing that helps me forgive myself is that it's just so easy to forget. It's my favorite thing about life. And also my least favorite. When I was still seeing a shrink, we had an ongoing conversation about my fantasy of walking into a crowd of people and firing a gun into the air. I didn't want to hurt anyone, I just wanted to create a memorable moment for myself and for everyone else, and I knew that, whatever happened after that gunshot, we would remember it. It would be an instance set apart, like nothing else from the rest of our lives, which were passing in a blur.

Recently, a friend reminded me about a summer in college when I worked at a clothing store. "I remember you were embroiled in a whole thing there."

I had no idea what she was talking about.

"You don't remember this? Something about an abortion?"

"Oh my God, that's right!"

It had to do with a guy I worked with. I couldn't remember his name, only that he wore an orthodontic retainer. He had gotten his girlfriend pregnant, and they had gone to get an abortion despite their supposed religious objections. They had encountered protesters there who had forced into their hands little plastic models of their unborn baby. Could I have been confusing this with a plotline from the TV show *Degrassi High*? I lent the couple money for the procedure, and the guy cried in the stock room about how much he loved his girlfriend, but how he wasn't ready to be a father.

How can I learn anything or do anything other than the same stupid things I've always done, if I can't remember the abortion drama that ate up weeks of that summer? I can't even remember the guy's name. I thought I'd know him forever after that experience, but today if I saw him in public, I'd probably pretend not to recognize him at all.

53

I WENT TO A PORN SHOP ATTACHED TO A REGULAR newsstand. I discovered the place while searching for a difficult-to-find arts magazine. The newsstand was listed as a vendor on the magazine's website. The fact that it doubled as a pornography store was an unanticipated bonus that I discovered upon my arrival.

A few racks were, in fact, devoted to a fairly impressive inventory of newspapers, weeklies, and journals. But just beyond them stood row upon row of shelves, all of them bearing more than their share of pornographic DVDs. The walls were covered in magazine racks, stuffed with the most artless and low-quality skin mags imaginable. The covers were not concealed like the newsstand nudie publications of my youth. Nor were they merely suggestive, as they once had been. They were sufficiently explicit that anyone learning about sex for the first time could acquire a more-than-complete education merely by taking a brief stroll among the aisles.

The room swam in flesh tones, and I almost missed the only other living person in the area as I scanned it. But a slight movement caught my attention and my eye hung on him. He had already seen me. We traded nods then looked away to the carnival of sex on all sides of us.

I had only seen him for a second, but I caught it all. In dirty jeans and a feed store work shirt, the man looked like a slightly demented farmhand—a more frightening version of Lennie from *Of Mice and Men*, and that's remembering that Lennie actually killed someone. The man was about forty-five years old, not fat but broad, the type who could pick up a bale of hay and toss it into the bed of a pickup with no problem. He had a few days beard growth and, significantly, only one eye. It was impossible to tell if there was an eyeball in there or not, but his right eyelid was swollen completely shut, and there was no sign of bruising, which led me to believe it was a permanent condition and not the result of some barroom brawl, as attractive as that fantasy might have been.

It didn't matter. Moments after we acknowledged one another, we were looking at straight porn in separate parts of the store. My whole life, I had treated encounters with straight pornography the same way, as opportunities to retrain my brain, thinking things like, "Just look at those breasts. What luscious, luscious breasts. Her vagina is really glistening. I guess that means she's really excited. I'd sure love to get my hands on that shiny, wet pussy." And so on.

I never looked at the gay porn DVDs at the arcade. No one did. That one aisle was always utterly vacant. Historically, I had been satisfied in porn shops just perusing three-way porn, which at least enabled me to see more men than women. I wasn't gay, I told myself. I was going through a phase that involved a few somewhat quirky interests. A college friend of mine had been obsessed with Asian women and looked exclusively at pornography that featured them prominently. He even knew the names of several of the Asian porn actresses, and could list his favorites among their performances. I felt buoyed by news of his transformation when I learned that, years after graduation, he had married a blonde Caucasian attorney from Arkansas.

After looking at the cases of the threeway DVDs for a while, I decided to check out the gay porn section for the first time in my life. I made my way slowly, looking at everything else before winding up there. A big sign overhead said "Gay." I stood beneath it looking at the covers and spines. It felt strange, and I was aware that it was part of a progression. Even six months before, it would have been impossible. Whether it was good or bad, I didn't know.

Standing there, I became aware of the one-eyed man moving in my peripheral vision. He was on the next row over, just behind the rack I was looking at. Then he was on the far end of my aisle, looking in the section marked "Amateur." Though I would normally have left my post, I flashed back to the instance of recognition that flickered between my two eyes and his single eye when I entered, and I found the courage to remain in place. He browsed his way down the long aisle with increasing urgency until I understood that we were magnetized. I was aware of nothing but him until he was beside me.

After all the motion that had led him to my side, he was surprisingly still once he reached his destination. He didn't do anything except breathe audibly and stare along with me at the DVD covers. Or pretend to, anyway. After a few minutes of standing next to one another, I somehow mustered the nerve to squat down and begin picking up DVD cases with titles that might signal something to him. *Nasty Daddies 7. Hard at Work. Forty Plus Stud 3.* I picked up the boxes and held them so he could see them, but behaved as if I was looking at them myself, nodding in consideration of their synopses and the pictures that covered them. Then, as if realizing how impolite I was being, blocking his view of the shelf, I rose—nearer to him this time—and went back to looking at the titles from a standing position, my arms crossed over my chest. He reached down and shifted himself in his pants.

"Lotta big cocks," the Cyclops growled quietly, his accent thick and country.

One has to wonder how those drawls survive in a world of television and all of us moving from place to place. I'm sure hundreds of dialects are disappearing daily and that the *New Yorker* has done the most fascinating coverage of the brilliant mind, whosoever it is, that's working to preserve each of them, mapping them in the moments before they vanish forever. However fast they might be disappearing, one can always find those accents in use by the people with whom I grew up and people who resemble the people with whom I grew up and now wish to screw. Such is the trick of one's hometown. It leaves its sticky residue on you no matter how hard you scrub.

"I'm sorry?" I said, just to hear the Cyclops say it again.

"Lotta big cocks on them boxes."

"Oh," I said. "Yeah, there sure are."

"You live close?"

"I do, but I don't live alone."

"You got a girl?"

"Yeah," I said. "I'm not even supposed to be here. I'm supposed to be out running an errand. Do you live nearby?"

"Naw," he grunted, "I live way far away. Bet they got motels round here though."

"I'm sure they do, but I don't have time for that today, unfortunately. Maybe you could give me your number."

The Cyclops made a sudden gesture with his arm like he was skipping a rock. "Nope. Gotta be today. Today's the only day."

The truth was that no one was waiting at home for me. I had planned to run errands while I was out, but there were no particular demands on my schedule. Still, I felt the situation should be moderated somehow and slowed down. I didn't know how we had gone so quickly from idle browsing to discussing lodging options. I wanted another layer between us. I would have been happier on a staticky phone call with him.

"I'd sure like to," I said. "Maybe we could meet another time."

"Ain't no other time," he said. "This is the only time."

I knew I shouldn't go with him to a motel, and I'd never take him to my place. An impasse had been reached. We both stood before the shelves, neither of us getting what we wanted. He rubbed his erection through his pants to show me what I was missing. The tension was so pleasurable and open, I wished I could pause time, but the clerk had begun to look at us, and there was no good reason to stand there any longer. The Cyclops shook his head at me ruefully, and I did the same, raising my eyebrows in what I hoped was an expression of regret and hypermasculine wistfulness. He stood next to me for a moment longer and then left, making straight for the door without looking back.

Though I hung around the store for a few minutes longer I spotted the Cyclops the moment I stepped outside. He was sitting in the cab of a filthy junkyard pickup that looked barely operational. Built in the 1960s, it hadn't been painted in decades, and what paint remained was peeling off. He kept it up himself, I could tell. A shadetree mechanic. He probably kept things in place with bent wire hangers. The mouth of the gas tank was stuffed with a red rag like a bomb.

I looked every bit the part of the dandy, no doubt, making my way to my own pickup with its leather, heated seats—a last artifact of my real estate career. Safely ensconced, I let myself stare at the Cyclops for the first time. In the store, we had been side by side. This felt better. Our windshields were between us, and he was across the lot. I touched myself over my pants, and imagined he might be doing the same. To stall a moment longer, I pretended to search the cab of my truck for something. I pantomimed finding my sunglasses at last, then I gave him a small goodbye wave and reversed out of my parking spot. As I exited the lot, I could see him leave just behind me. I got onto the highway and drove, heading to a store several miles away. What a funny episode. I felt as if the arcade's energy had clung to me, following me out into the real world.

At first, I assumed we were merely going in the same direction, and he would soon pass me with a final farewell glance. He never got right on my tail, but stayed a car or two back as though trying to avoid detection. He was following me. I recalled car chases from movies in which the person being followed did something dramatic like running a red light or performing an abrupt U-turn. I considered the evasive driving techniques I had read about or seen on TV, though I doubted my ability to execute them in my aroused and increasingly terrified state.

When I exited the highway, the one-eyed man's pickup took the same exit. I pulled into the Home Depot parking lot. The truck was behind me. I found a spot away from the other cars, at the far end of the lot, and the Cyclops pulled up next to me. I tried to appear calm as I got out of my truck, but the adrenaline was loose in me, and I could feel the jerkiness in my movements. He was smoking a cigarette and he opened his truck door, which creaked loudly. I took out a cigarette of my own and leaned against his pickup.

"It's too bad I don't have time to connect today," I told him. "Why don't you give me your email address so we can get together another time?"

"I don't do email," he said.

"What's your name?" I said. "I'll tell you mine."

"I just wanna get you naked and suck you," he said. "Why don't you come on? There's a place right there. I'll pay for it if that's the hold up."

He was right, I saw. There was a motel just next door.

"I only wish I could, man, but I'm just supposed to run this errand and be home."

"Well, shit, how long you think it's gonna take for me to suck a load outta you? That sound like something that's gonna take all day?"

"Wish I could, buddy," I said. My dick was so hard I could already feel a drip in my underwear.

I finished my cigarette, rubbing myself through my pants when there was no one to see us, and, once or twice, touching him through his.

"I've really got to go now," I said at last. I reached out and shook his rough hand. He held mine a bit too long, acted as if he wasn't going to let go, then grinned slyly and released me.

I took off in the direction of the entrance. As the electronic doors parted, I turned and saw his truck pull out of the parking lot, heading in the direction of the highway. It was a relief seeing the Cyclops go.

Inside, I killed some time in the nursery looking at plants, and asking one of the employees about which one might be good in my apartment. I described its total darkness and asked what might thrive there. It was as the plant expert gave his reply that the Cyclops came into view behind him. He was stalking through the place, looking down every aisle with his one eye. At first he didn't see me, but then he did. He halted suddenly, looked at me, and then slowly proceeded in the direction he had been heading. My expression changed so abruptly that the plant expert looked at my face and then looked behind himself to see what it was I was reacting to.

Though he went on at some length after turning and finding nothing and no one behind him, I didn't hear another word he said. As soon as he was finished, I made my way to the front of the store with the vigilance of a soldier, scanning the terrain before me and whipping my head around to look down every passage, lest I become the victim of an ambush. Every denim-clad hoss received a double-take.

When I stepped through the doors of the store, I spotted his pick-up parked next to mine once again. I considered going back into the store to discuss my dilemma with the security guard on duty. "There's a man outside who wants to blow me," I could have said.

Opting for decisive action, I racewalked in the direction of my truck imagining that he might still be in the store, and that I could escape before he realized what had happened. But, as I drew near, his driver's side door creaked open.

"I left, but I come back," the Cyclops said. "Okay if I sit in your truck?"

"I just got a call when I was inside wondering what's taking me so long."

"What difference five minutes gonna make?"

"You can sit with me, but just for a minute, okay?"

In my pickup, I could smell him. He didn't stink, but he wore an invisible cloud of cheap tobacco and grease. I knew I'd have to ride with my windows down to get rid of the scent. I could see the bizarre jumble of junk in the bed of his truck beside us. Nothing about it made sense. There were auto parts and what looked to be a paint spraying rig and folding outdoor chairs. Each item looked as if it had been in there for a long time.

As soon as he was certain there was no one in our immediate vicinity, he surprised me by saying, "Okay if I kiss you?"

"Oh," I said. "Okay."

As soon as the words left me, his mouth was over mine.

The world is filled with repressed gay men who have strict stances against kissing. Many men won't even consider it. I've literally been inside of men, their hairy legs over my shoulders, who, if I leaned down to kiss them would reply, "I don't do that, man."

Only rarely have I run into this other breed of closeted men, who have no greater desire than to kiss another man, and have almost no actual knowledge of how to go about it. The usual complaints apply. In his case, the Cyclops seemed to think kissing meant filling my mouth with his entire tongue, pinning my own inside of my mouth with nothing to do but taste his cheap rolling tobacco.

He kept trying to mouth me even as I pushed him away. "I've got to go now," I said, feeling the first inklings of genuine fear.

"Just show it to me," he said, rubbing me through my jeans. It was amazing, I was as hard as I have ever been in my life.

"I don't want to get caught out here," I said, looking around anxiously.

"That ain't gonna happen. My truck's blocking us," he said. "I done that on purpose."

He was right. I took it out. Upon first sight, he grasped it with such frenzied titillation and pleasure that I could hardly help but mirror his enthusiasm. He removed his own dick from his pants, lost though it was in a sea of never-trimmed pubic hair. I touched it a little for him, but he was much more interested in mine than I was in his. He lowered his head to take it in his mouth, but I stopped him.

"Just for a minute," he said.

I let him do it for a few seconds but didn't let him go further. "You have to stop," I said. "I'm going to put it away if you don't."

"Just lemme touch it then," he said, collecting himself.

I let him. He sighed and moaned looking at it, alternately touching my cock or my balls or my stomach or himself with his free hand.

"You've got to stop," I said. "I'm getting too close."

"Oh, lemme see it," he said, jerking at me with renewed fascination.

I was closer than I realized. I pulled his hands off and yanked my underwear over my dick just in time for everything to pulse out. He watched, grinning and enthralled as the fabric darkened and grew transparent.

I did my best to contain the orgasm, and tried behaving as though nothing had happened, managing instead to look like a mental patient stifling a yawn or someone feigning composure after eating something incredibly sour. I was instantly awash in shame, appalled by what I had done and by the figure of the Cyclops in my space. The smell of him seemed stronger than before now that it was mixed with the scent of my cum.

"I've got to ask you to let me get out of here, man," I said, zipping my pants over the growing wetness.

His dick was still out and stiffer than ever. With one hand, he jerked himself, and with the other, he petted the dampening surface of my jeans. I swatted his hand away, checking myself to be sure I didn't come across as excessively aggressive. I could imagine his hands around my throat if I made the wrong move or said the wrong thing.

For a moment, I didn't think he would leave, but slowly, begrudgingly, he began to put himself away. When at last he opened the passenger door, it was with great reluctance.

His feet touched the parking lot, and I said, "Okay, man. Maybe we'll see one another again sometime." That gave him pause, and he hesitated again, turning to give me a long look with his one eye. I thought for a moment he was going to get back in with me, but instead he stood and shut the door.

I was out of the parking lot before he could open the door to his own rusty heap.

54

I HAD TO TELL SOMEONE ABOUT THE CYCLOPS, AND THERE was no one to tell but Malcolm.

"God, I'm jealous," he said. "Of course, like any reasonable person, I would have gone to the motel with him."

I'd left out the part about blowing my load in my pants. The story Malcolm heard ended with the Cyclops sucking me off in the parking lot until I stopped him and the two of us parted ways.

"I don't know how you resisted. I assume you haven't gotten laid much lately, though I imagine you haven't exactly been celibate these past few months."

"Well, I mean, practically. But, no, I haven't been celibate."

"No? Good for you! I'm glad to hear it."

"Ha. Thanks."

"So tell me about it. Do you have someone regular you've been playing around with?"

"I don't have a regular person, no. More like a regular place."

"A place? Oh, Sam, please don't tell me you're doing it in parks. Or rest stops. I mean, no judgment, but…"

"No. God."

"The bathhouse?"

"Are you kidding? I'm terrified of that place."

"That's probably good. I haven't been to that one in years, but it was pretty bleak last time I went."

"You've been there?"

"Sure. It's right next to the mall, so I used to drop in after buying shoes. But that was ages ago."

"Have you been to one in Boston?"

"I don't think they have one here. If they do, I've never heard of it. Anyway, I've been too busy to look. There's one in Chicago where I could probably spend a week. I'll tell you all about it, but now I'm really curious. Where is it you've been going?"

"Now I'm embarrassed to tell you."

"You're not embarrassed to tell me about the contents of the cop's emails, but you're embarrassed to tell me about how you've been getting laid?"

"I haven't been getting laid exactly. It's not even that big of a deal. It's an arcade on the outskirts of town."

"You've been going to an arcade? You're kidding. That's even weirder than the bathhouse."

"Is it?"

"Yes."

"I don't do much out there. Mostly I just watch."

"Guys let you watch them?"

"Yeah, sometimes."

"Do you ever fuck anyone out there?"

"No. Not at all."

"This is the one way south of town?"

"No, it's west of the city."

"Oh, that place. By the time they built that one, I was way past my arcade days. The one I knew was south."

"So you used to go to one too?"

"When I was a lot younger. Like pre-internet, before there were other halfway decent options. Hey, do they still use the same tokens?"

"I don't know. What did they look like back when you were going?"

"On one side it had a topless woman and it said, 'Heads you win' and on the other side it had her bare ass and it said 'Tails you lose.'"

"Yeah. They're the same. But they say, 'Heads I win, tails you lose.'"

"Oh, right. Pretty fucking iconic actually."

"Right. Like the Campbell's soup can."

"So you go out there a lot?"

"Not a lot, no. But, yeah, I've been going out there from time to time."

"I can only imagine the kind of people going to an arcade now. You're probably the toast of the town."

"Hardly. Like I said, I don't do much out there. I don't fuck or do oral or anything."

"Surely you at least let them blow you."

"I have once or twice, but I'm too paranoid about diseases. I get all stressed out."

"There's not much you can catch from a blowjob."

"People say that, but then you hear horror stories."

"The arcade. It's just so…quaint."

"Quaint might not be the right word."

55

THE COP AND THE KID WERE TRYING OUT NEW RESTAURANTS. They were having a great time, emailing each other little notes about how they should return to that new favorite place and be sure to remember the name of this server or that one. It seemed like they were having a wonderful, perfect life.

Together they navigated questions from family and coworkers, claiming to most of them that the kid was renting the guest bedroom while he attended the nearby college. They staged the spare room with the kid's possessions, even leaving the bed unmade to give the impression that the room was in use.

It was nothing like the life I had envisioned for myself. The frozen margarita machine was only the start of it. They also bought a pair of jet skis to use on the nearby lake. They had threeway sex with another of the police officers in town, and then another time with someone they met online. My heart raced and I grew sweaty reading these things. I cried. I logged out of his account, went to the other room, then went back to my computer to log in and read everything again.

They took a weekend road trip, and the kid got some bad tattoos: a series of stars across his chest like the tail of a comet, and his last name in one of those ornate, Gothic fonts some Mexican guys use for that purpose.

They fell asleep watching movies in bed and talked about how much fun they were going to have on the cruise they'd bought tickets for.

The kid debated whether or not he wanted to go back to school after that semester. He had gotten a part-time job working at a movie theater, and he figured if he went full-time he could be management in no time.

56

ONE NIGHT, I STEPPED OUT OF THE ARCADE TO GET A PACK of cigarettes, and ended up smoking one in my car while listening to my phone messages. The ex-bouncer was the clerk on duty, and I didn't think he'd care. While smoking a cigarette, I noticed two people, a man in his fifties and a boy in his early twenties, also both sitting in their cars. They were eyeballing one another in the parking lot.

The boy's posture, clothes, even his car suggested that he was of the straight world. I imagined he had driven out to the arcade having learned about it as I did, from the Missed Connections ads.

The older man and the twenty-ish kid were looking at one another through their open car windows. The older man noticed me but dismissed me after a single glance. As I carried on smoking my cigarette, he grew more and more courageous with the kid in the next car. He got out and asked the boy a question, then went back to his own car. Then he repeated the process. Then he took his dick out of his pants and walked around his car as if inspecting it after a fender bender, his penis waggling semi-erect out his fly. The young man made a comment to the older man, squirming in his driver's seat in a way that made me think he was jerking off. The man walked up to the boy's open window, and I watched as the boy—reluctantly at first, then enthusiastically—grasped the dangling penis. A moment later, he pulled it towards him and drew it into his mouth. The man pressed himself against the boy's open car window, looking as though he were being sucked in.

They were still at it when I snuffed out my smoke and went back inside. Later, when I left, having had no luck at the arcade, I found that both their cars were gone. I imagined them adjourning to another location, the older man's house maybe—where he had lived alone since his wife of 15 years left him five years earlier—where he still displayed photographs of his family at various vacation spots.

I imagined the boy and the man at the start of a long relationship, a combination of paternal mentorship, lustful sex, and a sincere emotional bond. I envisioned the fun they were having and the memory each of them would carry of that day in the parking lot, how ballsy and insane, both of them saying to the other, "I have never done anything like that in my life," and meaning it.

I drove home from the arcade horny and unsatisfied, thinking about these things, projecting the relationship between the older man and the younger man many years into the future. I wondered why the man had picked the other kid over me. He had seen me, after all. I didn't like thinking about it, but I felt I had to. I thought about it for a long time.

57

THERE HAD TO BE A WAY TO TAKE OVER THE KID'S POSITION in the cop's life. I pictured myself as an ant crawling on the surface of a sphere suspended in space, searching for a way in. My little ant brain knew there must be a way, that there was some passage that others before me had taken. I covered the same ground over and over in my mind, examining the problem from every possible angle, hopeful that my dedication would eventually yield an answer. I couldn't stop thinking about it, wondering what they were doing, checking the cop's email, congratulating myself on my rigor.

Over lunch, I showed Joan a picture of the kid on my phone where I had saved it. She looked closely at the photograph, zooming in and out and squinting at the image. Then she turned and looked at me with the same scrutiny.

"Your skin is better than the kid's," she said at last, "but it could still be better. It could be really smooth and have a great glow."

"My skin?"

"You have some blackheads, you know. And some oil issues in your t-zone. Which is totally normal, but maybe you should go see the girl who does my facials. It makes such a difference. And it makes you feel good too. It really does. You leave feeling like you've had a massage."

Grateful for a piece of advice I hadn't heard, I made an appointment and went to the aesthetician Joan recommended, a pretty girl with long hair, the hippie-born-too-late type, with a linen tunic and a pleasing, earthy aroma. She put me on an electric gurney and covered me with a blanket almost as heavy as the lead shield dental assistants use during x-rays.

As she methodically inspected my face and directed a steam machine at it, she asked why I had come to see her. I told her about Joan's referral. Then I told her about the kid's skin. Then I had to tell her about the cop. I wept through extractions of age-old blackheads.

"Keep talking," the girl said. "All these feelings are held in your skin as toxins we have to get rid of."

Later she said it had been a lucky thing she had seen me crying because had it revealed to her that what my skin needed most was a Paprika Lifting Mask.

"This will feel intense," she said, slathering goop onto my face, "but it will solve some of your problems."

"I would never normally say this," she said, "but try not to cry for the next fifteen minutes. The mask has to harden."

At the end of the session, the aesthetician booked me another appointment for six weeks later and told me to wait while she dug around in her purse for a business card. She handed it to me at last and said, "I really think you should go see this man."

The card listed a name, beneath which were the words "Palmist, Psychic, and Consultant."

I went, of course, putting the one-hundred-fifty-dollar, forty-five minute session on a credit card, along with everything else I bought during my reckless period of recovery.

The psychic was an unexpected figure in a three-piece suit, but his office was filled with all the cliché trappings of the trade, including what looked to be a genuine crystal ball. He read my palm, my face, and a tarot deck, which I shuffled, cut, and dealt according to his instructions.

I told him I was really only interested in what would happen to the cop and me.

He closed his eyes and drew a slow breath. "I see you as friends," he said at last. "That's it."

"You don't see us involved in a romance again?" I asked.

He squinted, peering thorough the psychic fog. "I'm sorry, but I'm getting that he's occupied with someone else."

"Yes, I know that. But when will that end?"

"I don't think you will be together with this man in the future. I think you should focus on using this time to improve yourself. You can still change your relationship with him into a friendship."

"But what can I do to move our relationship in the direction of a romance?"

Growing frustrated, he said, "I don't think you can do that, I'm sorry to say. I think this is just where things are from now on."

"But there's a twenty-four year age difference between them."

"I hope I'm wrong," he said, "but I don't think I am. Would you like to talk about other things, like your career path? There might be some interesting developments there."

"No, I'd just like to talk about this, please."

"I'm afraid I don't have anything else to say on this subject. I'm very sorry. I do think things are going to get better for you, though. I hope that helps."

"I guess it does," I said. "Can you tell me something about their lives that I don't already know?"

"I have a feeling you already know more than you should," he said, "but I can tell you this: The three of you have been linked in past lives many times. And you will all meet again in future incarnations."

When I left, the psychic gave me a CD recording he had made of our conversation. I took it home and smashed it underfoot against the tile floor in my kitchen. If for no other reason, I regretted our meeting because from then on I had to wonder about the absurd notion that the three of us had been linked in our past lives. Had we been husband, wife, and son? Siblings? The Three fucking Stooges?

I planned to see another psychic in town for a second opinion, but my credit card company called to ask if it had been stolen. There had been some very strange charges in the past few weeks, they said, and the card was over its limit.

58

THERE WAS A MAN I SAW AT THE ARCADE A FEW TIMES,
a tough-looking white thirtysomething, whom I had pegged as
military. I entered a booth to find him with three other men. The
military guy was naked, but the other three men were half dressed,
their pants around their ankles and their shirts lifted from their
stomachs and pinched beneath their chins. When I walked in,
he was going down on them in turn. I watched him do that for a
while. Then he stood and turned away from the men so that their
wet dicks were now at the same level as his ass.

He leaned close to me and whispered, "Can I?"

Then he raised his arms like he was going to hug me.

I understood that what he wanted was to lean on me. So I let
him. He put his arms around my neck and hung his head so that
the top of his skull was against my cheek. The three guys were behind him, grabbing his dick and theirs.

"Are you gonna let me?" one of the guys kept saying. "You gonna let me?"

The military guy appeared drugged or as if he was having a religious experience. His face was three inches from mine. "Should I
let him?" he whispered.

"Do you want him to?" I whispered back.

"Don't ask me. It's up to you."

"Yes, you should let him."

He nodded, as if a grave finality had been reached. "Okay," he
said over his shoulder.

I can't remember whether or not the guy put on a condom. I
couldn't see what was being done to the military man. He was leaning on me with most of his weight. I could tell when the man was

inside of him. That guy finished quickly, then another of the men did it, and he got off fast too.

I wanted to go, but the military guy was holding on to me. "Don't leave until it's over," he said.

While the third guy fucked him, the military guy looked straight into my eyes with his arms around my neck. Then the third guy left, and we were alone.

When the other men were gone, he seemed to come out of his spell a bit. He dressed himself slowly.

"Thanks for being there," he said.

"Sure. Thanks for letting me watch."

He left the booth, and I walked out a minute later, after standing in the smell for a while, taking it all in.

I walked around the hallways feeling drunk and uneven. Then I saw him in the opposite corridor, cruising another guy. I'd assumed he had left. I couldn't imagine what he was looking for or when it would be finished. I watched the two of them go into a booth, and I followed them. I pressed against the door, and found it unlocked. Though they had only bumped into one another two minutes earlier, when I opened the door, I saw the military man bent over and the other man behind him licking his ass.

A couple of days later, by chance, I ran into the military man at an electronics store. We were on opposite sides of a display when we noticed one another. At first, I didn't remember how I knew him. But then I remembered his blissed-out eyes as those strangers took him from behind. We lifted our chins at one another. Guys like that, you don't know whether to pity them or what. People would say the same thing about me if they could have seen me in that booth, maybe, even though I was only watching.

Normally, I only pushed against the door of an occupied booth when I knew exactly who I would find inside, but I suspended that rule when it was clear that it was occupied by a group of men rather than an individual. When I could manage to be included, groups at the arcade were my best-case scenarios. As someone who mostly watched, it meant a chance to see a lot more than I might otherwise have seen. As long as my dick was out of my pants, no one cared that I wasn't participating as much as the others. I'd let them touch me a little, but when they tried to suck me or direct me to their rear ends, I'd shake my head no. No one minded as long as there were plenty of alternatives present.

At the arcade, sometimes you'd knock on the door of a booth filled with people, and they'd open it a crack, take a look at you, and then grant you entry like nightclub bouncers. Sometimes they'd just leave the door unlocked and when they saw who it was coming in, they'd all nod their heads like, "Yeah, man. Come join the fun."

Sometimes, I'd walk into a booth and recognize that everyone was looking at me with a who-the-fuck-is-this-guy expression. Or they wouldn't let me in at all. Sometimes, I'd be the only man out there not crammed into a single booth with the rest of the crowd.

It sometimes happened that, having pulled into the parking lot to find it half full, I'd buy my tokens confident that I wouldn't pass the evening alone. But, upon entering the hallways, I'd discover only one red light lit. Though I could hear several people inside, I'd press against the door and find it locked. Confident that there must be others that I hadn't yet come across, I'd walk around seeking other possibilities. Then, finding none, I'd circle back and test the door again to see if it had been unlocked in the interval. In desperation, I'd try the doors on either side and find them locked too, even though their lights weren't lit. Some perverts were already in there watching everything under the wall.

59

THE NEXT TIME MR. GRATE AND BENCH CHECKED IN, everything was as usual. He asked, as always, to borrow one of the irons and miniature ironing boards we kept at the front desk. Actually, he didn't have to ask. I remembered to give it to him without prompting, which I hoped would help my case somehow.

He didn't say anything about the job or about his pregnant employee before he went to his room. And I was alone again in the motel lobby, the fishbowl room where people looked in from outside and saw me at all times, reading, eating, and watching bad television on the tiny TV set beneath the counter.

He had to give me the job. I'd treat it with wry irony, but really it would be the end of shame for me, the way an action hero backed into a corner has to use whatever is at hand to make his escape. At the end of the film it doesn't matter that he wore a dress for five minutes to blend into a crowd. What matters is that he is free and has completed whatever task he set out to complete, even if in an unconventional and unexpected way.

I'd buy new clothes with the money. Expensive shoes with leather soles. If you can afford them, you actually save money in the end. Maybe I'd hire a stylist who would understand what looks good on me. I'll feel silly at the time, but I'd always remember his sharp observations about what fits and cuts most suited my build, his tips about the best way to roll up my shirtsleeves. I'd learn which brands were scoffed at by people in the know.

I'd subscribe to all the magazines I wanted and pay for two years up front to get the biggest discounts. And I'd have nights free to read them and to become a smarter and better-informed version of myself. Maybe I'd take private lessons and learn French or something even more frivolous like Swedish.

I'd go out to dinners like a normal person. I'd run into my clients, who would appear in the landscape of the city as if materializing from nothing. They would have been there all along, of course, but now that I knew them as serious consumers of high-quality outdoor products, they would stand out from the crowd.

I'd be easy to spot too, because of my classic and stylish clothes that fit me better all the time thanks to biweekly sessions with my personal trainer, and the great haircuts I'd get at a salon that I'd always wondered about, with its expensive-looking branding and their hair care line displayed in their windows visible from the street. My hair stylist would know the best person in the state for that hair transplant, if I ever got serious about it.

"Trust me," she'd say, looking at me in the mirror as she touched my hair, "it's totally worth the cost, and this guy is so good no one will ever be able to tell. Not in a million years."

Mr. Grate and Bench came to the lobby and asked me to call him a cab. He had read about a restaurant and he wanted to try it out.

I observed, as he waited for his cab, that he was very good at pressing his shirts. "Maybe you can teach me your trick sometime."

He laughed. "It must be my special talent."

I could tell he wasn't going to say anything about it, so I said, "How's your pregnant employee doing?"

"I'll find out tomorrow," he said. "She says she's showing now."

"Wow," I said, "that must be weird, huh?"

"Yeah, it always is for my wife. It kind of makes everything real."

"I bet."

"Yeah. Anyway, we'll see what she's thinking tomorrow, I guess."

Then the cab came, and he told me to have a nice night and to take care. I said the same to him, and then I was alone in the fishbowl again.

One of the day clerks had forgotten to log out of her Facebook account, so I looked up Mr. Grate and Bench. His profile picture was of him and his wife and kids, taken professionally, it appeared. They were seated on a bench on the front porch of their upper middle class tract home in Connecticut. The wife, pretty and brunette, the kids—maybe four and six years old—dressed like their father, in light-colored polo shirts and loafers.

It resembled in no way the life I had envisioned for myself, but it appeared to have its charms. More than the lobby, anyway, where I had to keep a vanilla-scented candle lit around the clock to mask a mysterious odor the source of which no one had been able to locate over the past three-and-a-half years.

A couple of hours later, I watched through the window as my future employer was dropped off by another cab. He took a while figuring out how to pay, and I could see he was slightly drunk. He made a gesture of surrender that I took to mean that he had chosen to overtip tremendously rather than do the math.

He waved at me as he passed the lobby on the way to his room. I waved back, but then opened the door and called out, "How was it?"

"Great!" he said, still walking away from me. "You've got to try it!"

60

I WAS STILL A PART OF THE COP'S LIFE EVERY DAY. WHETHER he knew, it didn't matter. What mattered was that I was there, a minor character in the movie of his life, knowing and knowing and knowing that I'd move from background extra to leading actor if I could only hold on. Maybe he could sense my presence somehow, a friend and protector, watching over something as minor as his daily email correspondence.

I knew what greeted him each day before he did, what he had to dread and look forward to. At first I only read the messages he'd already read himself, but that quickly began to seem like a meaningless ethical technicality. I soon found I couldn't resist, and I began reading the messages he hadn't read yet, always remembering afterwards to highlight them and click "Mark as Unread" before signing out, only to sign in five minutes later to see if anything had changed.

In the weeks just after he ended things with me, he replied to my emails right away. I could see he had read them, and then I would get a reply. But it wasn't long before I found that he would read my emails without responding immediately. Sometimes days would pass. It was as though he was too exhausted of me even to send a quick note. I could understand why. Even a short reply would result in an astonishingly disproportionate response from me. I read an article during that period about how people who have recently been broken up with have reduced blood flow to the parts of the brain in command of reasoning. It made perfect sense, but when I thought of it, I was only reminded to go check his email again.

Sometimes I would send an email to him, then log in to read how it looked from inside his inbox. I could don his moustache and his holster and his self-assurance and read as though I were him.

Often, I'd then think better of it and delete the just-sent missive from his inbox and trashcan, pulling the words back before he could ever read them.

Once, I read a particularly exciting email that had just been sent by the kid minutes earlier. It was about some of the problems they had been having at home and the kid's promises to try to get better about keeping the house clean and taking better care of the cat. But the kid said that the cop had to make changes too, like being more fun when the kid had friends to the house. And not being such a grump when he was tired, which he often was. The kid also griped that the house did not contain a sufficient number of things representing himself, and that he felt that he was living in the cop's world, which was very nice in some ways, but awful in other ways, because, though he loved the cop more deeply than he could possibly say in some stupid email, he wanted to be young too, and to play music at high volumes and have posters of his favorite musicians on the walls if he wanted.

I logged out of the cop's account in something like a state of euphoria.

Nothing in months had made me feel as good as that list of their problems, and after only a few minutes had passed I logged in again to revisit the litany. But I saw that the email had been marked as read. That worried me. I knew the cop was at a work meeting he had been dreading all week, so he definitely wasn't looking at his email. I was almost certain I hadn't forgotten to mark it unread, but it was possible. I read the email again, then carefully marked it unread, checked it and double checked it, then read another email that had just come in from the cop's travel agent about the cruise he and the kid were going to take.

When I returned to the main screen, the email from the kid was grayed-out again, as if it had been read. A moment later, I refreshed the page, and the email was gone. I looked in the trash, and found it there. Then I refreshed once again, and saw that it had disappeared.

The kid was reading the cop's email too. It almost made me wonder if the psychic had been right about all of us being connected in some past life, the way the cop had chosen the two of us, both of us so sneaky and insecure and scared and dumb.

61

STR8 ITALIAN VISITING. MARRIED COACH TYPE IN TOWN FOR
*biz. Other str8 guys looking for a massage? I give good ones. Safe and
clean here. Average build. Prefer 18-24 yo. Discreet.*

Though I was past his target age range by a few years, I emailed
him. When he replied asking for pictures, I took a few photos of
my dick with my phone. He replied with photos of himself and his
room number at the Radisson Hotel downtown. I liked the way he
looked, like someone my grandfather would have called "a genuine Yankee." He was an Italian guy in his mid-forties with a gold
chain around his neck and a pinkie ring. He looked like he could
have been a gangster and not a commercial property appraiser in
town for a conference.

I went to his room, which he had set up for me as a little massage
studio, with the bed all covered in towels and the pillows arranged
so I'd feel like I was on a real massage table. He even had massage
oil. We shook hands, and he went to the bathroom and turned on
the shower for me.

"Get undressed," he said. "If you take a shower first, your mus-
cles will be loose for the massage."

I had assumed that the massage was just a Craigslist pretext, but
it appeared he was serious. I didn't know then that innumerable
men advertise for massages every day, that these amateur massages are themselves a type of fetish, and that many, many men like to
begin sexual encounters in this way.

I didn't mind. At least he gave me something to do after walking
in the door other than immediately having sex. I got undressed in
front of him and he looked at me as a doctor would a patient.

"You're very fit," he said.

"Thanks."

I went to the bathroom.

"I hope it's not too foggy in there," he called from the other room. "I just showered before you arrived."

"It's fine," I said.

"Open the curtain so we can talk," he said.

I opened the curtain and showered so he could see me, but we didn't speak. I just showered and he watched, occasionally nodding in approval of my careful and exhaustive bathing.

"Would you mind bringing me a towel?" I said. "There aren't any in here."

"Of course," he said, taking one from the table nearby and bringing it to me.

But instead of handing it to me as I stepped from the tub onto the bathmat, he wrapped it around me and began to dry me himself.

I hadn't experienced anything like it since I was a very small child. No one had dried me off. He even dried my hair. It felt good. He was wearing his gold chain even then. It was funny and endearing, the chain.

He had a tattoo on his left bicep of a baseball bat with a word inside of it.

"What does your tattoo say?"

"Nothing," he said. "It's the name of my son's little league team. I coach for them."

"That's nice. He must like that tattoo."

"Yeah, he does."

"I bet you're a good dad," I said.

He smiled at that, then he led me to the bed, where he laid me down on my stomach and slowly began rubbing my back. It felt great. I had never had a massage before that. I had always said I didn't want to be touched that much by any stranger, but it felt terrific.

He had told me to close my eyes at the start, so I didn't see when he took his shirt off. But I could feel the hair of his chest brushing against parts of my back when he reached over me.

Later, I flipped over and he saw that I was hard.

"I think I'd feel more comfortable if you took your pants off too," I told him.

I was somehow able to shed all my inhibitions with the little league coach. It was even better than it had been with the cop. I let him do whatever he wanted. We kissed and kissed. Once, he got up to check his phone to see if his wife had called him, but she hadn't. That made him happy when he came back to bed, and he laughed and snuggled me. There was no rush.

"If my wife calls, I'm going to go to the other room and speak with her briefly, then I'm going to come back here and be with you. I don't want you to worry about it."

"I won't," I told him.

I didn't think about the cop. I only thought about the little league coach.

We'd get close to climaxing, then stop. We did this several times, each time slowing down and stopping before crossing over the edge. It was dark out now. A couple of hours had passed.

His phone rang. He got up to look at it and said, "This is what I told you about earlier. I'll be back in a moment."

"Okay," I said.

He went to the other room and shut the door. I lay in bed thinking, and for the first time I thought about the cop. I tried not to, but there he was. It was a little scary finding that I could have forgotten him at all.

I was glad when the man returned.

"I'm sorry about that," he said.

"No problem," I said.

"Do you have time to stay a bit longer?"

"Yes."

"Good."

He got back into bed, still naked, and he put his arms around me and squeezed me like he adored me, like he was so proud of me he couldn't even put it into words.

"Boy, I'm lucky tonight," he said.

"I am too," I said. And I meant it, even without knowing how truly lucky I had been, how rare those sorts of connections are.

We played until we got close again, and we stopped and kissed a while.

"I want to ask you if you'd be willing to try something," I said.

"Ask me."

"You don't have to say yes if you don't want to."

"I know that."

"How would it be if maybe…when we decide to finish, maybe we could look at one another and say, 'I love you.' Would that be okay? I know it's really weird."

The little league coach smiled at me. "I don't think that's weird at all, I think that's nice. We'll do that."

"You sure?"

"I'm one hundred percent sure. You know I've never said that to another guy before."

"Really? Me neither," I said. "At least, not like in a romantic or sexual situation or whatever."

"Right. That's what I meant too."

After that, we started again, kissing more passionately, moving towards our goal. At the last moment, he said, "Are we going to?"

"Yes."

"I love you," he said.

"I love you," I said.

Then we said it again. And again. Then we lay there a while longer just breathing and being against one another. Then he stood up and got the damp towels from the bathroom for us to clean up with.

"That was great," he said.

"Yeah, I can't tell you how much I needed this."

I met with him the next day, and we did it all again. Without discussing it, we looked into one another's eyes and said that we loved each other.

The next day he went home to his wife and kid.

I got one last email from him.

"Hey Squirt. Made it home. In a cab now. Hope you're okay today. Wish I was still in town."

62

I RARELY WONDERED WHY I WAS ATTRACTED TO THE MEN who most appealed to me. What mattered was that it was such a powerful feeling. It was a thrill connecting with a man who had the exact thing I liked. It was a thrill getting to put my hands in his pants. I couldn't believe my luck when it worked, that we both happened to want one another.

There were men who made me feel great about the way I looked. They told me how sexy I was, how I was exactly what they wanted. And I could tell it was true by the way they kissed or touched me. They felt lucky being in my presence. That meant something to me. I felt better about myself because of it. I probably remember every compliment anyone ever gave me about the way I look, which is embarrassing.

I've always despised people who have self-assurance and pride, especially about their looks. I can't imagine why anyone should get to feel good about something they have so little control over. Like the guys at the arcade who were so proud of their dicks. The bigger his dick, the prouder he'd be, as if he had made the wise choice of being well endowed, while the rest of the world's morons chose average and small dicks for themselves.

You could tell that a guy was going to have a big cock by the way he'd remove himself from his pants, as if he were pulling back the curtain on the most fantastic stage show you'd ever see. By the way they undressed themselves, men always disclosed what they liked best about their bodies. When he loved his chest, the first thing he'd do after entering a booth was take off his shirt and hang it on the hook. The guy would ask you to touch his chest, to play with his nipples. You see these men on the running trails all the time. It's freezing out and though he might be wearing long pants or even insulated leggings, his shirt is off. If there is an excuse in the world, it's always off. If a man at the arcade loved his legs, he'd wear shorts, or he'd have his pants around his ankles as soon as he could get them there.

My aversion to pride and self-satisfaction is life-long. In college, I had an incredible hatred of the Greek system, the world of fraternities and sororities on my campus. I complained about how disgusting it was that people became friends on the basis that they had wealthy parents, how they all dressed alike and talked alike and projected an air of superiority even though they seemed to everyone else to be such complete assholes. What bothered me most was that, even if they had been able to grasp how they appeared to the rest of the campus, they wouldn't have cared. What mattered to them was their insular club of moneyed, privileged kids born into something luckier even than a big dick or a nice chest. They felt proud of themselves for nothing.

It was the same for all sorts of pride. American pride, pride in your college team, pride in our soldiers, black pride, gay pride. Being from Texas, I heard a lot about being a proud Texan. Everywhere I saw bumper stickers boasting "Native Texan." But how can this type of pride be explained? It's not as if they sat surveying the options and chose to be born in the United States or Ireland or Afghanistan or Belize, so how could anyone be proud to be from those places? You could just as easily have been born anywhere as anyone. I've always felt repelled by those people who discover with such satisfaction that their bloodlines can be traced to the American Revolution or the Mayflower. It's like being proud of a roll of the dice. Not even a roll you made yourself. A roll someone else made hundreds or thousands of years ago.

The Apologizing Man was the counter archetype to the Big Dicks. "I'm sorry about my stomach," the Apologizing Man would say glumly. "I'm working on it, believe it or not." God, I found them endearing. They appeared not to know that there were men on the internet making videos of just their stomachs, rubbing them, and feeding themselves constantly to make them continue to grow so that their fans would continue to watch. The guys in those videos—"gainers" they call them—could be seen stuffing themselves, eating enormous meals, entire pizzas, downing three liter bottles of soda, stroking their enormous, engorged guts, which look as if they have somehow become impregnated, their owners saying over and over again to the invisible viewing audience, "You like that? You like that?"

You heard that a lot from the non-apologizers. *You like that?* Usually they were asking because they could tell you did like it, whatever it was. That hairy ass. Those incredible pectorals. The way they kissed or blew you or wore a pair of cowboy boots.

Other Apologizing Men were guys with small dicks. There is such insane variety within the world of male genitalia, I hardly remember, looking back, which belonged to who. Most of them were perfectly terrific, frankly, smallest to largest. Given the choice, I'd rather date a guy with a small dick than a very large one. Though of course I'd rather have a very large one myself.

Men are never ashamed about the things they should be ashamed of. If any man asking forgiveness for his little dick or potbelly had extended the invitation, I probably could have prepared a lengthy list of things he should have worried about instead.

Bad breath, for instance, was not merely an occasional problem. At the booths, where one was more apt to notice, it was an epidemic that thwarted many a fun sexual encounter. Escapades I thought were done deals fell apart as soon as I got close enough to smell or taste the foulness of another man's mouth. One wondered how they failed to taste it themselves and feel tortured by it.

I was astonished at how often it was a problem, at how often it was *the* problem that prevented things from moving forward. It made me so compulsively self-conscious about my own breath I could only wonder why everyone else in the place didn't adopt a similar stance, why breath spray and mints weren't sold at the counter next to the condoms and lube.

It happened once at the arcade that before I realized my partner was thusly afflicted, he began going down on me. The smell rose to my nostrils as the spit accumulated, forming not just a lubricant, but a multi-layered stench on my privates. I broke from him in a state of dizzy repulsion and left the booth as quickly as I could put myself away. I wandered the halls for a minute or two, unsure what to do next, though I knew I couldn't remove myself from my pants in the presence of anyone else. Finally, I pushed through the heavy exit door and into the night. I sped home and ran to the shower, stripping and standing beneath the spray without even waiting for it to warm up.

63

MALCOLM'S TIME IN BOSTON, WHICH HAD BEGUN AS A three-month stint, kept getting extended. I think he was bored talking about the cop and the kid after all those weeks and months. Or maybe it was because I had told him about the arcade and the Cyclops that he took me into his confidence.

"I've been fucking one of the bellboys," he said.

"Oh yeah?" A little spurt of jealousy entered my bloodstream.

"Yeah. For a few weeks now."

"You've been keeping secrets."

"Well, he's young. Which I know is a trigger for you."

"Don't be silly." My face was hot. "Of course he's young. Bell-boys are young, right? That's why they're boys. He's not twelve or something, is he?"

"He's twenty-two."

"Oh, nice. Just under half your age.

"We're not in love or anything like that. It's just…he's got this accent. This Boston accent, like Matt Damon in *Good Will Hunting*."

"I guess I can see how that would be appealing."

"I wouldn't have thought so, but it really is."

"Are you supposed to be doing that? I mean, are you allowed to have sex with your employees?"

"No, Sam, I'm not."

"So it's a secret. Like you can't get caught, right?

"Right."

"Those are the best."

"You think?"

"Absolutely. He sneaks into your room at night, right?"

"Yeah."

"You touch him surreptitiously when the two of you pass in the hallway."

"We've done that maybe once."

"When you're alone together and someone walks in, you act like everything is normal and pretend like you're in the middle of an innocent conversation."

"That's never happened."

"But it's the spirit of the thing, Malcolm. When it's a secret, it's like this little egg that the two of you protect together."

"Maybe. I don't think that's why it's fun though. Or if it is, that's just a small part of it."

"So what's fun about it then?"

"I don't know. Just being attracted to one another. Having fun sex. Making out with someone new. The whole thing."

"Does Ron know?"

"No. Although I assume he's fooling around with people while I'm gone. Which is fine."

"Are you in love with Ron?"

"Absolutely."

"Do you like having sex with the kid more than you like having sex with Ron?"

"Let's not start calling him 'the kid,' okay?"

"The bellboy then."

"That's better, but he has a name. It's Ethan."

"I think I'd rather just call him the bellboy."

"Having sex with Ronald is completely different than having sex with Ethan. And I wouldn't say that one is substantially better than the other. Just that they're different."

"So you wouldn't give one an eight and the other a nine? Like on a scale of ten?"

"No, I wouldn't."

"He's a bottom? The kid? The bellboy?"

"I'd say he's versatile."

"You fuck him and he fucks you."

"That's pretty much how it works, yeah."

"What's his dick like?"

"It's really huge actually. Too big for it to be comfortable. He likes to top more, but I just can't do that all the time."

"Of course he has a giant dick. And let me guess, he's straight."

Malcolm laughed. "Goes home to his girlfriend every night."

"All you guys are the same."

"You mean all *us* guys, right, Mr. Arcade? Anyway, don't be jealous. You know I'm going to be home visiting in a couple of weeks. We could meet for a beer or something."

"I'm afraid I wouldn't stack up after your experiences with the bellboy."

"Well, he's a lot less jaded than you, but I still think you're handsomer."

"You've never even seen my face."

"Yeah, but I have a feeling about you."

"So corny."

"You're never going to meet me, are you?"

"I might."

"I don't believe you."

"I should probably let you go. You're probably expecting the bellboy any minute."

"Ethan is going to a movie with his parents and his girlfriend tonight."

"Gag."

"I know. But it's kind of adorable, right?"

64

A BIG BULL OF A MAN APPEARED AT THE ARCADE. HE LOOKED like a teenager's stepdad, the kind who would never be ripped off by a mechanic or intimidated by pretty much anything or anyone. He strutted up and down the aisles wearing khaki pants with an XL polo stretched over his chest. In the store, he picked up DVD covers and considered them. He looked like a straight guy killing time while his lawnmower blades were being sharpened. But eventually he went to the counter and bought a handful of tokens.

It wasn't long before he caught on with the other men at the arcade. He wasn't good-looking—or not in the Cary Grant sense, which is what I always think people mean when they ask me if someone's good-looking. I think of Cary Grant. Or George Clooney. If the person I'm describing doesn't resemble one of those people, when someone asks me "Is he good-looking?" I always say no. So he wasn't good-looking like that, but he was good-looking to me. I was among a small group of men stalking him while trying to play it cool. He wouldn't acknowledge any of us. No one could draw more than a momentary glance from him. He went into a booth and locked the door. Everyone tried it one after the other, thinking that like *The Sword in the Stone*, the Chosen One might be able to do that which had been impossible before. Then the bull came out of the booth and walked around again. None of us could rest as long as he was out there.

It was always like that. No one wanted to settle down until he was certain he'd found the best he was going to get. It was perfectly acceptable to say to someone, "I just got here. I don't want to come yet." It was perfectly acceptable to say that you were going to walk around and see who else was there. That's why it felt so good when a guy bought his tokens and then came straight to you without reviewing the options. He knew you were exactly what he wanted.

But then it also felt good when someone had made the rounds and seen all the possibilities and then came back and found you. Which explains the burst of pride I felt when the bull lowered his head in my direction and indicated the door to a particular booth. It was as if he was the coach, who, after surveying all his players on the bench, selected me as the one best equipped for the job.

He went into the booth first, and I followed behind him a moment later. He faced the screen with his back to me. I let him get a look at me before I locked the door. I wanted there to be no mistaking the situation. He turned around after a second and lifted his chin in a gesture of recognition. As I turned to engage the lock, another man slipped into the booth with us. I had noticed him outside. He, too, had been pursuing the bull, though his advances had been absolutely devoid of style. He was furtive, awkward, and creepy. He was at least twenty years older than me.

"Get out," I whispered to him.

He pressed himself against the wall and shook his head, an eerie grin fixed on his face. The bull didn't see what was going on behind him or hear over the volume of the porn flick he'd selected.

"Get out," I said again, but the man didn't move.

I got the attention of the bull by tapping his shoulder. "He won't leave," I said, pointing to the man behind us.

The bull behaved exactly as you would expect. He turned and looked at the guy. He didn't waste a syllable. "Out," he said, gesturing with his thumb over his shoulder. The sneak, given no choice, exited, and I quickly locked the door behind him.

I joined the bull. We stood side-by-side watching the video. We both undid our pants. I looked at him and he looked at the screen. I reached over and took hold of him. He nodded. "Yeah," he said. He didn't touch me. He watched the screen. "Yeah," he repeated, as I got to know him down there, tugging lightly.

"Now suck it," he said.

I hadn't even had time to say, "I don't do that much out here" or to confirm and reconfirm his disease-free status.

I thought about trying it out on him, but I knew it would be the end of things. There wasn't going to be the shared time in the booth together touching and playing, watching one another and getting excited, possibly even climaxing together, possibly even at the same time, or roughly the same time.

I bent down and tried to get a look at it in the dim light to see if it was covered in sores or scars or unusual bumps or ridges. It seemed normal, from what I could tell. I opened my mouth and put it in. He was silent. I sucked for a minute or two. He put his hand on my head and was mostly quiet. Occasionally, he reached over my head to adjust the volume of the video or scroll through the available options when he got bored with what was happening on screen.

I took him out of my mouth and looked at his face. I stood up and jerked him, looking at the screen and wondering what would happen next, wondering if it was my turn. He looked at me, and I could tell he was going to say something. I thought it would probably be something really nice. Guys had already said a lot of nice things to me out there. It might have been the real reason I went out there at all, to hear all the nice things guys had to say when they got you alone, when they earned their shot in a booth with you.

"You gonna suck it or what?" he said.

For a second I imagined he must be joking, but I saw just as quickly that this was not a person who made ironic jokes in which he pretended to be an insensitive jerk as a way of breaking the ice. I could imagine that scenario. I could imagine connecting with someone intelligent and funny who could acknowledge the strangeness of our situation—who might look down and see that I was a person too, and within me a complex world of memories and feelings and pleasures and fears—and say, in a joking way, "You gonna suck it or what?"

But that wasn't this guy. This guy didn't make ironic jokes. More likely, he made racist or sexist jokes.

I didn't say anything else. I put myself away and left. Just outside waited the man who had refused to leave the booth. He slinked in like an insect before the door could swing shut on its springs, and I heard the door lock behind him.

65

THE COP DEIGNED TO SPEAK WITH ME LESS AND LESS. FOR weeks, I'd hardly contact him at all, white-knuckling it on Malcolm's advice. I recorded each of our interactions religiously on my calendar. The end of the six months was nearing.

I learned from their emails that my existence had become perhaps the only point of contention between the cop and the kid. Their agreement was that if the cop spoke to me, the kid had to be told, which meant a conversation about our conversation, and maybe an argument. It was hardly worth the trouble to the cop, particularly since phone calls with me had degraded to little more than a bizarre, rapid cycling between badly acted indifference and total desperation, as I repeatedly fell out of character.

During this period, I began getting allergy shots twice a week to cope with my allergy to the cop's cat—a supposed reason why I had never spent the night at his house, and a barrier, I saw, to our eventual happiness together. He'd be so impressed by my thoughtfulness in the end.

I panicked when I realized the two of them were emailing about the kid getting his passport for the cruise, which would enter international waters. If they were to split up before then, the cop was going to have an extra ticket, and I wouldn't be able to drop everything and join him unless I had a passport too.

I cooked up a phony travel agenda and went to a passport expediter, who would be able to acquire my passport far sooner than the eight weeks that were then standard for a new one. It cost me an extra $400, but I had my passport just two weeks later, with the most fittingly crazed and maniacal passport photo imaginable.

The focus on the kid and the cop, all the errands and tasks associated with getting him back, had the single great advantage that it made it easier for me to cope with reactions to news of my homosexually. My sister called as I arrived at my allergist's office one afternoon. When I answered, she said, "Well, you've always wanted to ruin the family, and now you've done it."

"I can't talk right now," I was able to say. "I have a doctor's appointment."

66

MY FRIEND GREG LOST HIS JOB WHEN HIS EMPLOYER
discovered he'd been spending hours of every shift looking at porn
on his work computer. I guess because I was the only other sexual deviant he knew, I was the one he asked to accompany him to
a twelve step meeting for sex addicts. He picked me up early on
a Saturday and drove us to a church not far from where I lived.
We rode an elevator filled with other sheepish men deep into a
basement, and followed signs printed with arrows and the letters
"SAA." Greg had told me on the ride over that there was another
organization called SLAA, which stood for Sex and Love Addicts
Anonymous. He didn't know the difference between the two, but
this one was more conveniently located, and anyway love wasn't
his addiction.

It was a big open room with a bunch of stackable plastic chairs in
a circle. We were among the last to arrive.

"Welcome, welcome," a guy with a clipboard said to everyone.
"Please get coffee and a donut and find a seat."

I stood by Greg while he got a cup of coffee, then we found two
chairs next to one another. The man with the clipboard said, "Hello, everyone. I'm Dave, and I'm a sex addict."

"Hi, Dave," we all said.

"Hi. First I want to say welcome to all these new faces. We're very
glad to see you today. Thank you for coming. If you have any questions or need help, please reach out to me or Bob after the meeting."

Bob raised his hand.

"Many of you knew coming in today that this is a special meeting. A fifth step meeting. Which is when a single individual under-
takes the completion of his or her fifth step."

Reading from his clipboard: "In which we admit to God, ourselves, and other human beings the exact nature of our wrongdoing."

"As you might imagine, the fifth step can only take place after the completion of the fourth step, in which the addict"—again reading from the clipboard—"makes a searching and fearless moral inventory of himself or herself."

The leader spoke for a moment longer while my attention was drawn to the anxious-looking man sitting next to him. He was a handsome guy with a good haircut in his early forties, wearing fitted black jeans and an expensive-looking button-up shirt. While Dave wrapped up his introduction, the man removed a few stapled-together pages from a worn backpack at his feet.

"Now I'll pass the floor to Don."

The handsome man with the pages said, "Hi, everyone, my name is Don, and I'm a sex addict."

In chorus: "Hi, Don."

Looking at the pages in his hands, we could all see how badly Don's hands were shaking.

It wasn't until he began to speak that I understood what we were witnessing. Essentially, it was to be an extended, public confession of all his sexual sins.

"When I was eleven, I had the family dog lick my penis until I reached orgasm. I don't know how many times I did that. Several times.

"When I was twelve, I began taking my mother's underwear from the laundry hamper and masturbating with them. Soon after that, I started doing the same thing with my sister's underwear. Sometimes I smelled and licked them. Sometimes I just used them for masturbation.

"That same year, I convinced my twelve-year-old friend, who was also a male, to put his mouth on my penis. After that, we traded oral sex several times, sometimes more than once a day."

The list droned on and on. It seemed like ages before Don even arrived at the depravities of his actual adulthood. When he did, he didn't mention sexual encounters he'd had with his girlfriends or his wives. He talked about all the women he'd had sex with outside of those relationships. He talked about picking women up at bars and having sex with one of his cousins when she was drunk and possibly blacked out. He talked about being a musician and how women sometimes threw themselves at him. He said the reason he got into music in the first place was that in high school, he realized it would help him get laid. He talked about having sex with unattractive women and women he knew to be carriers of one or another social disease when he was at his most desperate. He talked about all the times he'd had gonorrhea and syphilis and how many times a girl had called and told him he had given her chlamydia. He talked about how often he had had sex with women knowing he had an STI. He talked about the occasions when he had sex with men, though he was straight.

I had tagged along with alcoholic friends to a few AA meetings in the past, so I had imagined I knew what to expect. This was something very different. There was an electricity in the air, and it grew more and more intense as the man spoke. Everyone in the room was so rapt, I couldn't help wondering if there was a voyeuristic dimension to it for everyone, or if I was the only one sick enough to have a prurient curiosity about what the man might confess to next. I wondered if the men in the room were concealing erections. Don, still reading his list, was obviously ashamed and desperately regretful. I couldn't imagine how he was doing what he was doing. It seemed unbearably courageous and unbearable in general.

As a kid, I had a particular vision of Judgment Day that I worried about all the time. I still envisioned it even in adulthood. I thought that God reserved judgment until everyone was dead, and that we all arrived in the afterlife at the same moment. I imagined all of mankind together in one place and that we'd take turns being judged. When it was my turn, all the people I had ever known would come to the front of the crowd, with the other members of humanity behind them. I would stand on a platform facing them, with God beside me. Then He would call out every sin I had ever committed for everyone to hear.

I'd have to admit to each transgression and then repent in front of everyone. It would last for months, except that the concept of months wouldn't exist in eternity. I had the idea that it wouldn't be enough merely to say I was sorry. I would have to mean it. I would have to honestly believe that, given a chance to revisit the moment of sin, I would make a different choice, to live differently, in absolute purity of spirit, completely free of immorality. Of course, God would be able to see my heart. There was no way He was going to let me move on to the next item on the list unless my regret was complete and heartfelt. And if I couldn't repent in earnest, then I'd have to go to hell. There, standing before me, would be everyone I had ever loved and hated and met once at a party, and even Abraham Lincoln and Christopher Hitchens and the cop who was my first love and his teenage boyfriend. And I would have to change everything I had ever done.

I worried about the sins that led me to meet some of them and how those people would recede into the crowd once I gave up the sins that had brought us together, all the loves and friendships and days and nights of excitement and pleasure and giddy fear. I thought about all the memories that would fade and then vanish. I wondered if I'd be able to do it. I didn't see how I could. It seemed like too much to ask, to take so much of it back.

And here was this guy trying to do it all by himself in this room full of sex addicts and me, a spectator as always. You had to give him credit. You have to give the whole recovery culture credit, I swear. I'm sure there are all sorts of things I wouldn't like about it if I was immersed in it myself, but I do admire it. Where else in the world are people taking "searching and fearless moral inventories"?

At the end of the meeting, Don turned the last page in his sheaf and said, "Okay, that's it. Thank you for listening."

"Thank you, Don," everyone said.

Whatever ambivalence I felt about the process, I was glad to have been there for it, to be an audience for his redemption. Before we left, the leader of the group, who had introduced the fifth stepper said, "Does anyone have anything they need to say before we call it a day?"

It seemed that no one was going to speak, but then a man in his late 60s in a purple golfing shirt and tan shorts stood up. He looked like someone's grandfather, a retiree who would give you preachy advice about buying American-made cars and have a pool table at his house. As soon as he was on his feet, he was sobbing.

"My name is Larry. And I might be a sex addict. I don't really know."

"Hi, Larry."

The man stood there barely able to speak. Finally he said, "Last night, my wife and my family found out who I really am. I don't know where I'm sleeping tonight. They all hate me. I didn't know where to go. I hope you can help me. I need help. I need you to help me however you can."

He stood there and cried trying to say more, but he couldn't figure out what else to say. I couldn't imagine what else there could be to say. He had said it all.

Dave, the leader said, "We can help you. We'll find a place for you tonight. Don't worry about that. Maybe a couple of guys can stay late and talk to Larry with me?"

A few guys, obviously veterans, nodded their heads that, yes, they would stay and take care of Larry. I got the feeling that they would, and that he would be okay, even though he was clearly at the beginning of something very dark, or at the end of it.

When we got in the car, Greg said, "Man, I was surprised to see him there."

"Who?" I said.

"The guy who was talking. The fifth step guy."

"Don?"

"That's not his real name."

"You know him?"

"No, not personally," he said. "You really didn't recognize him? He's pretty famous."

Greg didn't tell me who the guy was, and I didn't ask. I looked at the dashboard clock. It was something like 10:00 a.m. on a Saturday. It was a strange start to the weekend.

67

MR. GRATE AND BENCH DIDN'T SHOW UP FOR A RESERVATION.
When I clocked out at eleven, I thought it was strange that he hadn't
appeared yet. I couldn't remember another time he had checked in
so late. But sometimes people landed and then met up with friends.
I thought maybe he had gone out with old college buddies who happened to be in town. Maybe his rolling carry-on bag was next to him
in one of our city's many strip joints.

Our policy was to charge people when they didn't show up for
their reservations. But when the night auditor went to charge Mr.
Grate and Bench's card, he found that I had not gotten one when
I took the reservation. The auditor told the manager, and then the
manager did a bit of investigating and found that I had failed to get
a card for any of Mr. Grate's several reservations.

When I arrived for my late afternoon shift as usual, my manager
called me to her office and explained what had happened and what
she had discovered. It was clear that much of her day had been spent
on an internal audit, scanning through a sample of the reservations I
had taken to see whether I routinely bucked policy or if I had made
a special exception for Mr. Grate.

"I guess I was just sort of being lazy," I said. "He's a regular. He's
never failed to show up before, so I thought it'd be okay not to get a
card. He was in a rush that day, and I let it slide."

I'd been a good and reliable employee, so she was satisfied with
that, but she said that I'd have to find the money for the missed reservation somehow. The owner of the motel had been alerted to the
situation, and she wasn't going to be happy unless that revenue was
accounted for in the next batch-out.

"If it was me, I'd just call the guy and explain what happened, see
if he'll pay. I mean, even if he thinks he's in the right or whatever,

some people will give you a card number just to put the issue to rest. Otherwise, I'm afraid you'll have to pay it yourself."

I thought about it for most of my shift. I thought about calling him to see what he'd say. Maybe he'd say that he had never booked the reservation in the first place, that I had fucked up, and that the whole thing was my fault. I wondered if maybe something terrible had happened. Maybe his mother had died, or one of his kids. Maybe he was dead, and I'd never get a new job.

Everyone who worked at the motel hated no-shows. They inevitably represented a chain of events that circled back in a variety of other ways: chargebacks from the credit card company when the cardholder disputed the charge, people who showed up on the wrong date only to learn they'd already been charged for a missed reservation they had mistakenly booked for the wrong time. They meant unpleasant phone calls and bad reviews online. No-shows weren't good for anyone.

I came up with the smartest, most succinct way of explaining the situation to my future employer, and practiced my calm and helpful delivery. Twice, I picked up the phone to call him, and twice I returned it to its cradle without dialing.

Just before the end of my shift, long after I'd made the decision, I went to the computer and swiped my own card for the $150 charge, thinking all along about how broke I was. So fucking broke, so fucking broke, so fucking broke. *I prefer not to spend my money this way.*

I could barely hold out until the end of my shift, when I could leave the lobby and convert the five-dollar bill in my wallet into sixteen tokens and a one-dollar tip. I could go straight from work. I didn't even have to go to my apartment first. No one was waiting for me. I didn't have so much as a dog awaiting my return. I spent the rest of my shift thinking about the arcade.

68

IN A MOMENT OF DESPERATION, I WOUND UP IN A BOOTH with a guy I had a bad feeling about. Late at night especially, one's standards could slip unimaginably. It never happened to me during the day, at least not with the same sweaty fervor. In the daytime, I might have ended up in a booth with a fallback in the absence of someone more appealing. But after midnight, a man I'd walked past ten times, and with good reason, gradually began to seem like a viable option.

So it was that I found myself in a booth with a skinny speed freak wearing too much gel in his spiky, bleached hair after 1:30 a.m. one night. We both pulled down our pants. He wore earrings in both ears and had bad tattoos, including a barbed wire armband around his right bicep. I'd been told that an armband of that type on the right arm signaled that its wearer prefers to be the receptive partner in sexual situations, which in this case proved to be accurate.

"You gonna fuck me?" the tweaker said. He was twitching, and he kept narrowing his eyes and then bulging them open as if being repeatedly shocked. "Can you just fuck me?"

Close Encounter of the Fourth Kind: Sex with an Alien

"I don't do that out here," I said. "I actually don't do much out here at all."

"You do too," he said. "Come on. You can do whatever you want. I'm clean."

"I just watch," I said.

"You do not," he said. "You do not just watch."

The speed freak didn't whisper the way everyone else at the arcade did. He spoke at a slightly-louder-than-normal volume, the arcade equivalent of shouting.

He appeared agitated and continued squinting and popping his eyes open.

"Come on," he said, stepping closer to me. "Quit fucking around."

I needed to exit the booth as quickly as possible. As I pulled myself together and began doing up my pants, he took his hand from around his member and, before I knew what was happening, reached up and ran his finger across my cheek, applying the kind of pressure you might use to test the ripeness of a pear. He stopped right at the corner of my eye. I understood instantly that he had just spread a snail streak of precum across my face. Whether he had actually made contact with the mucus membrane of my eyeball, I couldn't tell.

I reached up to knock his hand away and wiped my face in the same motion. In the process I touched my eyeball myself, which wasn't something one ever wished to do at the arcade, where it would be impossible to overestimate the multitudinous microbes, bacteria, and germs on every surface imaginable.

The tweaker backed away, and reached again for his penis, cracking a crazed and unhinged smile like one of the lunatics from *The Texas Chainsaw Massacre*. I was rubbing my face, first with my hand and then with my t-shirt. I felt certain he was infected with something horrible and that, however ineffectual and bizarre the attempt, he had just tried to infect me too.

I reeled out of the booth without speaking another word to the man. I went straight to the counter and asked for the key to the bathroom, where I scrubbed my face with the pink liquid soap from the hot air balloon-shaped dispenser mounted on the wall. Afterwards, I raced home and showered for ages.

It turned out I had been lucky. I walked away without so much as conjunctivitis.

69

A SHORT LIVED PORN SERIES CALLED *TRUE COUPLES* FOCUSED on real-life masculine, older men and their much younger partners. Each sex scene in the *True Couples* series is preceded by an interview with the couple in question, in which they discuss how they met and ended up together.

A memorable moment unfolds in *True Couples 2*. Before their sex scene, fifty-three-year-old attorney, Dennis Mansfeld is interviewed with his twenty-two-year-old boyfriend, Eric Bell. Mansfeld explains that, before things between them went too far, he revealed to Eric that he was HIV positive. Mansfeld pauses to collect himself, then gets choked up as he recalls the occasion. Before he can continue, the attorney actually begins to cry.

"Aww, man," his young boyfriend says comfortingly. "It's okay."

Mansfeld tearfully recounts Eric's reaction to the news. "He said, 'I'm not worried about that. That's just part of life.'"

Eric hugs his aged attorney, and soon after, the two of them get naked and have impassioned, protected sex.

When young Eric enters him, Mansfeld, can be heard saying with the surfer inflection of *Fast Times at Ridgemont High's* Jeff Spicoli, "Dude, dude. You know what daddy likes." They kiss and seem genuinely affectionate.

Googling Dennis Mansfeld, the fifty-something attorney from *True Couples 2*, one discovers claims that he's a lunatic who spits when he speaks. Allegations that he talks so fast in court that some think he's on speed. That he has appeared before at least one judge wearing wrinkled clothes and looking disheveled. That he's frightening. Claims that he brags about his pornography career. Claims that he should be investigated and disbarred.

When I first saw *True Couples 2,* I thought he was probably a nice guy, a man caught up in an impulsive moment, deeply involved in one of those older/younger relationships that never work. I could imagine him saying, "Yeah, maybe I'll regret it one day. But I love Eric, and I don't care who knows it or who sees it, now or in the future." ·

Dennis Mansfeld probably *was* a nice guy, actually. But also kind of an unstable nutcase. What I found when I looked him up bothered me. It bothered me that everything that seemed clear at first grew cloudy when exposed to the slightest bit of scrutiny.

Mansfeld was the first thing I thought of when Malcolm told me he would be back in town for a week, and this time he really did want to meet. He said he wasn't taking no for an answer.

"Seriously, stop being such a chickenshit about this. It's ridiculous."

"What's the advantage of meeting in person?" I said. "Everything is perfectly nice the way it is."

"You're not at all curious to meet me after all this time?"

"I know you already. Maybe meeting would mess things up."

"What could it possibly mess up?"

"Why do you need another friend, anyway? You've got your teen-age bellhop. Aren't you ever satisfied?"

"Don't change the subject, Sam."

"What if I meet you somewhere and you write down my license plate number and find out my real name and address and start stalking me and ruin my life?"

"Now that's just fucking insulting. And don't even remind me about the name thing at this point."

"I'm kidding."

"We're meeting. I'll be home for a week. I'm not going to tell Ron about it, obviously, so we'll have to schedule it sometime when he won't be around."

"Does Ron know about me?"

"No."

"Okay."

"Okay, you'll meet me?"

"No, just 'Okay, Ron doesn't know about me.'"

"Why do you have to make everything so difficult?"

"I have no idea, Malcolm."

"Well, just stop then."

"Maybe we can meet. But no promises."

"We're meeting."

70

IT WAS THE KID'S TWENTIETH BIRTHDAY, AND THE COP turned forty-three just two weeks later. They liked the way their birthdays were close together. They had the same astrological sign, which they took to mean they were a perfect match.

The cop ordered a slew of gifts for the kid. I watched in disbelief as the receipts came rolling in. It was a whole new way of thinking about the kid, seeing the video games he wanted to play, and the kinds of t-shirts he'd wear, and the gift certificates to Red Lobster and Golden Corral. Did he really like eating at those places? It was unimaginable.

That's also when I learned that the kid collected things related to Spiderman. He loved Spiderman, apparently, and kept anything related to the superhero. One of his gifts—the one he loved the most, as it turned out—was a teddy bear from the Build-A-Bear Workshop wearing a Spiderman costume. After his birthday, he took a photograph of the bear on the guest bedroom bed that was supposedly his. It was surrounded by his various other Spiderman-related dolls and toys.

How could the cop want this child, this moron who collected cartoon memorabilia the same way my favorite hooker had collected all things Tweety Bird-related? What did they want from these pretend characters anyway? However much I watched, however closely I paid attention, I couldn't figure out which parts of the kid I should adopt to make the cop love me. Did I have to abandon all rational thought?

I decided to send the cop a birthday gift, against Malcolm's pleading counsel. Despite his objections, I knew I had to somehow remain at the fore of the cop's mind. The cruise for which I had secured my expensive passport was only weeks away.

I knew better than to send anything serious. Along with a peppy greeting card, the box contained only a beach towel with a chalk outline of a person on it, in the style of a crime scene. It seemed like an ideal fit—he loved the beach and was an actual crime fighter. I could imagine the two of us using the towel on the cruise, and the way that, years later, we'd acknowledge that, though the towel was threadbare and stained, we hated throwing it away because of its sentimental value.

I knew how the gift landed before I heard from the cop. It enraged the kid, who emailed in all caps that I had ruined their special day entirely. He requested permission to destroy the towel and the card, and the cop said he didn't care one way or the other. The kid did it while the cop was at work that evening, then sent a photo of the tattered remains at the bottom of a trashcan. The subject of the email was "Done."

Later that evening, the cop called to say thanks for the towel and the card but that it would be better if I didn't send presents.

"Oh, I understand," I told him. "Absolutely. I just thought you might like it, that's all."

I picked up the phone to call Malcolm, but he had warned me against sending it, and he wouldn't want to talk about it any more. I sat in my apartment smoking cigarettes and wondering what to do next.

71

MR. GRATE AND BENCH REPEATED HOW MUCH HE HATED
the thought of getting my hopes up.

"Who knows what'll happen?" he said.

"Oh, don't worry about me," I told him. "I know how it goes. I'm not counting on anything."

He showed up for his next reservation, thank God. It didn't occur to me until the date had almost arrived that he might not show up again, and I'd end up paying for that room too.

When he appeared, a guest was yelling at me about her toilet being clogged. She wanted me to know that this was her fourth stay at the motel, and three of those times her toilet had become stopped up.

"Sometimes people put more paper into the commode than the system can handle," I said.

"I'm not an idiot," she said. "I don't use any more here than I do at my house, and the toilets at my house practically never get clogged."

"This is a really old property," I said. "Maybe our plumbing can't handle as much as you're used to."

I tried not to look at Mr. Grate and Bench, who had entered the lobby shortly after the woman did. He stood behind the woman, waiting patiently, playing with his phone.

"Could you just try flushing more often?" I said.

"Not that that's any of your business, but I don't particularly enjoy the sensation of flushing while I'm sitting on the pot," she said.

At that, I accidentally made eye contact with Mr. Grate, and the two of us instantly smiled so broadly that neither of us could contain a short burst of laughter.

The woman whipped around to look at him, then glared at me.

"I'm going to dinner," she said. "My toilet had better be unclogged by the time I get back. And don't drip toilet water on the seat."

"Absolutely. Sorry for the trouble. Have a nice night."

Mr. Grate and Bench held the door for her, and then laughed and shook his head at me when she was gone. "Hope she eats light," he said, "for your sake."

"Thanks a lot."

"I bet you wouldn't miss that kind of thing if you came to work for me."

"If she comes back, I might quit this job and come volunteer for you, whether your pregnant rep leaves or not."

"Haha. Hopefully it won't come to that."

We talked for a few minutes about the job, and he said that if it ever looked like the position was actually going to open up we would have a real sit down over lunch one day and he'd tell me what it was all about.

When he was gone, I locked up and went to the woman's room where the toilet was so close to overflowing that shit and water splashed on my shoes while I plunged it. The diarrhea smell mixed with the smell of her hairspray and powdery deodorant was so strong I thought I might throw up, topping off the already-flooded bowl.

I imagined all the traveling Mr. Grate and Bench did and wondered for a minute if he might have been playing the same game with clerks across the country, following the narrative of their rising hopes.

72

I RAN INTO A STRAIGHT COUPLE AT THE ARCADE, A RARE sight. They were looking at videos, and the woman was giggling quietly, as they often do in porn stores, unable to believe what they're seeing, the monuments men have built to vaginas and to the very notion of sex. In my experience women seldom grasped the being-private-in-public basics of porn browsing. Years before she was married and with-child, I took my friend Joan to a porn shop without first explaining what I assumed were the self-evident fundamentals of porn store etiquette. I was looking through the videos piled on the discount table when I heard her call my name. I looked up and saw her next to a man looking at pregnancy porn. "Check this out," she yelled, holding a video aloft. "Pregnant nuns! What the fuck, right?" The man was gone in a flash, the bell on the door tinkling behind him.

The straight couple I saw at the arcade was discreet enough, whispering and flipping through DVDs. But they muddied the vibe out there just by their presence. I found myself watching them. Once in a while, the husband looked up at me and then said something to his wife, who would look up at me and reply to her husband. Then she would giggle again. I couldn't tell if they were quietly ridiculing me, or if she was just laughing at the whole scene. Or if they were flirting.

I crossed the store and went down the smoking hallway just to see how they'd react if I passed close to them. We all looked at one another, and a moment later, I heard them following behind me.

"Psst!" the man said.

I stopped and looked back at him. He was drunk and cheery, smiling and holding his wife's hand. She looked drunk too, the redness in her cheeks visible even in the darkened hallway. She was pretty and blonde and in her early forties, her husband a few years older.

"Hey," I whispered. "What are you guys up to?"

"Do you want to come with us?" he said.

"Sure."

"Take his hand, honey."

She took my hand, so we were all three in a line together. I pointed to a door a couple of feet away with my free hand and we all went inside and locked the door.

The woman was wearing a thin dress in a floral pattern that covered just the tops of her thighs. Her husband moved behind her and lifted her breasts up and down.

"See how nice they are?" he said.

His wife laughed and shook her head. "Bobby loves to show men my tits."

"I'm proud of 'em," Bobby said. "Ain't they nice?"

"They're perfect," I said.

"You're damn right. See, honey? This guy knows."

"Mind if I feel?" I said.

"Do you mind, hun?"

"I don't mind," she said.

Her husband's hands were still on her breast as I moved towards her. He reached out and took my hand in his and guided me to her tits. I felt her up as if I were his puppet. I liked having his hand on my hand and mine on her.

"You like that?" he said.

"Sure I do."

"That's not even the best part."

He let go of my hand so I could see what he meant. He put his hands on her hips and slowly lifted the fabric of her dress until I could see that she wasn't wearing any panties. She had a perfect little patch of hair, and I watched the husband slide his hand down and rub her from behind. After a minute, I could smell it. It was a nice, different smell from the smell I was used to in the booths.

She looked down at his hand and then up at my face, appearing to enjoy herself. She seemed happy and confident like an amateur model showing off. She smiled at me.

"Mind if I touch?"

"That okay, hun?" he said.

"You clean?" she said.

"You bet."

"Alright then."

I reached out and slipped my fingers down with her husband's. We were rubbing her together, sliding in and out. It felt almost perfect, like we had planned it or practiced beforehand. The wife moaned and stretched her neck so that her head was tilted back, pressed against her husband's.

"Kiss her on the neck," he said.

I kissed her on the neck, from her throat to her ear. Her husband did the same on the other side. Then we switched sides.

"Go slow," he said. "We got time."

Funny, but after he said that, things began moving faster. He lifted her dress off so that she was naked except for a pair of white canvas sneakers.

She wanted to be on all fours on the bench. The husband slipped off his cargo shorts and unbuttoned his Hawaiian shirt revealing a hairy chest and paunch and one of the biggest dicks I'd ever seen. All he wore was a pair of flip-flops.

"She wants for me to be behind while you're in front."

"Sounds good to me," I said.

I stood in front of her. When I started to thrust into her mouth, her husband said, "Don't do it like that. She don't like that. Just let her be in control."

"Oh, sure. Sorry."

So I stood still while she sucked me and moaned. Bobby slammed her from behind.

After a while, he was fucking her hard enough that she stopped sucking my dick to focus on taking his. So I moved to the back and watched his cock going in and out of her. It never got boring. The wife was moaning louder and louder.

I could hear men gathered outside. They kept trying the door.

I couldn't resist. I reached down and wrapped my hand around the base of his dick. He tensed up when I did it, but he didn't stop me. He kept fucking her. I couldn't even come close to encircling it with my hand. It was as fat as a beer can.

The wife looked over her shoulder and saw what I was doing. "You're scaring my husband," she said. "I like that."

"You're the one who should be scared," I wanted to say to her.

"Wish I could be in there too," I said instead.

"You kiddin'? There ain't even room for him," she said.

She was moaning and laughing and squealing, making more noise than I'd ever heard anyone make at the arcade. I touched her husband, feeling his dick and balls and his chest. With my other hand I rubbed his wife, sliding my fingers in when he pulled out.

Her moaning grew louder until finally she came at the top of her lungs. Then her husband came inside of her. Then, with my hand still around his dick, I came on the floor.

We started getting dressed. The husband had a handkerchief in the pocket of his shorts, and he handed it to his wife who cleaned up between her legs.

"You want this back, or toss it?" she said.

"You can toss it, hun," he said. She dropped it in the trashcan before pulling her dress over her head.

"Boy," I said. "Thanks a lot."

"Thank *you*," he said. "That was fun. Maybe we'll run into one another again sometime."

"I hope so."

The three of us left at the same time. In the hallway, a few men were gathered. I'd heard them knocking and trying the door, but greeting them that way was strange and surprising. They looked like a crazed reception line of zombies.

We exited to the parking lot together and all said "goodnight" one last time. On the highway, we rode alongside one another for a mile or two, them in a big white pickup. Before we separated at last, the wife rolled down her window and lowered the top of her dress so I could get a final look at her breasts. I could see her husband in the driver's seat craning his neck to see my reaction, having the time of his life.

73

A DARK CLOUD FORMED OVER THE COP'S HOUSE. HE started taking my calls again as everything began to go wrong for him and the kid. I thought maybe my crying and obsessing and praying had finally roused God like a sleepy old man waking from a nap to finally join the fight.

The first thing He did was kill the cat. The cop and the kid had been worrying about it lately. It had been vomiting, and then it stopped wanting to jump up onto the furniture. They took him to the vet who said they could take the little guy home for one last night and bring him in first thing in the morning to be put to sleep. They cried together and stayed up all night telling the cat how much they loved it, thanking it for being such a good friend. Then it was dead and they were in sorrow together. I sympathized, but also worried about the potential for them to be further bonded by the loss of their pet. At least I could stop getting allergy shots twice a week.

They were still grieving when the next ordeal struck. The kid awoke in pain, and had to be taken to the ER where an emergency appendectomy was performed. That wasn't so bad really, except for the expense and the way the incision fucked up one of his already-horrible tattoos. In a sense, crisis had been averted. But just a week later, he had to return to the hospital, this time with a painful, unidentified skin infection. The cop had it too, on his hands and shoulders.

The appearance of the first sores marked the beginning of a weeks-long fight against a persistent staph infection that passed between them, to all different parts of their bodies. It was painful and upsetting, and they started freaking out because no matter how careful they were, new spots kept appearing. Something as minor as sharing a towel could lead to another agonizing infection on a new and unexpected location. Sex was out of the question.

Then the kid was in a car accident. His car totaled, he wore a neck brace for a week. They took photos in case of a lawsuit. Frowning and wearing the collar, I almost felt bad for the kid. He even had a black eye. When he took a few days away from work to get things sorted out, there was a misunderstanding about who was covering his shifts, and he lost his job at the movie theater.

It was an ugly scene. The sores and the dying cat especially recalled a modern Job story recast with gay guys in present-day small-town Texas.

74

ONE OF THE GIRLS WHO WORKED THE FRONT DESK IN THE mornings spoke with Mr. Grate and Bench while he was checking out. I'd made the mistake of complaining to her about paying for his missed reservation. Naturally, I hadn't mentioned anything about the possibility of becoming employed by him, so it made no sense to her that I should have paid for his room because of a simple mistake.

"I asked if he knew he missed a reservation," she said, "and you know what? He said he did know. He said it slipped his mind after one of his trips got rescheduled. Then he didn't bother calling because he said you knew he'd be back soon."

"You didn't mention the money thing, did you?" I said.

"I hope that's okay. I just said that it was between the two of you, but that I thought he should know that you had to pay for his room yourself because you had trusted him enough to take his reservation without getting a credit card number."

"What did he say?"

"He just said that it hardly seems fair. And I said that I thought it was unfair too, because us clerks don't make that much money that we can afford to pay for other people's rooms whenever they forget to cancel their reservations."

"Did he say anything else?"

"No, just thanks for telling him. I hope it's alright that I said something. You never said not to."

I was anxious in advance of his next reservation. I hoped he'd take a money clip from his pocket and insist, *insist* that I take the money.

"Please!" he could have said. "Are you kidding me? Take the money! It was my mistake!"

I would have taken it. I decided in advance that I would. The truth was that I needed it.

He was polite and affable at check-in. I gave him an iron and miniature ironing board to take to his room like always. But he didn't say anything about the missed reservation or the money. He didn't say anything about his pregnant employee or the job either. I called his room later that evening.

"Hey, it's me at the front desk. Sorry to bother you, but is your TV working okay?"

"Seems fine to me."

"Okay, good. One of your neighbors is having a problem with the cable, and I just wanted to make sure it wasn't the whole building."

"Nope. All clear here. Still wish you got ESPN2 though."

"Yeah, I mentioned that to the owner. I think they're working on it."

"Sounds good."

Either his guilt would make him want to hire me as compensation, or his guilt would prevent him from hiring me, or he felt no guilt at all.

75

"THIS GUY SOUNDS LIKE AN ASSHOLE," MALCOLM SAID, WHEN I told him the story of Mr. Grate and Bench. "You should never have paid for the room in the first place, but at least now you know. You definitely don't want to work for someone like that. Just look for a job like a normal person if you want something else."

"Like what? It took me months to get this job."

"Looking for a job is easy. Especially if you already have one. You just have to get used to people turning you down a lot. Then something always works out unexpectedly."

"God, I feel like I get rejected all the time as it is."

"Oh, please," Malcolm said.

But it was true. The longer I went to the arcade, the more it felt like a study in rejection. It certainly wasn't a place one went to forget one's shortcomings.

"By the way, we're set for Saturday night at seven o'clock," Malcolm said. "I fly in on Wednesday, so we can email, but no phone calls. Saturday night. Don't forget."

"How are you managing it with Ronald?"

"He has a dinner and book club thing with some friends. He'll be out late."

"Maybe we shouldn't. I'm worried it might be weird."

"I think that because you are weird, it might be weird. But we're still meeting."

"I just hope you won't get mad if I get sick or something."

"Don't even think about standing me up, Sam. Seriously."

"I wouldn't do that," I said. "I mean, I probably wouldn't. I don't think I would."

76

I MET AN IRRESISTIBLE HEDGEHOG OF A MAN. IRRESISTIBLE because he found me so attractive. He carried himself as though everyone at the arcade wanted him, and I confess it did make me want him a little, even though every time I saw him, he was wearing a button-up shirt unbuttoned and untucked over an untucked white undershirt. It was exactly the style in which I dressed in the seventh grade. He came in while I was pretend-perusing DVDs, and looked at me and smiled, even as he was purchasing his tokens at the counter. He put the tokens in his pocket and walked directly over to me.

"Would you like to see a movie with me?" he said.

No shopping around. No seeing who else was there. I'd never had anyone ask me that way. I was accustomed to looks and head nods. I'd had guys brush against me, then give me sly grins. But no one had ever walked up to me and asked if I·wanted to see a movie with him.

Alone in a booth together, I said, "I have to warn you, I don't do very much out here."

"That's okay," he said. "We don't have to do anything you don't want to."

He undid my pants and I undid his. We reached in and touched one another. Then he began to lift my shirt. "I don't want to take my shirt off," I said.

"Please," he said. "Do it for me. You're so sexy."

I let him take my shirt off and hang it on one of the clothes hooks.

"You smell like pot," I said.

"I smoked on the way over," he said. "I'll smoke you out if you want."

"That's okay."

Once my shirt was off, the hedgehog's hands were all over me. I didn't get the sense that he'd hurt me or do anything especially weird, but he was much stronger than I was, and he seemed to be blissing out into some kind of touch-induced trance amplified by the weed he'd smoked. He put one hand on my shoulder and rubbed my chest with the other.

I didn't like having my shirt off because it meant I couldn't leave in an instant. When I stopped his hand from making the rounds of my torso again, he knelt on the ground and tried putting my dick in his mouth.

"No," I said. "Stop."

"Come on, bud. I want to make you feel good. I want to make you feel so good."

"I don't do that out here."

"That's okay. You can trust me."

He opened his mouth and put my dick inside.

Over his head, I grabbed my shirt and put it on. I pulled it over my head and was still putting my dick in my pants as I fled the booth. I went to the sales floor and pretended to look at DVDs. He walked out of the hallway and straight over to me.

"Would you please come back and watch a movie with me?" he said.

"No, thanks."

"Why?"

"You're too grabby and you don't listen when I say no. I told you I don't do much out here, and then you tried to force me. Forget it. I'm sure you can find someone else."

"I'd never find someone else out here like you," he said. "Because you're what I like. You're exactly what I like. All my boys have been like you."

I don't know why I went back with him. I must have liked the idea of being one of his boys, the newest one in line. I was probably flattered he thought of me as a boy at all, though he wasn't more than ten years older than me. This time he was more courteous, though he was still passionate in a way that made me feel I had less control than I preferred.

"Sit on my lap and make out with me," he said.

He pulled down his pants so they were around his ankles, then sat down and patted the tops of his thighs. "Take down your pants and sit on my lap."

I did it. I don't know why. I could feel his dick pressing against my thigh, and I let him kiss me. He was a fantastic kisser. We kissed for a long time stopping only to put tokens in the slot when the movie stopped.

"Tell me your name," he said.

I thought it over then said, "Honestly, I'd only make one up."

"Then make one up," he said. "Next time I see you, I'll remember it. You'll see."

And the next time I saw him, he did remember.

"Hey, Sam," he said. "Would you like to come see a movie with me?"

He was stoned and too handsy again, and I found that I wanted more and less of him at the same time. He was still a terrific kisser.

"Let me bring you to my house," he said. "I don't live far from here."

"That's the last thing I'd do."

"You don't trust me?"

"Not at all," I said.

"Well, you should," he said. "I'm very trustworthy."

"You look stoned."

"I am stoned," he said. "Come out to my truck, and we'll get you stoned too."

"I have stuff to do later," I said.

"So do I. I'm going back to work here in just a little while."

He looked at me and smiled and said, "You're exactly what I like. Have I told you that? You're just like all my boys. Every one I ever had."

This time, I was less taken with the notion of being one of his boys. Maybe I was thinking about John Wayne Gacy, who had boys of his own that he eventually buried in the crawlspace beneath his house.

The hedgehog didn't get off either time I saw him, but he made sure I did.

When he was getting dressed and pulling up his pants, I noticed a bottle of cough syrup protruding from the pocket of his jeans.

"Why do you have cough syrup in your pocket?"

He gave me a sideways grin. "I've had a little cough lately."

"And you bring the cough syrup with you into the arcade?"

"You want a sip? Just say so. You can have some."

Were I to list the highs I found most absurd and lowbrow, the one offered by cough syrup would be very near the top, in the vicinity of gasoline huffing and the canned air people use to clean their keyboards. I could understand a little pot smoking, but, hell, we already had the arcade. How many drugs could the hedgehog possibly need?

I wondered if his other boys drank cough syrup with him or if they preferred getting drunk on hand sanitizer, as I'd read was being done. I was sure it wouldn't be hard to find someone like that, some boy so trashy and young he wouldn't know that the hedgehog wasn't any kind of salvation from anything.

The cop thought he was saving the kid, setting him on the right track. I could tell from their emails. It was all coming into focus now, how that's what they all liked. The boys liked being set on the right track, and the men liked setting them on it. God knows I would have done anything to find someone who could tell me how to make a little sense of my life.

If you wanted someone to save you, I saw, it was a cinch finding someone willing to try. Same if you wanted to save someone else. It was an undiagnosed fetish, some kind of mutual need that drew people together and then locked them in place like shopping carts, so that life had to yank hard to separate them, even long after it should have been clear that no one was doing any saving.

Before we parted for the last time, the hedgehog said, "I could take such good care of you if you'd let me. All you need is someone to help you out a little. I like to help people when I can. And, honest to God, you're just what I like. You've got exactly that thing that I like."

I wanted to believe him. I surprised myself when he gave me his number and I actually saved it in my phone.

"You'll call," he said. "Maybe not tomorrow, but you will."

77

I WANTED TO TAKE THEIR OCCASIONAL BICKERING AS A hopeful sign, but it was growing obvious even to me that I probably wouldn't be going on that cruise in the kid's place.

I mentioned my despair about this to Jack, who had come to my house to take me to lunch. After all those months, I was still being treated as an emotional invalid. Though friends conspired to organize semi-regular meals to get me out of the house, I could see they were all growing tired of me.

"The cruise is just a couple of weeks away," I told Jack. "If the staph infection is cleared up by then, they'll be on a vacation together. They'll be drinking and having sex. And then everything will be good between them again."

"I can't believe he tells you all this stuff," Jack said. "It's really sick in a way. It just keeps you so involved with everything."

"He only tells me some things. I get a lot of it from his email. I told you that."

"I thought you got into his email once early on. Or that it was a joke even."

"No. You obviously have no idea how upset I am."

"You're reading it regularly?"

"Yes, Jack. Do you not listen to me at all?"

"Are you kidding? What the fuck, man?"

Jack sat there shaking his head and thinking about it.

"Oh, don't be so judgmental," I said. "It's no tragedy. We're talking about stupid little notes they send one another. I'm not stealing government secrets."

"I honestly don't think I can go on being your friend if you keep doing this."

"You're so extreme," I said. "I can't just stop now. I'll never see how it ends."

"It's not ending. Obviously. And if it does end, it's none of your fucking business. You can't just rationalize doing anything you want."

"It's not that bad," I said. "You're being dramatic."

"I'm not. I think there's something seriously wrong with you."

After that, we were quiet until Jack finally calmed down enough to take me to lunch. We both drank beer and ate sandwiches and didn't talk about the cop and the kid again until he dropped me off.

"Think about what I said before," he said, as I got out of the car.

I did think about it, but I logged in to the cop's email when I got home. The kid had sent some information about an excursion he wanted to take during the cruise. A day of snorkeling. I followed the link to a website that showed pictures of that incredibly blue water and bright-colored fish and turtles and smiling people wearing those stupid masks.

I could see the cop and the kid there, mentally superimposed in the photographs. Like the ones I'd have to log in and see for myself a month hence. The frustration welled up in me until it was all I could feel. I read the email one more time, then deleted it. Then I deleted it from the trash and logged out.

78

SOMETIMES IT FELT LIKE EVERY MAN AT THE ARCADE
wanted something from me. They wanted me not to be there competing for the same people. Or they wanted me to come into a booth
with them. Or not to come into a booth with them. To leave them
alone. To stick around as an alternate in case something didn't work
out with the other guy they were trying to cruise, or were hoping
would arrive. They wanted me with my shirt off, with my shoes
off. To look them in the eye, or not to. They wanted me in a suit, or
a pair of running shorts, or Levi's. They wanted me with long hair
that fell over one eye like a skateboarder from the early 1990s, or
they wanted my hair buzzed like a military man. They wanted to
see the way my hard dick pushed against my jeans. They wanted
me in boxers or briefs or boxer briefs. Or they wanted me not to
wear underwear under my jeans. They wanted me to be ten years
younger or older. Ten pounds lighter or fatter. They wanted me to
be a way I wasn't. To stand with my hip cocked or to subtly roll my
r's. They wanted more from me than they realized they wanted.

If I paid attention, I could see how much they wanted because
I could see when I'd gotten off track. My eye became attuned to
their nearly imperceptible micro expressions, the slight narrowing
of their eyes, the withdrawing of the corners of their mouths.

They wanted me to do more than I wanted to do. They wanted
to persuade me, to cajole me. They wanted me not to want to do
anything other than what they wanted from me. Or they wanted
me to resist and then concede. Or they wanted to be submissive
and for me to dominate them.

They wanted to see me come, even when they weren't going to
come themselves. Because if they got off, it would be over. If they

came, they had to go home. Or, they'd tell me, it was because they just loved to give pleasure. Like those men who are always bragging to anyone who'll listen that they love to go down on women, that they get off on getting her off.

If they didn't want me to come, they wanted me to make them come. And they wanted it in a very particular way. They wanted me to suck them this way or to fuck them slow or hard or at alternate speeds. They wanted the door unlocked so someone else could come in. Because they wanted me to suck another guy while we fucked.

They wanted me to squeeze their nipples.

Harder. Not that hard.

That felt good. What did you just do? Do it again.

They wanted me to precome.

Do you precome a lot? When you're really excited? Oh, yeah, I bet you really leak.

They wanted me to come.

Do you come a lot?

No one asked if I came just a little. They wanted a gusher. They wanted me to come like I meant it. And they even knew where they wanted it. They wanted me to come on their faces, their chests, their beards. Come in their hands. Come in their mouths.

It was a lot to want from someone who had just walked in the door. Maybe they wanted me to be like someone they were with once, or someone they wanted but could never have, a fantasy to which they'd jerked off a million times.

Of course I wanted things from them too. Once I saw that, I had to think about the whole list and why I wanted those things, all while trying to stay hard and have something resembling a good time.

79

I WAS SUPPOSED TO MEET MALCOLM AT THE BAR OF THE
Old San Francisco Steakhouse, a place famous for a swing dangling from its thirty-foot ceiling where an attractive girl performed
at intervals, swinging until she made it high enough to ring a bell
hanging from a roof beam. It had also earned some renown for
providing each table with an enormous block of Swiss cheese upon
being seated. Malcolm and I had spoken about the place on the
phone one night. I told him I had read it was closing down. We
agreed that it was a kitsch institution, although I'd never been
there, and he had only been once years earlier for a business lunch,
when the swinging girl had been out with the flu. It seemed like a
perfect place to meet, where it was a given that neither of us would
run into anyone we knew. And it seemed nice to go right before it
closed forever.

I felt anxious and reluctant, but I envisioned an air of festive
abandon at The Old San Francisco Steakhouse in its final days that
I hoped would carry over to us and fill us with the same. I arrived
on time, and saw Malcolm already seated at the bar. All day I had
taken comfort in the fact that he didn't know what I looked like.
But he happened to be looking at me the moment I saw him, and
he recognized me recognizing him. He raised his eyebrows and
smiled, and I smiled back.

I walked over to him, and he held out his hand and shook mine.
Then he rose and put his arms around me. Malcolm was taller than
I had imagined him. He was wearing a pressed white shirt, tailored
black pants, expensive leather shoes, and a beautiful wristwatch.
He smelled like sophistication itself, something very subtle, a light
cologne, or maybe he had just been burning a candle at his house.

I felt silly by comparison, in dark jeans and a buttoned-up short-sleeved shirt, smelling of Irish Spring and Speed Stick deodorant.

"You should have shown me your face sooner," he said, pulling away to look at me. "You're handsome, you know it?"

"You just have low standards," I said.

"Oh, please. Follow me. I've got a table waiting."

I followed Malcolm and saw his nice back and broad shoulders. He weighed about twenty pounds more than I expected, but he wore it well. He was an attractive guy. It was true that he seemed different than the cop and the guys at the arcade. But he was handsome and kind.

I looked around and saw that The Old San Francisco Steakhouse wasn't a bustling carnival in its final days. Though a pianist pounded out lively music on a big, black piano near the bar, the famous swing hung limp. The cavernous restaurant was less than a quarter full, and the wait staff wore what were obviously the toned-down who-cares versions of their usual uniforms. Vests without ties. Ties without vests. Their white dress shirts dirty or with sleeves rolled to the elbow.

We sat down at a table, and a waiter came and dropped a giant cutting board with Swiss cheese and two big menus.

A few minutes later, we both ordered beer and steaks, and looked at one another smiling and unsure how to proceed.

"Is this as bad as you thought?" he said.

"Worse."

"Not really."

"No, it's fine. I'm glad to meet you. I just hope it doesn't change things."

"Everything changes everything. But I'm glad to meet you, Sam. I really am."

"I'm glad to meet you too. Do I look how you thought I would?"

"Not exactly. I like the way you look more than I thought I would. I mean it, you're handsome."

"I am not. Not as handsome as Ethan the bellboy, I bet."

"Let's not get into that again. Tell me, are there any updates about the cop and the kid?"

"Not really. The cruise is next week, and they seem to be getting better, so I guess they're going. I did something I shouldn't have done and deleted an email from the kid to the cop."

He shook his head. "What could you be thinking when you do this stuff, Sam?"

"I don't know. I just got so frustrated the other day. It was really stupid."

"You definitely can't go on like this."

"I know. It felt really bad."

"Is the six months up?"

"Practically, yeah."

"You think you'll be able to move on soon?"

"I guess I might not have a choice. I thought if I held on hard enough something would change and things would swing in my favor, but now it looks like it'll never happen."

"Yeah, that's the way it goes sometimes. I'm sorry."

"It's okay. I just have to figure out what to do next."

"I think it'll be good."

"Yeah, maybe."

"Like maybe you'll get another job. Something that requires more of your brain."

"That would be good. Anyway, let's not talk about me the whole time. Is everything going okay in Boston?"

"Yeah, things are great actually. I can finally see the light at the end of the tunnel. It's been such a huge project, but I'm feeling good about it, and I'm going to get a big bonus, which is always good."

"So it's almost over?"

"Yep. Which is perfect because Ron is really tired of living in different places. Neither one of us are cut out for the long distance thing."

"You still feel good about Ron?"

"Absolutely. Ron's great. I'd really like to introduce the two of you sometime."

"Like that would ever happen."

"Why shouldn't it?"

"How would you explain how we know one another?"

"There's always a way. I'm not worried about that. At the very worst we could tell the truth. You'd like Ron. He's an interesting guy. He's funny and cynical like you."

While we ate, a girl in a frilly vaudeville dress came out and stood on the bar. The man on the piano said into a microphone, "Please put your hands together for Missy!"

We clapped.

The girl sat on the swing and began to rock to and fro, back and forth until she was so high she could kick a bell attached to the ceiling. She kept swinging until she could twist the opposite direction on the backswing and slap another bell on the opposite side of the restaurant. Malcolm and I watched and cheered, as did everyone in the place, including the waiters.

The man at the piano spoke into a microphone. "Tonight is the last performance for Missy, who is moving on to bigger and better things. Please give her a big round of applause."

Everyone clapped, and Missy—still swinging back and forth—waved.

"As many of you know, this is our last weekend here at The Old San Francisco Steakhouse. We've had a great time here, acting like a bunch of big kids. I'd probably get fired any other time for saying this, but please tip your server generously tonight, and if you know of anyone who's hiring, let them know."

Missy performed twice more before the check came.

Malcolm insisted on paying, even though I kept saying we should split the check.

While the waiter was away with his credit card, I said, "I hope you know how much I appreciate you. You might have saved my life."

"Oh, now you're giving me too much credit. But I'll take it. I like you, Sam. And I really do think you're going to be fine. I'm glad we're friends."

"Me too," I said.

In the parking lot, I assumed we'd hug and part ways, but Malcolm said, "I've been trying to work up the nerve to ask you to show me the arcade. It's been ages, and you piqued my interest. Do you have time to take me there?"

"Seriously?"

"I could follow you out in my car. Ron's not going to be home for a couple of hours."

"I don't know," I said. "Should we?"

"Why not?"

"Okay," I said. "I guess."

I drove, and Malcolm followed in a black BMW. There were only five or six other vehicles in the lot. It was early for a Saturday night.

"This is it," I said. "It's still pretty quiet. It'll pick up later."

"This looks a lot nicer than the one I used to go to," he said.

"We can't talk a lot inside, you know."

"This isn't my first rodeo, Sam."

We pushed through the doors. The bouncer was at the counter. I bought three dollars worth of tokens and Malcolm did the same. We walked around the store.

I whispered a few things to him, about how there was a smoking hallway and a nonsmoking hallway. The guys who were out there must have been in booths, because we didn't see anyone in the store.

"I want to check out a movie," Malcolm said.

"You want me to come with you?"

"What, are you kidding? Come on."

I followed Malcolm into the nonsmoking hallway. There were a few lights lit, but he chose a booth away from the others.

He knew what to do when we got inside. He locked the door behind us then put a couple of tokens in the slot. The movie started loud, and he quickly turned it down. Then he turned around and kissed me. He was a great kisser, and my dick hardened instantly. I reached down and felt his pants. His dick was stiff too. I could tell he was wearing briefs because of the way his hard-on was bent and curled under.

We kissed for several minutes without removing our clothes. It felt so good that I wondered if I was in love with Malcolm, and if I was at the start of something as complicated and difficult as whatever I was emerging from.

"Wait here," he said suddenly. He left the booth.

I didn't lock it after him, and a man in a John Deere cap poked his head inside. "No thank you," I whispered to him. "I'm already with someone else. He'll be right back."

When Malcolm returned he had a condom and a little bottle of lube from the front counter.

"You just bought these?"

"Yeah."

He kissed me, and this time he pulled at my shirt, looking for the buttons. Malcolm got my shirt off, then we took his off. Then we paused to take off our shoes, and get out of our pants and underwear. A minute later we were completely naked except for his long black socks and my white gym socks. It was the first time I'd been undressed in one of the booths.

He lay back on one of the benches and I lay on top of him. I reached down and felt his dick. I held it together with mine and jerked us off while we kissed.

"Put it on," he said, pressing the condom into my hand.

I stood up and tore open the rubber package while he put lube on his dick and ass. When I had the rubber on, he put lube on my dick, and said, "Come on."

He lifted his legs for me, and I pressed them back with my hands. He reached down and found my cock and pushed it against his ass.

"Slow," he said.

I didn't move until I felt him relaxing a little at a time. A few seconds later, my dick had disappeared into him completely and I was kissing him, feeling my balls against his rear end.

"Go on," he said.

I started to fuck him, holding his legs. I looked into his eyes and he smiled like he was containing a laugh. Then the movie stopped, and it was black in the booth. I felt him beneath me and regretted that I had delayed meeting him for so long.

I tried to take it slow, but I felt like I was going to come after just a couple of minutes.

"I'm going to come," I whispered. "Sorry."

"That's okay," he whispered. "Kiss me. I'm about to come too."

Then we did, and I could feel it pulsing out of him, dripping off my stomach as we kissed. Then we both exhaled, and I rested my head on his chest. He wrapped his arms around me and kissed me on the top of my head.

80

SOMEONE CAME INTO THE LOBBY WHILE I WAS ON THE PHONE taking a reservation. I didn't pay him any attention at first. He only glanced at me before turning his back to look at some maps and fliers that were set out on a table in the lobby.

Before I was off the phone, a woman and her daughter arrived to check-in. Then a man in a suit lined up behind them. When I hung up, I started checking in the woman, and a Norwegian guest came in to ask why he might be having trouble with the wi-fi.

I helped him with the wi-fi on his phone, and I got the woman to sign her paperwork and directed her to her room.

I checked in the man in the suit. Then the phone rang while he was signing his paperwork. I put the phone call on hold and directed the man in the suit to his room.

All along, the guy who had entered earlier stood at the table. When I bothered focusing my attention on him, I recognized something familiar—the distracted air of someone pretending to look at something but actually just stalling.

"Can I help you with something?" I said.

He turned and looked at me.

It was the kid.

"No," he said. "You can take your call."

"You sure?" I said.

"Yeah."

I picked up the phone, and took a reservation from a woman. Normally, I detested lengthy conversations with guests, but I spent much longer than necessary on the phone with her in hopes that another person would enter the lobby. I pretended to be ridiculously friendly and helpful so that he would hear me. I hoped I wasn't about to be murdered or even confronted.

The call ended at last.

Even after I hung up, the kid stayed there at the table, pretending to examine a bus schedule and a flyer for a company offering double decker bus tours.

"Let me know if there's anything I can do for you," I said.

He turned around and looked at me. I thought he was about to say something, but he just kept staring. The seconds ticked past, and I could feel my face turn red and my throat close up.

His face was red too. It was the first time I was able to get a good impression of him. I could almost see what the cop would want with him. Maybe there was something handsome in him. Beneath the baby fat, I thought I could see something dignified. A jawline. Broad shoulders.

The map in the kid's hands shook. It seemed likely that he would remove a gun or a knife from his pants and that would be the end of me. But after staring at one another for several seconds, he nodded. Then, with trembling hands, he folded the bus map, put it back on the table and left.

81

FANTASIZING WAYS TO ESCAPE THE LOBBY, I IMAGINED THE possibility of a career at the arcade. But the more I thought about it, the more I saw that I didn't really want to work out there so much as I wanted to have an arcade of my own.

I thought about getting into the industry, the newsletters I never would have known existed, the catalogs and invitations to sleazy conventions where I'd meet guys who'd seen it all. Maybe one would make a project of me, teaching me the business the way Burgess Meredith taught Sylvester Stallone how to box in *Rocky*. Maybe I'd speak at his funeral and inherit his chain of arcades and car washes, the son he'd never had.

I'd be like Bruce Mailman, the owner of the New St. Marks Baths in New York. Like the St. Mark's, we'd never close. I read that, though the building had been open and operating as a bathhouse for more than seventy years, the city had been forced to buy a lock when they shut it down in 1985 because no one who worked there—not even the owners—had a key to the place. They'd never closed up before, not even for holidays.

My employees and I would all have horror stories about cleaning up booths and the bathroom. We'd have favorite regulars and guys we wanted to sleep with, and guys we absolutely loathed, and guys we banned. We'd have an endless supply of anecdotes for one another about the things we had seen and the conversations we'd had, and no one would understand except for those of us who worked there.

Maybe manning the counter, I'd meet fascinating and fun people, and maybe when I did, I could join them in a booth, leaving the front desk unattended like a sidewalk newsstand from the 1950s, with a stack of tokens and a note reading "Honor System."

82

I EMAILED MALCOLM TO TELL HIM ABOUT THE VISIT FROM the kid. I couldn't talk about it out loud yet.

His reply arrived just a few minutes later.

"Sounds to me like that's finished. And like maybe it's time for you to move on. Since it seems like you're never going to ask, you know I could get you a job, right? A pretty good one. All you have to do is say the word. Of course, you'd have to tell me your real name."

83

IT WAS A QUIET NIGHT. I WAS DOING MY USUAL ROUNDS, walking from here to there, looking at DVD covers, waiting for something to happen. I wasn't interested in anyone out there, and no one was interested in me.

I went to the hallway and entered an empty booth. The second I dropped a token in the slot, I recognized a powerful stench. I searched around for its source and spotted on the floor a pile of human excrement. I jumped back, I was so startled. I didn't think for a second before pushing out of the booth. I felt so revolted, I wanted to leave the arcade right away, but I was afraid that if I did the staff might see me entering the booth and then leaving abruptly on the security footage, and assume I was the culprit. Maybe they'd freeze frame a picture of me and hang a wanted poster on the premises. Maybe they'd wait until the next time I came in to confront me. Surely they'd see what a short time I'd spent in there. But, then, maybe if you really had to go, you could be in and out in no time at all.

I walked around for a few minutes trying to behave normally but not feeling normal. I no longer felt like finding someone to connect with. I thought the arcade must be falling apart and becoming the kind of weird and disgusting underbelly that anyone might imagine when thinking of a place like that.

I left after I felt enough time had passed to clear me as someone who had shat and run. Walking past the clerk on my way out, I debated telling him what I'd seen, but I feared it would make me look like someone trying to avoid suspicion.

Driving home, I didn't know what to think about the place. I wasn't sure why I had been going or where it was all leading. I wondered about my best-case scenario at the arcade, and if there had ever been one at all. I wondered what, if anything, would finally make me stop going there. Maybe it would take a big scare or a real crisis. I imagined that the whole place was in decline. I thought about the broken windows theory, and wondered if I had seen the first broken window, or maybe just *a* broken window. Maybe it wasn't the first shit on the floor. Maybe it was just the first one I had encountered.

I remembered Holden Caulfield at the end of *The Catcher in Rye*, when he discovers the words "fuck you" written on the wall at his younger sister Phoebe's school, how he imagines the way it threatens to destroy the innocence of the children there. "I kept wanting to kill whoever'd written it," he says.

84

I WENT OUT TO THE ARCADE ONE NIGHT A FEW WEEKS LATER, and found it closed. The building was dark. There was another man out there. We circled the place in our cars. I got out and tried the door. The guy parked next to my car, and I went to his window after I found the door locked. He was a good-looking, middle-aged Latino.

"It's locked," I said.

"That's strange," he said. "Was there a note on the door?"

"I didn't see one."

I walked back to the door to see if I had missed a note, or if one had fallen on the ground.

"No note," I said.

I went back to his window, and we appraised one another for a second.

"All the lights are off," I said. "Maybe they're closed for a staff meeting or something."

"Huh," the guy said. "Well, you wanna sit in my car with me for a minute?"

"Thanks, but I think I'm going to head out. Playing in public makes me nervous. Besides you could be an axe murderer."

He laughed. "Yeah, you too."

"Maybe I'll see you next time."

"Okay, man."

Another car was pulling in as I was leaving. We drove past one another very slowly, but I wasn't able to get a look at the driver.

The day I found the arcade I knew that it couldn't last forever. It seemed too old fashioned to survive, the buttons on the wall, the porn on disks instead of online. The lit-up coin slots. It was like discovering a pinball arcade.

The next time I went, a week later, the place had been completely emptied out. No note.

However much the arcade seemed like an artifact from some lost era, I had never imagined it would close that way—with no warning, no clearance sale, no heads-up from the clerks, no sign on the front door made in Microsoft Word.

I experienced the same reaction as when the cop ended things with me. Not the hysterical sadness, but the incredulity at not having a vote about something that pertained to me so directly. Like a kid told by his parents that the family is moving across the country, I couldn't believe other people were permitted to make these decisions about my life unilaterally.

I pictured the other men from the arcade like satellites cut loose in space with nothing to orbit. There was no chance I'd see the Marine again, or the bull, or the hedgehog, or the guy who said I should read *The Better Angels of Our Nature*. I wished I could phone some of the other men who went there in order to gauge the appropriate response. Maybe they had received news of the arcade's closing with a shrug.

Even after seeing it all emptied out and vacated, I drove out there one last time a couple of weeks later, just to be sure. In my fantasies, they'd had to close the place down and remove the inventory for some kind of temporary mold or asbestos remediation, after which it would reopen exactly the same as before.

ABOUT THE AUTHOR

DREW NELLINS SMITH grew up in a small town in Texas and wrote *Arcade* while working at a motel in Austin. He has written, reviewed, and interviewed for many of the usual literary places.